Step into the world of murder, mayhem, crime, and detection with today's bestselling writers!

HOMICIDAL ACTS

D0034166

Other Mystery Anthologies
Edited by Bill Pronzini and Martin H. Greenberg

POLICE PROCEDURALS
WOMEN SLEUTHS
THE ETHNIC DETECTIVES
GREAT MODERN POLICE STORIES
PRIME SUSPECTS *
SUSPICIOUS CHARACTERS *

*Published by Ivy Books

HOMICIDAL ACTS

EDITED BY BILL PRONZINI AND MARTIN H. GREENBERG

IVY BOOKS · NEW YORK

Ivy Books
Published by Ballantine Books
Copyright © 1988 by Bill Pronzini and Martin H. Greenberg

Library of Congress Catalog Card Number: 88-91242

ᵀSBN-0-8041-0294-5

Printed in Canada

First Edition: January 1989

Acknowledgments

"Blond and Blue," by Loren D. Estleman. Copyright © 1985 by Loren D. Estleman. Originally published in *New Black Mask, No. 4*. Reprinted by permission of the author.

"Moving Spirit," by Arthur C. Clarke. Copyright © 1957 by Arthur C. Clarke. Reprinted by permission of the author and the author's agents, Scott Meredith Literary Agency, Inc., 845 Third Avenue, New York, N.Y. 10022.

"Address Unknown," by Joyce Harrington. Copyright © 1982 by Joyce Harrington. Originally published in *Ellery Queen's Mystery Magazine*. Reprinted by permission of the author and the author's agents, Scott Meredith Literary Agency, Inc., 845 Third Avenue, New York, N.Y. 10022.

"Charlie's Game," by Brian Garfield. Copyright © 1976, 1981 by Brian Garfield. Originally published in *Alfred Hitchcock's Mystery Magazine* as "Joe Cutter's Game"; revised version first published in *Checkpoint Charlie* by Brian Garfield, Mysterious Press, 1981. Reprinted by permission of the author.

"The Curious Facts Preceding My Execution," by Donald E. Westlake. Copyright © 1960 by Donald E. Westlake. First published in *Alfred Hitchcock's Mystery Magazine* as by Richard Stark. Reprinted by permission of the author and Knox Burger Associates, Ltd.

"The Jail," by Jesse Hill Ford. Copyright © 1975 by Jesse Hill Ford. Originally published in *Playboy*. Reprinted by permission of Harold Ober Associates, Inc.

Acknowledgments

Grateful acknowledgment is made to the following for permission to reprint previously published material:

"The Arrow of God," by Leslie Charteris. Copyright © 1954 by Leslie Charteris. Reprinted by permission of the author.

"Dagger," by John Jakes. Copyright © 1956 by Star Publications, Inc. First published in *Hunted*. Reprinted by permission of the author.

"Skin Deep," by Sara Paretsky. Copyright © 1986 by Sara Paretsky. Originally published in *New Black Mask, No. 8*. Reprinted by permission of the author.

"Buried Treasure," by John Lutz. Copyright © 1982 by Davis Publications, Inc. Originally published in *Alfred Hitchcock's Mystery Magazine*. Reprinted by permission of the author.

"The Candy Skull," by Ray Bradbury. Copyright © 1948 by Popular Publications. Copyright renewed 1975 by Ray Bradbury. First published in *Dime Mystery*. Reprinted by permission of Don Congdon Associates, Inc.

"The Killer," by Norman Mailer. Copyright © by Norman Mailer. Reprinted by permission of the author and his agents, Scott Meredith Literary Agency, Inc., 845 Third Avenue, New York, N.Y. 10022.

"The People Across the Canyon," by Margaret Millar. Copyright © 1962 by The Margaret Millar Survivor's Trust u/a 4/12/82. Originally published in *Ellery Queen's Mystery Magazine*. Reprinted by permission of Harold Ober Associates, Inc.

"Iris," by Stephen Greenleaf. Copyright © 1984 by Stephen Greenleaf. Originally published in *The Eyes Have It*, Mysterious Press, 1984. Reprinted by permission of the author.

Contents

Introduction

The crime story has undergone numerous refinements and updatings during this century. It reflects its times perhaps better than any other form of popular writing, and therefore has not only flourished but has taken its rightful place as a major facet of world literature. Today its popularity is at an all-time high, owing in no small part to the growing number of innovative writers working to stretch the once-confining limits of the genre.

Homicidal Acts is the fourth in a series of anthologies designed to bring the contemporary reader some of the most unusual, finely crafted, and entertaining stories by today's crime-fiction specialists, as well as by important figures in other areas of popular and mainstream fiction. The first three volumes—*Prime Suspects, Suspicious Characters,* and *Criminal Elements*—contain the work of such luminaries as Stephen King, Ruth Rendell, Loren D. Estleman, Donald E. Westlake, John Jakes, P. D. James, John D. MacDonald, Lawrence Block, Ed McBain, Isaac Asimov, Robert Bloch, Marcia Muller, Brian Garfield, Jonathan Gash, Simon Brett, Edward D. Hoch, Sara Paretsky, John Lutz, Sue Grafton, Tony Hillerman, Richard S. Prather, Joseph Hansen, and Edward Gorman. In this volume you will find wholly different stories by some of the above, plus first-rate efforts by Arthur C. Clarke, Joyce Harrington, Jesse Hill Ford, Leslie Charteris, Ray Bradbury, Normal Mailer, Margaret Millar, and Stephen Greenleaf.

Future entries in the series will showcase different works by many of these writers, and by such others as Michael Collins, Stuart Kaminsky, Clark Howard, Dorothy B. Hughes, Eric Ambler, and Dorothy Salisbury Davis,—most if not all the very best writers producing modern mystery and suspense fiction.

Good reading.

—Bill Pronzini and
Martin H. Greenberg

Blond and Blue

•

Loren D. Estleman

Loren D. Estleman has been often—and justifiably—called the best modern writer of the traditional private eye novel. His Detroit-based detective, Amos Walker, has appeared in eight full-length works to date, among them Motor-City Blue *(1980),* The Glass Highway *(1983),* Sugartown *(1984, winner of the Private Eye Writers of America Shamus for Best Novel of that year), and* Downriver *(1988). He has also written two excellent pastiche novels about Sherlock Holmes, three tough books about a former Detroit hit man named Peter Macklin, and a dozen award-winning historical Westerns. "Blond and Blue" is Estleman and Amos Walker at the top of their short-story form.*

Ernest Krell's aversion to windows was a legend in the investigation business. It was a trademark, like his tie clasp made from a piece of shrapnel the army surgeons had pried out of his hip in Seoul and his passion for black suits with discreet patterns to break up their severity. During his seventeen years with the Secret Service he had spent so many public hours warning presidential candidates' wives away from windows that when it came time to open his own detective agency he dug into his wife's inheritance to throw up a building that didn't have any. Narrow vertical slits set eight feet apart let light into a black marble edifice that looked like a blank domino from anywhere along the Detroit River.

A receptionist with blue stones in her ears and that silver complexion that comes free with fluorescent lights took my hat and left me alone in Krell's office, a bowling alley of a room carpeted in black and brown and containing oak-and-leather

3

chairs and an antique desk in front of a huge Miró landscape, lots of blues and reds, to make up for the lack of a window. The walls were painted two shades of cinnamon, darker on the desk side of the office to keep the customers where they belonged. A lot of framed citations, Krell's license, and a square black-on-white sign reading "RELIANCE—Courtesy, Efficiency, Confidentiality" took care of the bare spots.

There were no ashtrays, so I took a seat near a potted fern and lit a cigarette, tipping my ashes into the pot. After five puffs the man himself came through a side door and scowled at the curling smoke and then at me and said, "There's no smoking in this building."

"I didn't see any signs," I said.

"You don't see any ashtrays either." He ran a hand under the edge of the desk. A second later, the silver-skinned receptionist came in carrying an ashtray used just for putting out smokes, and I did that. I couldn't decide if it was the way he had pushed the button or if I just had the look of a guy that would light up in the boss's office. When she left carrying my squashed butt, the man extended his hand and I rose to take it. His grip was cool and firm and as personal as a haberdasher's smile.

"Good to meet you, Walker. I don't think I've had the pleasure."

"This is the first time I've gotten any higher than the fourth floor," I said.

Krell chuckled meaninglessly. He was six three and two hundred pounds, a large pale man with black hair that looked dyed and wrinkles around his eyes and mouth from years of squinting into the sun looking for riflemen on rooftops. It was orange today, orange stripes on his black suit and jaunty orange sunbursts on his silk tie to pick it up. It softened the overall effect of his person like a bright bow tied to a buffalo's tail made you forget he was standing on your foot. The famous tie clasp was in place.

He waved me into one of the chairs but remained upright at parade rest with his hands folded behind him. "Spent last night reading the files on the cases you assisted us with," he said. "Despite the fact that you're anything but the Reliance type"

—his gaze lit on my polyester suit—"you show a certain efficiency I admire. Also you spend more time and effort on each client than a Reliance operative could afford."

"You can do that when they only come into your office one at a time," I volunteered.

"Yes." He let the word melt on his tongue, then pressed on. "The reason I asked you to come down today, we have a client who might best benefit from your rather unorthodox method. A delicate case and a highly emotional one. Frankly, I'd have referred her to another agency had she not come recommended by one of our most valued clients."

"She?"

"You'll meet her in a moment. It's a missing persons situation, which I believe is your specialty. Her son's been kidnapped."

"That's the FBI's specialty."

"Only in cases where ransom is demanded. On the statutes it's abduction, which would make it a police matter except that her ex-husband is the suspected culprit. The authorities consider that a domestic problem and approach it accordingly."

"Meaning it gets spiked along with the butcher's wife who threw a side of pork at her husband," I said. "How old is the boy?"

"Seven." He quarter-turned toward the desk and drew a typewritten sheet from a folder lying open on top. "Blond and blue, about four feet tall leaning to pudgy, last seen April third wearing a blue-and-white-striped T-shirt, red corduroy shorts, and dirty white sneakers. Answers to Tommy. One minute he was playing with a toy truck in the front yard of his mother's home in Austin, Texas, and the next there was just the truck. Neighbor thought he saw him on the passenger's side of a low red sports car going around the corner. The ex-husband owns a red Corvette."

"That's April third this year?" I asked. It was now early May.

"I know it's a long time. She's been to all the authorities here and in Texas."

"Why here?"

"A relative of the mother is sure she saw the father at the Tel-

Twelve Mall in Southfield three weeks ago. She flew in right after. Staying at the relative's place.''

"What makes it too hot to touch?''

He stroked the edge of the sheet with a meaty thumb, making a noise like a cricket. "The ex-husband is an executive with a finance corporation I sometimes do business with. If it gets out I'm investigating one of its employees—''

"Last stop for the money train,'' I finished. "What's to investigate? She should've gone back to court to start, put the sheriffs on his neck.''

"His neck is gone and so is he. He took a leave of absence from his company, closed out his apartment in Austin and vanished, boy and all. He probably had all his bags packed in the Corvette's trunk when he picked up Tommy and just kept driving. It's all here.'' He put the sheet back inside the folder and handed the works to me.

It ran just five pages, triple-spaced and written in Reliance's terse, patented preliminary-report language, but on plain paper without the distinctive letterhead. Very little of it was for me. The ex-husband's name was Frank Corcoran. He was a house investments counselor for Great Western Loans and Credit, with branch offices in seventeen cities west of the Mississippi. There were two numbers to call for information there. The name and number of the witness who had seen his car at the time of the boy's disappearance were there too, along with the 'Vette's serial number and license plate. It was long gone by now or the cops in Austin or Detroit would have had it in on a BOL weeks ago. I folded the report into quarters anyway and put it in a pocket and gave back the empty folder. "Can I talk to the mother?''

"Of course. She's in the other office.''

I followed him through the side door into a room separate from the one where the receptionist sat, a chamber half the size of Krell's, decorated in muted warm colors and containing a row of chairs with circular backs, like the room in a funeral home where the family receives visitors. "Charlotte Corcoran, Amos Walker,'' said Krell.

The woman seated on the end chair raised a sunken face to look at me. Her jaw was too long to be pretty, but it had been an attractive face before she started losing weight, the bones sculpted, not sharp like now, the forehead high and broad instead of jutting and hollow at the sides. The little bit of lipstick she wore might have been painted on the corpse in that same funeral home. Her hair was blond and tied back loosely with wisps of gray springing loose around her ears. Her dress was just a dress, and her bare angular legs ended in bony feet thrust into low-heeled shoes a size too large for her. She was smoking a cigarette with a white filter tip. I peered through the haze at Krell, who moved a shoulder and then flipped a wall switch that started a fan humming somewhere in the woodwork. The smoke stirred and began twisting toward a remote corner of the ceiling. I got out a Winston and sent some of my own after it.

"My boy Tommy turned seven last week," Charlotte Corcoran told the wall across from her. "It's the first birthday I missed."

Her speech had an east Texas twang. I twirled another chair to face hers and sat down. The connecting door clicked shut discreetly behind Krell. It was the only noise he made exiting. "Tell me about your husband," I said.

She snicked some ash into a tray on the chair next to her and looked at me. Seeing me now. "I could call him a monster. I'd be lying. Before this the worst thing he did was to call a half hour before supper to say he was working late. He did that a lot; it's part of why I divorced him. That's old news. I want my son back."

"What'd the police in Austin say?"

"They acted concerned until I told them he'd been kidnapped by his father. Then they lost interest. They said they'd put Tommy's picture on the bulletin board in every precinct, and maybe they did. They didn't give it to the newspapers or TV the way they do when a child's just plain missing. I got the same swirl of no action from the police here. Kidnapping's okay between relatives, I guess." She spat smoke.

"Skipping state lines should've landed it in the feds' lap," I said.

"I called the Houston office of the FBI. They were polite.

7

They test high on polite. They said they'd get it on the wire. I never saw any of them."

"So far as you know."

It was lost on her. She mashed out her butt, leaving some lipstick smeared on the end. "I spent plenty of time at Police Headquarters here and back home," she said. "They showed me the door nice as you please, but they showed me the door. They wouldn't tell me what they'd found out."

"That should have told you right there."

Her expression changed. "Can you find them, Mr.—I've forgotten."

"Walker," I said. "A lot rests on whether they're still here. And if they were ever here to begin with."

"Frank was. My cousin Millie doesn't make mistakes."

"That's Millicent Arnold, the relative you're staying with?" She nodded. "I'll need a picture of Tommy and one of Mr. Corcoran."

"This should do it." From her purse she drew a five-by-seven bureau shot and gave it to me. "I took it last summer on a trip to Corpus Christi. Tommy's grown several inches since. But his face hasn't changed."

I looked at a man with dark curly hair and a towheaded boy standing in swim trunks on a yellow beach with blue ocean behind them. "His father didn't get that build lifting telephone receivers."

"He worked out at a gym near his office. He was a member."

I pocketed the photograph next to the Reliance report and stood up. "I'll be in touch."

"I'll be in."

Krell was on the intercom to his receptionist when I reentered his office. I waited until he finished making his lunch reservation, then:

"How much of a boost can I expect from Reliance on this one?"

"You already have it," he said. "The situation is—"

"Delicate, yeah. I'll take my full fee, then. Three days to start."

"What happened to professional courtesy?"

"It went out of style, same as the amateur kind. What about it? You're soaking her five bills per day now."

"Four fifty." He adjusted his tie clasp. "I'll have Mrs. Marble draw you a check."

"Your receptionist has access to company funds?"

"She's proven herself worthy of my trust."

I didn't say it. My bank balance was stuck to the sidewalk as it was.

The report had Mrs. Corcoran in contact with a Sergeant Grandy in General Service, missing persons detail. I deposited half of the Reliance check at my bank, hanging on to the rest for expenses, and drove down to Police Headquarters, where a uniform escorted me to a pasteboard desk with a bald head behind it. Grandy had an egg-salad sandwich in one hand and a styrofoam cup of coffee in the other and was using a blank arrest form for a place mat. He wore a checked sport coat and a moustache healthy enough to have sucked all the hair from his scalp.

"Corcoran, yeah," he said, after reading my card and hearing my business. "It's in the works. You got to realize it don't get the same priority as a little boy lost. I mean, somebody's feeding him."

"Turn anything yet?"

"We got the boy's picture and the father's description out."

"That's what you've done. What've you got?"

He flicked a piece of egg salad off his lapel. "What I got is two Grosse Pointe runaways to chase down and a four-year-old girl missing from an apartment on Watson I'll be handing to Homicide soon as she turns up jammed in a culvert somewhere. I don't need parttime heat too."

We were getting started early. I set fire to some tobacco. "Who's your lieutenant?"

"Winkle. Only he's out sick."

"Sergeant Grandy, if I spent an hour here, would I walk out any smarter than I was when I came in?"

"Probably not."

"Okay. I just wondered if you were an exception."

I was out of there before he got it.

On the ground floor I used a pay telephone to call the Federal Building and explained my problem to the woman who answered at the FBI.

"That would be Special Agent Roseman, Interstate Flight," she said. "But he's on another line."

I said I'd wait. She put me on hold. I watched a couple of prowl-car cops sweating in their winter uniforms by the Coke machine. After five minutes the woman came back on. "Mr. Roseman will be tied up for a while. Would you like to call back?"

I said yeah and hung up. Out on Beaubien the sidewalks were throwing back the first real warmth of spring. I rolled down the window on the driver's side and breathed auto exhaust all the way to my office building. You have to celebrate it somehow.

The window in my thinking parlor was stuck shut. I strained a disk heaving it open a crack to smell the sweet sun-spread pavement three stories down. Then I sat down behind the desk— real wood, no longer in style but not yet antique—and tried the FBI again. Roseman was out to lunch. I left my number and got out the Reliance report and dialed one of two numbers for the firm where Frank Corcoran worked in Austin.

"Great Western." Another woman. They own the telephone wires.

I gave her my name and calling. "I'm trying to reach Frank Corcoran. It's about an inheritance."

"I'm sorry, Mr. Corcoran is on indefinite leave."

"Where can I reach him?"

"I'm sorry."

I thanked her anyway and worked the plunger. I wasn't disappointed. It's basic to try the knob before you break out the lockpicks. I used the other number, and this time I got a man.

"Arnold Wilson, president of Thornbraugh Electronics in Chicago," I said. Thornbraugh Transmissions on Livernois put out the advertising calendar tacked to the wall across from my desk. "We're building a new plant in Springfield and Frank

10

Corcoran advised me to call Great Western for financing. Is he in?"

"What did you say your name was?" I repeated it. "One moment."

I had enough time to pluck out a cigarette before he came back on the line. "Are you the private investigator who spoke to my partner's secretary about Mr. Corcoran a few moments ago?" His tone had lost at least three layers of silk.

"What's the matter," I said, "you don't have any walls in that place?"

I was talking to myself. As I lowered the dead receiver I could hear the computers gossiping among themselves, trashing my credit rating. The laugh was on them; I didn't have one.

My next trip was through the yellow pages. There were at least fifty public gymnasiums listed within a half hour of downtown Detroit, including Southfield, any one of which would suit Corcoran's obsession with a healthy body. We all have our white whales. I made a list of the bigger, cleaner places. It was still long. Just thinking about it made my feet throb.

I tried the number of the place where Charlotte Corcoran was staying in Southfield. A breathy female voice answered, not hers.

"Millicent Arnold?"

"Yes. Mr. Walker? Charlotte told me she spoke with you earlier. She's napping now. Shall I wake her?"

"That's okay. It's you I want to talk to. About the man you saw who looked like Frank Corcoran."

"It was Frank. I spent a week in their home in Austin last year, and I know what he looks like."

"Where did you see him at the mall? In what store?"

"He was coming out of the sporting goods place. I was across the corridor. I almost called to him over the crowd, but then I remembered. I thought about following him, see where he went, but by the time I made up my mind he was lost in the crush. I went into the store and found the clerk who had waited on him. He'd paid cash for what he bought, didn't leave a name or address."

"What'd he buy, barbell weights?" Maybe he was working out at home and I could forget the gyms.

"No. Something else. Sweats, I think. Yes, a new sweat suit. Does that help?"

"My feet will give you a different answer. But yeah. Thanks, Miss Arnold."

"Call me Millie. Everyone does."

I believed her. It was the voice.

After saying good-bye I scowled at the list, then raised my little electronic paging device from among the flotsam in the top drawer of the desk and called my answering service to test the batteries. They were deader than the Anthony dollar. I said I'd call in for messages and locked up.

The office directly below mine was being used that month by a studio photographer, five foot one and three hundred pounds with a Marlboro butt screwed into the middle of a face full of stubble. I went through the open door just as he finished brushing down the cowlick of a gap-toothed ten-year-old in a white shirt buttoned to the neck and blue jeans as stiff as aluminum siding and waddled around behind the camera, jowls swinging. "Smile, you little—" he said, squeezing the bulb on the last part. White light bleached the boy's face and the sky blue backdrop behind.

When the kid had gone, following the spots in front of his eyes, I handed the photographer the picture Charlotte Corcoran had given me of her ex-husband and their son. "How much to make a negative from this and run off twenty-five prints?" I asked.

He held the shot close enough to his face to set it afire if his stub had been burning. "Eighty-seven fifty."

"How much for just fifteen?"

"Eighty-seven fifty."

"Must be the overhead." I was looking at a rope of cobwebs as thick as my wrist hammocking from the ceiling.

"No, you just look like someone that wants it tomorrow."

"Early." I gave him two fifties and he changed them from a cigar box on a table cluttered with lenses and film tubes and wrote me out a receipt.

I used his telephone to call my service. There were no messages. I tried the Federal Building again. Special Agent Roseman had come in and gone out and wasn't expected back that day. He had the right idea. I went home and cooked a foil-wrapped tray for supper and watched the news and a TV movie and went to bed.

I was pulling a tail.

Leaving the diner I let fix my breakfast those mornings I can't face a frying pan, I watched a brown Chrysler pull out of the little parking area behind me in the rearview mirror. Three turns later it was still with me. I made a few more turns to make sure and then nicked the red light crossing John R. The Chrysler tried to do the same but had to brake when a Roadway van trundled through the intersection laying down horn.

I was still thinking about it when I squeezed into the visitors' lot outside Police Headquarters. My next alimony payment wasn't due for a month, and I hadn't anything to do with the Sicilian boys' betterment league all year.

Sergeant Grandy had a worried-looking black woman in a ratty squirrel coat in the customer's chair and was clunking out a missing persons report with two fingers on a typewriter that came over with Father Marquette. I asked him if Lieutenant Winkle was in today.

"What for?" He mouthed each letter as he typed.

"Corcoran, same as yesterday."

"Go ahead and talk to him. I had a full head of hair before people started climbing over it."

I followed his thumb to where a slim black man in striped shirt-sleeves and a plain brown tie was filling a china mug at the coffee maker. He wore a modest Afro and gray-tinted glasses. I gave him a card.

"I've been hired by Charlotte Corcoran to look for her ex-husband and their boy Tommy," I said. "The sergeant wasn't much help."

"Told you to walk off a dock, right?" His eyes might have twinkled over the top of the mug, but you can never be sure about cops' eyes.

13

"Words to that effect."

"Grandy's gone as high as he's going in my detail," he said. "No diplomacy. You have some identification besides a card?"

I showed him the chintzy pastel-colored ID the state hands out. He reached into a pocket and flipped forty cents into a tray full of coins next to the coffee maker. "Let's go into the cave."

We entered an office made of linoleum and amber pebbled glass, closing the door. He set down his mug, tugged at his trousers to protect the crease, and sat on the only clear corner of his desk. Then he pulled over his telephone and dialed a number.

"Hello, Miss Arnold? This is Lieutenant Winkle in General Service. . . . Millie, right. Is Mrs. Corcoran in? Thank you." Pause. "Mrs. Corcoran? No, I'm sorry, there's nothing new. Reason I called, I've got a private investigator here named Walker says he's working for you. . . . Okay, thanks. Just wanted to confirm it."

He hung up and looked at me. "Sorry. Department policy."

"I'm unoffendable," I said. "How many telephone numbers you keep in your head at any given time?"

"Last month I forgot my mother's birthday." He drowned his quiet smile in coffee. "We have nothing in the Corcoran case."

"Nothing as in nothing, or nothing you can do anything with?"

"Nothing as in zip. We run on coffee and nicotine here. When we get a box full of scraps we can hand over to the feds, we don't waste time trying to assemble them ourselves. The FBI computer drew a blank on Corcoran."

"Not unusual if he doesn't have priors."

"It gets better. Because of the exodus from Michigan to Texas over the past couple of years, a lot of local firms have been dealing with finance companies out there. So when it landed back in our lap, we fed Great Western Loans and Credit into the department machine. Still nothing on Corcoran, because only the officers are on file. But the printout said the corporation invests heavily in government projects. As investments counselor, Frank Corcoran should have shown up on that FBI report. He'd have had to have been screened one time or another."

"Some kind of cover-up?"

"You tell me. The word's lost a lot of its impact in recent years."

I opened a fresh pack of Winstons. "So why keep Mrs. Corcoran in the dark?"

"Don't worry. It's not rubbing off on us," he said. "We're just holding her at arm's length till we get some answers back from channels. These things take time. Computer time, which is measured in Christmases."

"So why tell me?"

He smiled the quiet smile. "When Sergeant Grandy gave me your card I did some asking around the building. If you were a bulldog you'd have what the novelists call 'acquisitive teeth.' Quickest way to get rid of you guys is to throw you some truth."

"I appreciate it, Lieutenant." I rose and offered him my hand. He didn't give it back as hastily as some cops have. "Oh, what would you know about a brown Chrysler that was shadowing me a little while ago?"

"It wasn't one of mine," he said. "I'm lucky to get a blue-and-white when I want to go in with the band."

I grasped the doorknob. "Thanks again. I guess you're feeling better."

"Than what? Oh, yesterday. I called in sick to watch my kid pitch. He walked six batters in a row."

I grinned and left. That's the thing I hate most about cops. Find one that stands for everything you don't like about them and then you draw one that's human.

The job stank, all right. It stank indoors and it stank on the street and it stank in the car all the way to my building. I had the window closed this trip: the air was damp and the sky was throwing fingers whether to rain or snow. Michigan. But it wouldn't have smelled any better with the window down.

The pictures came out good, anyway. It must be nice to be in a business where if they don't you can trace the problem to a bad filter or dirt in the chemicals, something definite and impersonal that you can ditch and replace with something better. I left the fat photographer developing nude shots for a customer on Adult Row on Woodward and went upstairs.

I lock the waiting room overnight. I was about to use the key when the door swung inward and a young black party in faded overalls and a Pistons warm-up jacket grinned at me. He had a mouth built for grinning, wide as a Buick with door-to-door teeth and a thin moustache squared off like a bracket to make it seem even wider. "You're late, trooper," he said. "Let's you come in and we'll get started."

"Thanks, I'll come back," I said, and backpedaled into something hard. The wall was closer this morning. A hand curled inside the back of my collar and jerked my suit coat down to my elbows, straining the button and pinning my arms behind me.

Teeth drew a finger smelling of marijuana down my cheek. Then he balled his fist and rapped the side of my chin hard enough to make my own teeth snap together.

"Let's you come in, trooper. Unless you'd rather wake up smiling at yourself from your bedside table every morning."

I kicked him in the crotch.

He said, "Hee!" and hugged himself. Meanwhile I threw myself forward, popping the button and stripping out of my coat. My left arm was still tangled in the sleeve lining when I pivoted on my left foot and swung my right fist into a face eight inches higher than mine. I felt the jar to my shoulder. I was still gripping the keys in that hand.

The guy I hit let go of the coat to drag the back of a huge hand under his nose and looked at the blood. Then he took hold of my shirt collar from the front to steady me and cocked his other fist, taking aim.

"Easy, Del. We ain't supposed to bust him." Teeth's voice was a croak.

Del lowered his fist but kept his grip on my collar. He was almost seven feet tall, very black, and had artificially straightened hair combed into a high pompadour and sprayed hard as a brick. In place of a jacket he wore a full-length overcoat that barely reached his hips, over a sweatshirt that left his navel and flat hairy belly exposed.

Behind me Teeth said, "Del don't like to talk. He's got him a cleft palate. It don't get in his way at all. Now you want to come in, talk?"

I used what air Del had left me to agree. He let go and we went inside. In front of the door to my private office Teeth relieved me of my keys, unlocked it, and stood aside while his partner shoved me on through. Teeth glanced at the lock on his way in.

"Dead bolt, yeah. Looks new. You need one on the other door too."

He circled the room as he spoke and stopped in front of me. I was ready and got my hip out just as he kicked. I staggered sideways. Del caught me.

"That's no way to treat a client, trooper," Teeth said. "It gets around, pretty soon you ain't got no business."

"Client?" I shook off the giant's steadying hand. My leg tingled.

Teeth reached into the slash pocket of his Pistons jacket and brought out a roll of crisp bills, riffling them under my nose. "Hundreds, trooper. Fifty of them in this little bunch. Go on, heft it. Ain't no heavier'n a roll of quarters, but, my oh my, how many more smiles she draws."

He held it out while I got my coat right side in. Finally his arm got tired and he let it drop. I said, "You came in hard for paying customers. What do I have to forget?"

"We want someone to forget something, we go to a politician," he said. "Twenty-five hundred of this pays to look for somebody. The other twenty-five comes when the somebody gets found."

"Somebody being?" Knowing the answer.

"Same guy you're after now. Frank Corcoran."

"That standard for someone who's already looking for him for a lot less?"

"There's a little more to it," he said.

"Thought there might be."

"You find him, you tell us first. Ahead of his wife."

"Then?"

"Then you don't tell her."

17

"I guess I don't ask why."

His grin creaked. "You're smart, trooper. Too smart for poor."

"I'll need a number," I said.

"We call you." He held up the bills. "We talking?"

"Let's drink over it." I pushed past him around the desk and tugged at the handle on the deep drawer. Teeth's other hand moved and five inches of pointed steel flicked out of his fist. "Just a Scotch bottle," I said.

He leaned over the corner to see down into the drawer. I grabbed a handful of his hair and bounced his forehead off the desk. The switchblade went flying. Del, standing in front of the desk, made a growling sound in his chest and lurched forward. I yanked open the top drawer and fired my Smith & Wesson .38 without taking it out. The bullet smashed through the front panel and buried itself in the wall next to the door. It didn't come within a foot of hitting the big man. But he stopped. I raised the gun and backed to the window.

"A name," I said. "Whose money?"

Teeth rubbed his forehead, where a purple bruise was spreading under the brown. He stooped to pick up the currency from the floor and stood riffling it against his palm. His smile was a shadow of a ghost of what it had been. "No names today, trooper. I'm fresh out of names."

I said, "It works this way. You tell me the name, I don't shoot you."

"You don't shoot. Desks and walls, maybe. Not people. It's why you're broke, and it's why I get to walk around with somebody else's five long ones on account of it's what I drop on gas for my three Cadillacs."

"What about a Chrysler?"

"I pay my dentist in Chryslers," he said. "So long, trooper. Maybe I see you. Maybe you don't see me first. Oh." He got my keys out of his slash pocket and flipped them onto the desk. "We're splitting, Del."

Del looked around, spotted my framed original *Casablanca* poster hanging on the wall over the bullet hole, and swung his fist. Glass sprayed. Then he turned around and crunched out behind his partner, speckling my carpet with blood from his lacerated fingers.

The telephone rang while I was cleaning the revolver. When I got my claws unhooked from the ceiling I lifted the receiver. It was Lieutenant Winkle. He wanted to see me at Headquarters.

"Something?" I asked.

"Everything," he said. "Don't stop for cigarettes on the way."

I reloaded, hunted up my holster, and clipped the works to my belt. No one came to investigate the shot. The neighborhood had fallen that far.

On Beaubien I left the gun in the car to clear the metal detectors inside. Heading there I walked past a brown Chrysler parked in the visitors' lot. There was no one inside and the doors were locked.

The lieutenant let me into his office, where two men in dark suits were seated in mismatched chairs. One had a head full of crisp gray hair and black-rimmed glasses astride a nose that had been broken sometime in the distant past. The other was younger and looked like Jack Kennedy with a close-trimmed black beard. They stank federal.

"Eric Stendahl and Robert LeJohn." Winkle introduced them in the same order. "They're with the Justice Department."

"We met," I said. "Sort of."

Stendahl nodded. He might have smiled. "I thought you'd made us. I should have let Bob drive; he's harder to shake behind a wheel. But even an old eagle likes to test his wings now and then." The smile died. "We're here to ask you to stop looking for Frank Corcoran."

I lit a Winston. "If I say no?"

"Then we'll tell you. We have influence with the state police, who issued your license."

"I'll get a hearing. They'll have to tell me why."

"That won't be necessary," he said. "Corcoran was the inside man in an elaborate scheme to bilk Great Western Loans and Credit out of six hundred thousand dollars in loans to a nonexistent oil venture in Mexico. He was apprehended and agreed to turn state's evidence against his accomplices in return for a new identity and relocation for his protection. You're familiar with the alias program, I believe.''

"I ran into it once." I looked at Winkle. "You knew?"

"Not until they came in here this morning after you left," he said. "They've had Mrs. Corcoran under surveillance. That's how they got on to you. It also explains why Washington turned its back on this one."

I added some ash to the fine mulch on the linoleum floor. "Not too bright, relocating him in an area where his wife's cousin lives."

Stendahl said, "We didn't know about that, but it certainly would have clinched our other objections. He spent his childhood here and had a fixation about the place. The people behind the swindle travel in wide circles; we couldn't chance his being spotted. Bob here was escorting Corcoran to the East Coast. He disappeared during the plane change at Metro Airport. We're still looking for him."

"It's a big club," I said. "We ought to have a secret handshake. What about Corcoran's son?"

LeJohn spoke up. "That's how he lost me. The boy was along. He had to go to the bathroom, and he didn't want anyone but his father in with him. I went into the bookstore for a magazine. When I got back to the men's room, it was empty."

"The old bathroom trick. Tell me, did Corcoran ever happen to mention that the boy was in his mother's custody and that you were acting as accomplices in his abduction?"

"He seemed happy enough," said LeJohn, glaring. "Excited about the trip."

His partner laid manicured nails on his arm, calming him. To me: "It was a condition of Corcoran's testimony that the boy go with him to his new life. Legally, our compliance is indefensible. Morally—well, his evidence is expected to put some important felons behind bars."

"Yeah." I tipped some smoke out my nostrils. "I guess you got too busy to clue in Mrs. Corcoran."

"That was an oversight. We'll correct it while we're here."

"What did you mean when you said it was a big club?" LeJohn pressed me. "Who else is looking for Corcoran?"

I replayed the scene in my office. Lieutenant Winkle grunted. "Monroe Boyd and Little Delbert Riddle," he said. "I had one or both of them in here half a dozen times when I was with Criminal Intelligence. Extortion, suspicion of murder. Nothing stuck. So they're jobbing themselves out now. I'll put out a pickup on them if you want to press charges."

"They'd be out the door before you finished the paperwork. I'll just tack the price of a new old desk and a picture frame on to the expense sheet. The bullet hole's good for business."

"How'd they know you were working for Mrs. Corcoran?" Stendahl asked.

"The same way you did, maybe. Only they were better at it."

He rose. "We'll need whatever you've got on them in your files, Lieutenant. Walker, you're out of it."

"Can I report to Mrs. Corcoran?"

"Yes. Yes, please do. It will save us some time. You've been very cooperative."

He extended his hand. I went on crushing out my cigarette in the ashtray on Winkle's desk until he got tired and lowered it. Then I left.

Millicent Arnold owned a condominium off Twelve Mile Road, within sight of the glass-and-steel skyscrapers of the Southfield Civic Center sticking up above the predominantly horizontal suburb like new teeth in an old mouth. A slim brunette with a pageboy haircut answered the bell wearing a pink angora sweater over black harem pants and gold sandals with high heels on her bare feet. Charlotte Corcoran might have looked like her before she had lost too much weight.

"Amos Walker? Yes, you are. My God, you look like a private eye. Come in."

I kept my mouth zipped at that one and walked past her into a living room paved with orange shag and furnished in green plush and glass. It should have looked like hell. I decided it was

21

Millie Arnold standing in it that made it work. She hung my hat on an ornamental peg near the door.

"Charlotte's putting herself together. She was asleep when you called."

"She seems to sleep a lot."

"Her doctor in Austin prescribed a mild sedative. It's almost the only thing that's gotten her through this past month. You said you had some news." She indicated the sofa.

I took it. It was like sitting on a sponge. "The story hangs some lefts and rights," I said.

She sat next to me, trapping her hands between her knees. She wasn't wearing a ring. "My cousin and I are close," she said. "More like sisters. You can speak freely."

"I didn't mean that, although it was coming. I just don't want to have to tell it twice. I didn't like it when I heard it."

"That bad, huh?"

I said nothing. She tucked her feet under her and propped an elbow on the back of the sofa and her cheek in her hand. "I'm curious about something. I recommended Reliance to Charlotte. She came back with you."

"The case came down my street. Krell said she was referred to him by one of his cash customers."

She nodded. "Kester Clothiers on Lahser. I'm a buyer. I typed Charlotte's letter of reference on their stationery. The chain retains Reliance for security, employee theft and like that."

"I guess the hours are good."

"I'm off this week. We're between seasons." She paused. "You know, you're sort of attractive."

I was looking at her again when Charlotte Corcoran came in. She had on a maroon robe over a blue nightgown, rich material that bagged on her and made her wrists and ankles look even bonier than they were. Backless slippers. When she saw me her step quickened. "You found them? Is Tommy all right?"

I took a deep breath and sat her down in a green plush chair with tassels on the arms and told it.

"Wow," said Millie after a long silence.

I was watching her cousin. She remained motionless for a moment, then fumbled cigarettes and a book of matches out of her robe pocket. She tried to strike a match, said "Damn!" and threw the book on the floor. I picked it up and struck one and held the flame for her. She drew in a lungful and blew a plume at the ceiling. "The bastard," she said. "No wonder he never had time for me. He was too busy making himself rich."

"You didn't know about his testifying?" I asked.

"He came through with his child support on time. That's all I heard from him. It explains why he never came by for his weekends with Tommy." She looked at me. "Is my son in danger?"

"He is if he's with his father. Boyd and Riddle didn't look like lovers of children. But the feds are on it."

"Is this the same federal government that endowed a study to find out why convicts want to escape prison?"

"Someone caught it on a bad day," I said.

"How much to go on with the investigation, Mr. Walker?"

"Nothing, Mrs. Corcoran. I just wanted to hear you say it." She smiled then, a little.

"What progress have you made?" asked Millie.

"I'm chasing a lead now. If it gets any slimmer it won't be a lead at all. But it beats reading bumps." I got the package of prints out of my coat pocket, separated the original of Corcoran and Tommy from the others, and gave it back to Mrs. Corcoran. "I've got twenty-five more now, and at least that many places to show them. When I run out I'll try something else."

She looked at the picture. Seeing only one person in it. Then she put it in her robe pocket. "I think you're a good man, Mr. Walker."

Millie Arnold saw me to the door. "She's right, you know," she said, when I had it open. "You are good."

Attractive, too.

There was a gymnasium right around the corner on Greenfield. No one I talked to there recognized either of the faces in the picture, but I left it with the manager anyway along with my card and tried the next place on my list. I had them grouped by area with Southfield at the top. I hit two places in Birmingham, one in Clawson, then swung west and worked my way home in a loop through Farmington and Livonia. A jock in Redford Township with muscles on his T-shirt thought Corcoran looked familiar but couldn't finger him.

"There's fifty dollars in it for you when you do," I said. He flexed his trapezius and said he'd work on it.

I'd missed lunch, so I stopped in Detroit for an early supper, hit a few more places downtown, and went back to the office to read my mail and call my service for messages. I had none, and the mail was all bills and junk. I locked up and went home. That night I dreamed I was Johnny Appleseed, but instead of trees every seed I threw sprang up grinning Monroe Boyds and hulking Delbert Riddles.

My fat photographer neighbor greeted me in the foyer of my building the next morning. He was chewing on what looked like the same Marlboro butt, and he hadn't been standing any closer to his razor than usual. "Some noise yesterday," he said. "Starting a range up there or what?"

"No, I shot a shutterbug for asking too many questions." I passed him on the stairs, no small feat.

I entered my office with my gun drawn, felt stupid when I found it empty, then saw the shattered glass from the poster frame and felt a little better. I swept it up and called my service. I had a message.

"Walker?" asked a male voice at the number left for me. "Tunk Herman, remember?"

"The guy in Redford," I said.

"Yeah. That fifty still good?"

"What've you got?"

"I couldn't stop thinking about that dude in the picture, so I went through the records of members. Thought maybe his name would jump out at me if I heard it, you know? Well, it did. James Muldoon. He's a weekender. I don't see him usually because I don't work weekends, except that one time. I got an address for him."

I drew a pencil out of the cup on my desk. It shook a little.

* * *

Blond and Blue

It was spring now and no argument. The air had a fresh damp smell and the sun felt warm on my back as I leaned on the open-air telephone booth, or maybe it was my disposition coming through from inside. Charlotte Corcoran answered on the eighth ring. Her voice sounded foggy.

"Walker, Mrs. Corcoran," I said. "Come get your son."

"What did you say? I took a pill a little while ago. It sounded—"

"It wasn't the pill. I'm looking at him now. Blond and blue, about four feet—"

The questions came fast, tumbling all over one another, too tangled to pull apart. I held the receiver away from my ear and waited. Down the block, on the other side of Pembroke, a little boy in blue overalls with a bright yellow mop was bouncing a ball off the wall of a two-story white frame house that went back forever. While I was watching, the front door came open and a dark-haired man beckoned him inside. Corcoran's physique was less impressive in street clothes.

"Tommy's fine," I said, when his mother wound down. "Meet me here." I gave her the address. "Put Millie on and I'll give her directions."

"Millie's out shopping. I don't have a car."

"Take a cab."

"Cab?"

"Forget it. You've got too much of that stuff in your pipes to come out alone. I'll pick you up in twenty minutes."

It was all of that. The road crews were at work, and everyone who had a car and no job was out enjoying the season. I left the engine running in front of the brick complex and bounced up the wrought-iron steps to where Millie's door stood open. I rapped and went inside. Charlotte Corcoran was sitting on the sofa in her robe and nightgown.

"That's out of style for the street this year," I said. "Get into something motherly."

"Plenty of time for that."

I felt my face get tired at the sound of the voice behind me. I turned around slowly. Millie Arnold was standing on the blind side of the door in a white summer dress with a red belt around

25

her trim waist and a brown .32 Colt automatic in her right hand pointing at me.

"You don't look surprised." She nudged the door shut with the toe of a red pump.

. "It was there," I said, raising my hands. "It just needed a kick. I had to wonder how Boyd and Riddle got on to me so fast. They couldn't have been following Mrs. Corcoran without Stendahl and LeJohn knowing. Someone had to tell them."

"It goes back further than that. I made two calls to Texas after spotting Frank at the mall. The first was to his old partners. I can't tell you how much they appreciated it. If I did, I'd be in trouble with the IRS. Then I called Charlotte. Throw the gun down on the rug, Mr. Walker. It made an ugly dent in my sofa when you were here yesterday."

I unholstered the .38 slowly. It hit the shag halfway between us with a thump. "Then, when Mrs. Corcoran arrived, you talked her into hiring the biggest investigative firm you knew. You figured to let them do the work of finding Corcoran. It probably meant a discount on Boyd and Riddle's fee."

"It also guaranteed me a bonus when Frank got dead," she said. "Krell giving the case to you threw me, but it worked out just fine. When I got back from shopping and Charlotte gave me the good news, I just couldn't wait to call our mutual friends and share it."

"My cousin," said Mrs. Corcoran.

Millie showed her teeth. Very white and a little sharp. "You married a hundred-thou-a-year executive. I'd have settled for that. But if it wasn't enough for him, why should what I make be enough for me? I met his little playmates that time I visited you in Austin. I had a hunch there was money to be made. When I called, they told me just how and why."

"What happens to us?" I asked.

"You'll both stay here with me until that phone rings. It'll be Boyd giving me thumbs up. I'll have to lock you in the bathroom when I leave, but you'll find a way out soon enough. You can have the condo, Charlotte. It isn't paid for."

"The boy had nothing to do with Corcoran's scam," I said. "You're putting him in front of the guns too."

26

"Rich kid. What do I owe him?"

"They won't hurt Tommy." Mrs. Corcoran got up.

"Sit down." The gun jerked.

But she was moving. I threw my arm in front of her. She knocked it aside and charged. Millie squeezed the trigger. It clicked. Her cousin was all over her then, kicking and shrieking and clawing at her eyes. It was interesting to see. Millie was healthier, but she was standing between a mother and her child. When the gun came up to slap the side of Mrs. Corcoran's head, I tipped the odds, reversing ends on the Smith & Wesson I'd scooped up from the rug and tapping Millie behind the ear. Her knees gave then and she trickled through her cousin's grasp and puddled on the floor.

I reached down and pulled her eyelids. "She's good for an hour," I said. "Call nine one one. Give them the address on Pembroke."

While she was doing that, breathing heavily, I picked up the automatic and ran back the action. Millie had forgotten to rack a cartridge into the chamber.

Approaching Pembroke, we heard shots.

I jammed my heel down on the accelerator and we rounded the corner doing fifty. Charlotte Corcoran, still in her robe, gripped the door handle to stay out of my lap. Her profile was sharp against the window, thrust forward like a mother hawk's.

There was no sign of the police. As we entered Corcoran/ Muldoon's block, something flashed in an open upstairs window, followed closely by a hard flat bang. A much louder shot answered it from the front yard. There a huge black figure in an overcoat too short for him crouched behind a lilac bush beside the driveway. His .44 magnum was as long as my thigh but looked like a kid's water pistol in his great fist.

"Hang on!" I spun the wheel hard and floored the pedal.

The Olds's engine roared and we bumped over the curb, diagonaling across the lawn. Del Riddle straightened at the noise and turned, bringing the magnum around with him. I saw his mouth open wide and then his body filled the windshield and I felt the impact. We bucked up over the porch stoop and suddenly the world was a deafening place of tearing wood and exploding glass. The car stopped then, although my foot was still pasted to the floor with the accelerator pedal underneath and the engine continued to whine. The rear wheels spun shrilly. I cut the ignition. A piece of glass fell somewhere with a clank.

I looked at my passenger. She was slumped down in the seat with her knees against the dash. "All right?"

"I think so." She lowered her knees.

"Stay here."

The door didn't want to open. I shoved hard and it squawked against the buckled fender. I climbed out behind the Smith & Wesson in my right hand. I was in a living room with broken glass on the carpet and pieces of shredded siding slung over the chairs and sofa. Riddle lay spreadeagled on his face across the car's hood and windshield, groaning. His legs dangled like broken straws in front of the smashed grille.

"Ditch the piece, trooper."

My eyes were still adjusting to the dim light indoors. I focused on Monroe Boyd baring his teeth in front of a hallway running to the back of the house. He had one arm around Tommy Corcoran's chest under the arms, holding him kicking above the floor. His other hand had a switchblade in it with the point pressing the boy's jugular.

"Tommy!" Charlotte Corcoran had gotten out on the passenger's side. She took a step and stopped. Boyd bettered his grip.

"Mommy," said the boy.

"What about it, trooper? Seven or seventy, they all bleed the same."

I relaxed my hold on the gun.

A shot slammed the walls and a blue hole appeared under Boyd's left eye. He let go of Tommy and lay down. Twitched once.

I looked up at Frank Corcoran crouched at the top of the staircase to the second story. His arm was stretched out full length with his gun in it, leaking smoke. He glanced at Tommy. "I told you to stay upstairs with me."

"I left my ball here." The boy pouted, then spotted Boyd's body. "Funny man."

Mrs. Corcoran flew forward and knelt to throw her arms around her son. Corcoran saw her for the first time, said "Charlotte?" and looked at me. The gun came around.

"Stop waving that thing," his ex-wife said, hugging Tommy. "He's with me."

Corcoran hesitated, then lowered the weapon. He surveyed the damage. "What do I tell the rental agent?"

I heard the sirens then.

Moving Spirit

•

Arthur C. Clarke

For close to forty years, Arthur C. Clarke has been in the top echelon of popular and influential writers of science fact and fiction. His 1968 original screenplay, 2001: A Space Odyssey, *resulted in a film of classic proportions; and such novels as* Rendezvous with Rama *(1973) have been bestsellers. He hasn't often turned his hand to the criminous tale, but when so moved the result has been something special. "Moving Spirit" is not only spirited and spirit-full: it contains a mad scientist to make it an even headier brew.*

We were discussing a sensational trial at the Old Bailey when Harry Purvis, whose talent for twisting the conversation to his own ends is really unbelievable, remarked casually: "I was once an expert witness in a rather interesting case."

"Only a *witness*?" said Drew, as he deftly filled two glasses of Bass at once.

"Yes—but it was a rather close thing. It was in the early part of the war, about the time we were expecting the invasion. That's why you never heard about it at the time."

"What makes you assume," said Charles Willis suspiciously, "that we never did hear of it?"

It was one of the few times I'd ever seen Harry caught trying to cover up his tracks. "Qui s'excuse s'accuse," I thought to myself, and waited to see what evading action he'd take.

"It was such a peculiar case," he replied with dignity, "that I'm sure you'd have reminded me of it if you ever saw the reports. My name was featured quite prominently. It all happened in an out-of-the-way part of Cornwall, and it concerned the best example of that rare species, the genuine mad scientist, that I've ever met.''

Perhaps that wasn't really a fair description, Purvis amended hastily. Homer Ferguson was eccentric and had little foibles like keeping a pet boa constrictor to catch the mice, and never wearing shoes around the house. But he was so rich that no one noticed things like this.

Homer was also a competent scientist. Many years ago he had graduated from Edinburgh University but having plenty of money he had never done a stroke of real work in his life. Instead, he pottered round the old vicarage he'd bought not far from Newquay and amused himself building gadgets. In the last forty years he'd invented television, ball-point pens, jet propulsion, and a few other trifles. However, as he had never bothered to take out any patents, other people had got the credit. This didn't worry him in the least as he was of a singularly generous disposition, except with money.

It seemed that, in some complicated way, Purvis was one of his few living relatives. Consequently when Harry received a telegram one day requesting his assistance at once, he knew better than to refuse. No one knew exactly how much money Homer had, or what he intended to do with it. Harry thought he had as good a chance as anyone, and he didn't intend to jeopardize it. At some inconvenience he made the journey down to Cornwall and turned up at the rectory.

He saw what was wrong as soon as he entered the grounds. Uncle Homer (he wasn't really an uncle, but he'd been called that as long as Harry could remember) had a shed beside the main building which he used for his experiments. That shed was now minus roof and windows, and a sickly odor hovered around it. There had obviously been an explosion, and Harry wondered, in a disinterested sort of way, if Uncle had been badly injured and wanted advice on drawing up a new will.

He ceased day-dreaming when the old man, looking the picture of health (apart from some sticking plaster on his face), opened the door for him.

"Good of you to come so quickly," he boomed. He seemed genuinely pleased to see Harry. Then his face clouded over.

31

"Fact is, my boy, I'm in a bit of a jam and I want you to help. My case comes up before the local Bench tomorrow."

This was a considerable shock. Homer had been as law-abiding a citizen as any motorist in petrol-rationed Britain could be expected to be. And if it was the usual black-market business, Harry didn't see how he could be expected to help.

"Sorry to hear about this, Uncle. What's the trouble?"

"It's a long story. Come into the library and we'll talk it over."

Homer Ferguson's library occupied the entire west wing of the somewhat decrepit building. Harry believed that bats nested in the rafters, but had never been able to prove it. When Homer had cleared a table by the simple expedient of tilting all the books off onto the floor, he whistled three times, a voice-operated relay tripped somewhere, and a gloomy Cornish voice drifted out of a concealed loudspeaker.

"Yes, Mr. Ferguson?"

"Maida, send across a bottle of the new whiskey."

There was no reply except an audible sniff. But a moment later there came a creaking and clanking, and a couple of square feet of library shelving slid aside to reveal a conveyor belt.

"I can't get Maida to come into the library," complained Homer, lifting out a loaded tray. "She's afraid of Boanerges, though he's perfectly harmless."

Harry found it hard not to feel some sympathy for the invisible Maida. All six feet of Boanerges was draped over the case holding the *Encyclopedia Britannica*, and a bulge amidships indicated that he had dined recently.

"What do you think of the whiskey?" asked Homer when Harry had sampled some and started to gasp for breath.

"It's —well, I don't know what to say. It's—phew—rather strong. I never thought—"

"Oh, don't take any notice of the label on the bottle. *This* brand never saw Scotland. And that's what all the trouble's about. I made it right here on the premises."

"Uncle!"

"Yes, I know it's against the law, and all that sort of nonsense. But you can't get any good whiskey these days—it all goes for

32

export. It seemed to me that I was being patriotic making my own, so that there was more left over for the dollar drive. But the Excise people don't see it that way.''

''I think you'd better let me have the whole story,'' said Harry. He was gloomily sure that there was nothing he could do to get his uncle out of this scrape.

Homer had always been fond of the bottle, and wartime shortages had hit him badly. He was also, as has been hinted, disinclined to give away money, and for a long time he had resented the fact that he had to pay a tax of several hundred percent on a bottle of whiskey. When he couldn't get his own supply any more, he had decided it was time to act.

The district he was living in probably had a good deal to do with his decision. For some centuries, the Customs and Excise had waged a never-ending battle with the Cornish fisherfolk. It was rumored that the last incumbent of the old vicarage had possessed the finest cellar in the district next to that of the Bishop himself—and had never paid a penny in duty on it. So Uncle Homer merely felt he was carrying on an old and noble tradition.

There was little doubt, moreover, that the spirit of pure scientific inquiry also inspired him. He felt sure that this business about being aged in the wood for seven years was all rubbish, and was confident that he could do a better job with ultrasonics and ultraviolet rays.

The experiment went well for a few weeks. But late one evening there was one of those unfortunate accidents that will happen even in the best-conducted laboratories, and before Uncle knew what had happened, he was draped over a beam, while the grounds of the vicarage were littered with pieces of copper tubing.

Even then it would not have mattered much had not the local Home Guard been practicing in the neighborhood. As soon as they heard the explosion, they immediately went into action, Sten guns at the ready. Had the invasion started? If so, they'd soon fix it.

They were a little disappointed to discover that it was only Uncle, but as they were used to his experiments they weren't in the least surprised at what had happened. Unfortunately for Uncle, the Lieutenant in charge of the squad happened to be the local exciseman, and the combined evidence of his nose and his eyes told him the story in a flash.

"So tomorrow," said Uncle Homer, looking rather like a small boy who had been caught stealing candy, "I have to go up before the Bench, charged with possessing an illegal still."

"I should have thought," replied Harry, "that was a matter for the Assizes, not the local magistrates."

"We do things our own way here," answered Homer, with more than a touch of pride. Harry was soon to discover how true this was.

They got little sleep that night, as Homer outlined his defense, overcame Harry's objections, and hastily assembled the apparatus he intended to produce in court.

"A Bench like this," he explained, "is always impressed by experts. If we dared, I'd like to say you were someone from the War Office, but they could check up on that. So we'll just tell them the truth—about your qualifications, that is."

"Thank you," said Harry. "And suppose my college finds out what I'm doing?"

"Well, you won't claim to be acting for anyone except yourself. The whole thing is a private venture."

"I'll say it is," said Harry.

The next morning they loaded their gear into Homer's ancient Austin, and drove into the village. The Bench was sitting in one of the classrooms of the local school, and Harry felt that time had rolled back a few years and he was about to have an unpleasant interview with his old headmaster.

"We're in luck," whispered Homer, as they were ushered into their cramped seats. "Major Fotheringham is in the chair. He's a good friend of mine."

That would help a lot, Harry agreed. But there were two other justices on the Bench as well, and one friend in court would hardly be sufficient. Eloquence, not influence, was the only thing that could save the day.

The courtroom was crowded, and Harry found it surprising that so many people had managed to get away from work long enough to watch the case. Then he realized the local interest that it would have aroused, in view of the fact that—in normal times, at least—smuggling was a major industry in these parts. He was not sure whether that would mean a sympathetic audience. The natives might well regard Homer's form of private enterprise as unfair competition. On the other hand, they probably approved on general principles with anything that put the excisemen's noses out of joint.

The charge was read by the Clerk of the Court, and the somewhat damning evidence produced. Pieces of copper tubing were solemnly inspected by the justices, each of whom in turn looked severely at Uncle Homer. Harry began to see his hypothetical inheritance becoming even more doubtful.

When the case for the prosecution was completed, Major Fotheringham turned to Homer.

"This appears to be a serious matter, Mr. Ferguson. I hope you have a satisfactory explanation."

"I have, your Honor," replied the defendant in a tone that practically reeked of injured innocence. It was amusing to see His Honor's look of relief, and the momentary frown, quickly replaced by calm confidence, that passed across the face of H. M. Customs and Excise.

"Do you wish to have a legal representative? I notice that you have not brought one with you."

"It won't be necessary. The whole case is founded on such a trivial misunderstanding that it can be cleared up without complications like that. I don't wish to incur the prosecution in unnecessary costs."

This frontal onslaught brought a murmur from the body of the court, and a flush to the cheeks of the Customs man. For the first time he began to look a little unsure of himself. If Ferguson thought the Crown would be paying costs, he must have a pretty good case. Of course, he might only be bluffing. . . .

Homer waited until the mild stir had died away before creating a considerably greater one.

"I have called a scientific expert to explain what happened at the vicarage," he said. "And owing to the nature of the evidence, I must ask, for security reasons, that the rest of the proceedings be *in camera*."

"You want me to clear the court?" said the chairman incredulously.

"I am afraid so, sir. My colleague, Dr. Purvis, feels that the fewer people concerned in this case, the better. When you have heard the evidence, I think you will agree with him. If I might say so, it is a great pity that it has already attracted so much publicity. I am afraid it may bring certain—ah—confidential matters to the wrong ears."

Homer glared at the Customs officer, who fidgeted uncomfortably in his seat.

"Oh, very well," said Major Fotheringham. "This is all very irregular, but we live in irregular times. Mr. Clerk, clear the court."

After some grumbling and confusion, and an overruled protest from the prosecution, the order was carried out. Then, under the interested gaze of the dozen people left in the room, Harry Purvis uncovered the apparatus he had unloaded from the Baby Austin. After his qualifications had been presented to the court, he took the witness stand.

"I wish to explain, your Honor," he began, "that I have been engaged on explosives research, and that is why I happen to be acquainted with the defendant's work." The opening part of this statement was perfectly true. It was about the last thing said that day that was.

"You mean—bombs and so forth?"

"Precisely, but on a fundamental level. We are always looking for new and better types of explosives, as you can imagine. Moreover, we in government research and the academic world are continually on the lookout for good ideas from outside sources. And quite recently, Unc—er, Mr. Ferguson, wrote to us with a most interesting suggestion for a completely new type of explosive. The interesting thing about it was that it employed *nonexplosive* materials such as sugar, starch and so on."

"Eh?" said the Chairman. "A nonexplosive explosive? That's impossible."

Harry smiled sweetly.

"I know, sir—that is one's immediate reaction. But like most great ideas, this has the simplicity of genius. I am afraid, however, that I shall have to do a little explaining to make my point."

The Bench looked very attentive, and also a little alarmed. Harry surmised that it had probably encountered expert witnesses before. He walked over to a table that had been set up in the middle of the courtroom, and which was now covered with flasks, piping, and bottles of liquids.

"I hope, Mr. Purvis," said the Chairman nervously, "that you're not going to do anything dangerous."

"Of course not, sir. I merely wish to demonstrate some basic scientific principles. Once again, I wish to stress the importance of keeping this between these four walls." He paused solemnly and everyone looked duly impressed.

"Mr. Ferguson," he began, "is proposing to tap one of the fundamental forces of nature. It is a force on which every living thing depends—a force, gentlemen, which keeps *you* alive, even though you may never have heard of it."

He moved over to the table and took up his position beside the flasks and bottles.

"Have you ever stopped to consider," he said, "how the sap manages to reach the highest leaf of a tall tree? It takes a lot of force to pump water a hundred—sometimes over three hundred—feet from the ground. Where does that force come from? I'll show you, with this practical example.

"Here I have a strong container, divided into two parts by a porous membrane. On one side of the membrane is pure water—on the other, a concentrated solution of sugar and other chemicals which I do not propose to specify. Under these conditions, a pressure is set up, known as *osmotic* pressure. The pure water tries to pass through the membrane, as if to dilute the solution on the other side. I've now sealed the container, and you'll notice the pressure gauge here on the right—see how the pointer's going up. That's osmotic pressure for you. This same force acts through the cell walls in our bodies, causing fluid movement. It drives the sap up the trunk of the trees, from the roots to the topmost branches. It's a universal force, and a powerful one. To Mr. Ferguson must go the credit of first attempting to harness it.''

Harry paused impressively and looked around the court.

"Mr. Ferguson," he said, "was attempting to develop the Osmotic Bomb."

It took some time for this so sink in. Then Major Fotheringham leaned forward and said in a hushed voice: "Are we to presume that he had succeeded in manufacturing this bomb, and that it exploded in his workshop?"

"Precisely, your Honor. It is a pleasure—an unusual pleasure, I might say—to present a case to so perspicacious a court. Mr. Ferguson had succeeded, and he was preparing to report his method to us when, owing to an unfortunate oversight, a safety device attached to the bomb failed to operate. The results, you all know. I think you will need no further evidence of the power of this weapon—and you will realize its importance when I point out that the solutions it contains are all extremely common chemicals."

Major Fotheringham, looking a little puzzled, turned to the prosecution lawyer.

"Mr. Whiting," he said, "have you any questions to ask the witness?"

"I certainly have, your Honor. I've never heard such a ridiculous—"

"You will please confine yourself to questions of fact."

"Very good, your Honor. May I ask the witness how he accounts for the large quantity of alcohol vapor immediately after the explosion?"

"I rather doubt if the inspector's nose was capable of accurate quantitative analysis. But admittedly there was some alcohol vapor released. The solution used in the bomb contained about 25 percent. By employing dilute alcohol, the mobility of the inorganic ions is restricted and the osmotic pressure raised—a desirable effect, of course."

That should hold them for a while, thought Harry. He was right. It was a good couple of minutes before the second question. Then the prosecution's spokesman waved one of the pieces of copper tubing in the air.

"What function did these carry out?" he said, in as nasty a tone of voice as he could manage. Harry affected not to notice the sneer.

"Manometer tubing for the pressure gauges," he replied promptly.

The Bench, it was clear, was already far out of its depth. This was just where Harry wanted it to be. But the prosecution still had one card up its sleeve. There was a furtive whispering between the exciseman and his legal eagle. Harry looked nervously at Uncle Homer, who shrugged shoulders with a "Don't ask *me*!" gesture.

"I have some additional evidence I wish to present to the court," said the Customs laywer briskly, as a bulky brown paper parcel was hoisted onto the table.

"Is this in order, your Honor?" protested Harry. "All evidence against my—ah—colleague should have already been presented."

"I withdraw my statement," the lawyer interjectedly swiftly. "Let us say that this is not evidence for *this* case, but material for later proceedings." He paused ominously to let that sink in. "Nevertheless, if Mr. Ferguson can give a satisfactory answer to our questions now, this whole business can be cleared up right away." It was obvious that the last thing the speaker expected— or hoped for—was such a satisfactory explanation.

He unwrapped the brown paper, and there were three bottles of a famous brand of whiskey.

"Uh-huh," said Uncle Homer. "I was wondering—"

"Mr. Ferguson," said the chairman of the Bench. "There is no need for you to make any statement unless you wish."

Harry Purvis shot Major Fotheringham a grateful glance. He guessed what had happened. The prosecution had, when prowling through the ruins of Uncle's laboratory, acquired some bottles of his home brew. Their action was probably illegal, since they would not have had a search warrant—hence the reluctance in producing the evidence. The case had seemed sufficiently clear-cut without it.

It certainly appeared pretty clear-cut now. . . .

"These bottles," said the representative of the Crown, "do

not contain the brand advertised on the label. They have obviously been used as convenient receptacles for the defendant's—shall we say—chemical solutions.'' He gave Harry Purvis an unsympathetic glance. ''We have had these solutions analyzed, with most interesting results. Apart from an abnormally high alcohol concentration, the contents of these bottles are virtually indistinguishable from—''

He never had time to finish his unsolicited and certainly unwanted testimonial to Uncle Homer's skill. For at that moment, Harry Purvis became aware of an ominous whistling sound. At first he thought it was a falling bomb—but that seemed unlikely, as there had been no air raid warning. Then he realized that the whistling came from close at hand; from the courtroom table, in fact. . . .

''Take cover!'' he yelled.

The court went into recess with a speed never matched in the annals of British law. The three justices disappeared behind the dais; those in the body of the room burrowed into the floor or sheltered under desks. For a protracted, anguished moment nothing happened, and Harry wondered if he had given a false alarm. Then there was a dull, peculiarly muffled explosion, a great tinkling of glass—and a smell like a blitzed brewery. Slowly, the court emerged from shelter.

The Osmotic Bomb had proved its power. More important still, it had destroyed the evidence for the prosecution.

The Bench was none too happy about dismissing the case; it felt, with good reason, that its dignity had been assailed. Moreover, each one of the justices would have to do some fast talking when he got home; the mist of alcohol had penetrated everything. Though the Clerk of the Court rushed round opening windows (none of which, oddly enough, had been broken) the fumes seemed reluctant to disperse. Harry Purvis, as he removed pieces of bottle glass from his hair, wondered if there would be some intoxicated pupils in class tomorrow.

Major Fotheringham, however, was undoubtedly a real sport, and as they filed out of the devastated courtroom, Harry heard him say to his Uncle: ''Look here, Ferguson—it'll be ages before we can get those Molotov cocktails we've been promised by the War Office. What about making some of these bombs of yours for the Home Guard? If they don't knock out a tank, at least they'll make the crew drunk and incapable."

"I'll certainly think about it, Major," replied Uncle Homer, who still seemed a little dazed by the turn of events.

He recovered somewhat as they drove back to the vicarage along the narrow, winding lanes with their high walls of unmortared stone.

"I hope, Uncle," remarked Harry, when they had reached a relatively straight stretch and it seemed safe to talk to the driver, "that you don't intend to rebuild that still. They'll be watching you like hawks and you won't get away with it again."

"Very well," said Uncle, a little sulkily. "Confound these brakes! I had them fixed only just before the war!"

"Hey!" cried Harry. "Watch out!"

It was too late. They had come to a crossroads at which a brand new HALT sign had been erected. Uncle braked hard, but for a moment nothing happened. Then the wheels on the left seized up, while those on the right continued gaily spinning. the car did a hairpin bend, luckily without turning over, and ended in the ditch pointing in the direction from which it had come.

Harry looked reproachfully at his Uncle. He was about to frame a suitable reprimand when a motorcycle came out of the side turning and drew up to them.

It was not going to be their lucky day, after all. The village police sergeant had been lurking in ambush, waiting to catch motorists at the new sign. He parked his machine by the roadside and leaned in through the window of the Austin.

"You all right, Mr. Ferguson?" he said. Then his nose wrinkled up, and he looked like Jove about to deliver a thunderbolt. "This won't do," he said. "I'll have to put you on a charge. Driving under the influence is a *very* serious business."

"But I've not touched a drop all day!" protested Uncle, waving an alcohol-sodden sleeve under the sergeant's twitching nose.

"Do you expect me to believe *that*?" snorted the irate policeman, pulling out his notebook. "I'm afraid you'll have to come to the station with me. Is your friend sober enough to drive?"

Harry Purvis didn't answer for a moment. He was too busy beating his head against the dash-board.

"Well," we asked Harry. "What did they do to your Uncle?"

"Oh, he got fined five pounds and had his license endorsed for drunken driving. Major Fotheringham wasn't in the chair, unfortunately, when the case came up, but the other two justices were still on the Bench. I guess they felt that even if he was innocent this time, there was a limit to everything."

"And did you ever get any of his money?"

"No fear! He was very grateful, of course, and he's told me that I'm mentioned in his will. But when I saw him last, what do you think he was doing? He was searching for the Elixir of Life."

Harry sighed at the overwhelming injustice of things.

"Sometimes," he said gloomily, "I'm afraid he's found it. The doctors say he's the healthiest seventy-year-old they've ever seen. So all I got out of the whole affair was some interesting memories and a hangover."

"A hangover?" asked Charlie Willis.

"Yes," replied Harry, a faraway look in his eye. "You see, the exciseman hadn't seized *all* the evidence. We had to—ah—destroy the rest. It took us the best part of a week. We invented all sorts of things during that time—but we never discovered what they were."

Address Unknown

•

Joyce Harrington

Joyce Harrington's first published fiction, "The Purple Shroud," was the recipient of a Mystery Writers of America Edgar for Best Short Story of 1972. Since then she has written dozens of equally fine stories, such as "Address Unknown," which deal with the conflicts and dangers not only of contemporary society but within the human mind. She also has to her credit three well-received crime novels: No One Knows My Name *(1980),* Family Reunion *(1982), and* Dreemz of the Night *(1987).*

It happened again today.

I couldn't remember my address. Well, that's nothing. Not a serious lapse. It could happen to anyone. Just a minor short circuit in the good old memory bank. Only it's happened several times lately, and each time it happens I feel peculiar afterward.

The first time, I'd been working late and decided to catch a cab home. It was almost ten o'clock when I finally let myself out of the office. The night guard must have been off on his rounds because the reception area was dim and eerie and deserted. The lobby of the huge building was pretty much the same, and I almost despaired of finding a cab before I dragged myself through the revolving doors and out onto the deserted and eerie but well-lit midtown street. But a cab was slowly nosing toward me from the end of the block and I flagged it down with my last ounce of strength. When it stopped, I crawled into its lumpy, foul-smelling back seat, gave the driver the address, and closed my eyes.

We jounced and rattled for a while, stopped and started, swerved and had a few near misses. I didn't open my eyes for any of it. I knew the passing scene well, too well. I was weary, disgruntled, hungry, and bored. All I wanted was to get home and fall into bed, and hope that Mitchell had walked the dog and wasn't too put out about my lateness. When I felt the cab pulling over to the curb and the driver said, "Four sixty," I opened my eyes and groped for my handbag. And then I looked out the window.

"But this isn't—I mean, how did we get here?"

Here. Here wasn't home. Not any more. It had been home in the pre-Mitchell days, the pre-big-important-job days, the days of wine and poets and spaghetti and going up on the roof to see the sun rise over Manhattan. Here was a funny little building in Greenwich Village where one room was all I could afford, but it was all I needed then.

"Driver," I muttered, embarrassed. "I made a mistake. I wanted to go to—" And that's when I couldn't remember.

"Four sixty, lady," the driver repeated. "If you want to go somewheres else I'll have to start the meter again. I already shut it off."

"Never mind," I said. I gave him a five-dollar bill and some change and got out.

The street looked the same. The same worn stoops, the same dented garbage cans, the same children's games chalked on the sidewalk. And the same battle-scarred orange tomcat slinking in the shadows. Or his son. Or grandson. How long had it been? Eight years? Nine? The front of the house that had once been home told me nothing. My room had been at the back, its single window overlooking the back yards and clotheslines. But I'd had a windowbox full of petunias in the spring, and chives and sweet basil. I never cooked spaghetti anymore and hadn't seen a petunia in years. Plants didn't seem to thrive in my apartment, our apartment. Maybe it's because there isn't time to talk to them.

I started walking. There were people on the street. There are *always* people on the street in the Village. Young people, casually dressed. Sandals, jeans, loose floppy dresses on tall rangy girls, tight leather trousers on slim young men walking thin nervous dogs. I felt overdressed in my lady-executive crisply tailored summer beige two-piece with my Crouch & Fitzgerald lady's briefcase hanging from its strap on my shoulder.

Around the corner then, more people, more dogs, idling away a summer night, gossiping, laughing, scratching fleas. And the coffee house, the same old coffee house with its wire-backed chairs and marble tables and the fading dingy murals of the last days of Pompeii. I went in and sat at the table, the very table where I used to sit for hours, sipping slow espresso and reading Rilke and Eliot and sometimes Baudelaire.

The waitress was new and young—well, waitresses come and go, don't they, and she didn't know me. She brought me espresso and a cannoli. Pastry had been out of bounds for me for years, but that night I dug into the sweet, thick creamy filling and the crisp outer shell as if diets had never been invented. The coffee was strong and thick and black, just the way I liked it. I sipped it slowly. There was plenty to read in my briefcase, none of it poetic, so I read nothing but tried to figure out what had happened.

Obviously I'd given the wrong address to the cab driver. My old address, and he'd faithfully delivered me there. A simple mistake brought on by stress, overwork, and a subconscious yen to return to simpler times. So far, so good. But then, when I tried to give him the correct address—the elegant, expensive condominium apartment where Mitchell was waiting for me—I couldn't for the life of me remember where it was. How about that? Must mean something. But what? sitting in the coffee house, dawdling over the dregs of my espresso, I knew perfectly well where I lived.

And I'd better get there quick. It was past eleven and Mitchell liked to get to bed no later than eleven thirty on week nights. It was part of his drinking-man's health routine. I considered calling him, but thought better of it. He might be sleeping already, and I didn't want to risk waking him. And I wasn't so very sure that if I picked up a telephone and started to dial, I would remember what number I was calling.

Back on the street a cab found me quickly. I thought it was because I looked so out of place and uptownish. I was home in ten minutes. Mitchell was asleep. Hank, the dog, a young but cagey black mutt from the pound, was pretending to be asleep on the white velvet sofa in the living room. Forbidden territory— he had a huge plaid pillow on the floor in my study, but I let him lie. Sleeping dogs, and all that. I crept into bed beside Mitchell as quietly as I could. He didn't stir.

That was the first time.

There was a second and a third time over the next few weeks. Not quite as jarring as the first time. Simple things really. Like sending out invitations to a cocktail party and coming up blank at the space for the return address. That was easy. I was sitting at my desk in my study at home, and I simply glanced at a piece of mail addressed to me. And shrugged it off. Or making reservations for our trip to Ireland in early September. I was at the office on the phone talking to the airline reservation clerk when the blankness struck. I'd had to scrabble in my handbag and finally had the presence of mind to look at my driver's license. The clerk must have thought I was balmy, or trying to hide something.

The vacation trip to Ireland was fine. Well, almost fine. I'd had to fly over to London for a couple of days on business. Despite Mrs. Thatcher, the British aren't quite accustomed to women making international deals, no matter how minor. But that's what I was there for, and that's how come Mitchell and I were vacationing in a stately thatched cottage on the West Coast of Ireland. So that I could be within leaping distance if anything should go wrong.

Mitchell hated Ireland. He said it was damp and boring and there was nothing to do but drink. He really wanted to go to New Zealand and ski. I hate skiing vacations. I never learned how and don't want to, so I get cold and bored and maybe drink a little too much.

The two days in London turned into three. It was about as hot as London ever gets and sticky as flypaper. The gentlemen I was dealing with were very gentlemanly and negotiations moved at a seemly pace. But I sensed a polite perplexity when evening came and it was time to entertain me. Obviously I couldn't be treated as one of the boys. Wives appeared, and they did their best. My answers to their cautious questions seemed to reassure them, somewhat. Yes, I was married. No, I had no children. Yes, my husband had a job, a rather important one in television. (I didn't tell them that Mitchell was an unsuccessful actor who had turned to writing soap operas.) Yes, I enjoyed my work, and no, I didn't find it difficult to be both wife and career woman. (Well, what else could I tell them? That Mitchell had turned silent and sullen lately, and that I was overtired and suffering lapses of memory?)

At last it was over, the papers signed, the celebration dinner eaten, and the telephone call to my boss back in New York made. He virtually assured me that there'd be a promotion and a substantial raise waiting for me when I got back. All I wanted to do was settle down for the next few days in that picturesque cottage by the seashore and read Keats and try to find out what Mitchell was thinking. About us.

Mitchell had brought along his portable typewriter and a ream of paper. His idea was that after five years of writing soaps, it was time he tried something more ambitious. A novel. And as long as we were spending two weeks in Ireland, where there was nothing else to do, he might as well get it started. Ireland seemed to inspire a lot of novel writing. Maybe some of it would rub off.

When I drove the rented car up the lane to the cottage (electrified and plumbed for the convenience of American visitors) in the misty twilight, it's windows were dark. I honked the horn, hoping for some help with my luggage. Not that there was a lot of it. One small suitcase and my ever-present briefcase. Nothing I couldn't handle myself, but it would have been nice. The cottage remained dark and quiet.

I got out of the car and pushed open the cottage door.

"Mitchell! I'm back."

No answer. I'd telephoned him twice from London. Once to tell him of the extra day needed to finish the deal, and again from the airport to let him know when I'd be arriving. And I'd hinted that it might be nice if he could somewhere in the village find a bottle of champagne to celebrate my victory. Maybe that's where he'd gone.

I switched on the lights and stood in the doorway, appalled.

The place was a mess. The cottage had only two rooms, a large one with a kitchen at one end and a collection of miscellaneous chairs and sofas at the other and a round dining table in the middle, and a smaller one that was our bedroom. Between the two, space had been carved out to accommodate a cranky bathroom. We'd rented the cottage from glowing descriptions furnished by the travel agent; the glow came after a sufficiency of Guinness stout had been swallowed.

And that, from the looks of it, was precisely what had happened. Stout bottles littered the floor, the table, and kitchen sink, the window sills, everywhere I looked. All empty. Among them were scattered the occasional empty whiskey bottle, dirty dishes used as ashtrays, wrinkled clothes, and, unaccountably, a goat. A nanny goat I gathered, as she bleated and clopped past me on her way to freedom through the open door. The smell was fierce.

Mitchell had apparently been having a party.

I looked in the bedroom. More of the same, around a tumbled unmade bed. The bathroom showed signs of someone having been sick.

Welcome home, I said to myself. Congratulations and all that. I was tempted to get back in the car and drive until I found a clean hotel with a cheap *single* room and have a nice clean bath and get into a freshly made bed. But what about reading Keats in the cool of the evening by a peat fire in a stone fireplace? The stone fireplace was there all right, and I began by clearing the stout bottles off its mantel.

An hour later I'd heaped most of the trash into a small mountain behind the house, cleaned the bathroom, and remade the bed. There was no sign of Mitchell. I took a bath, unpacked my suitcase, and sat down in the armchair by the fireplace with Keats in my lap, to wait.

Waiting is hard for me to do. It wasn't always. I can remember days that seemed to have no end while I was waiting for something important to happen to me. I wasn't impatient then. I always knew that there was time enough and important things didn't just come along every day. Mitchell was important. I knew that from the moment I met him.

It was at a party, a different kind of party from the ones I usually went to in those days. These were some friends of my parents who were celebrating the graduation of their son from law school. With honors. The crowd was mixed, both my parents' generation and my own, and I knew the young man slightly from joint attempts by both families to get us interested in each other. We weren't interested but had gone out together a couple of times, just to keep the peace.

That night he was shyly pleased with himself and accepted both the teasing and the congratulations of the guests with solemn grace. We sat together for a while and he told me how hard it had been for him in school but that the grind had been well worth it because now he'd been offered a fine position with a large corporation and the future was dazzling. His salary awed me.

I'd agreed to come to his party out of discontent. He gave me a focus for my malaise. I, too, could go back to school and make the important thing happen for me. I'd spent enough time with bearded poets and cheap wine, waiting for I didn't know what. Then and there I decided to take charge of my life. My parents would be only too glad to help me out, although my mother, I knew, still cherished notions of becoming a young grandmother. Anything would be better than the aimless drifting which was all I had done since leaving college. In the meantime I listened to the fledgling lawyer's modest boasting—he managed the balance quite nicely—and gazed around the room.

When my eyes met the dark ones of the man standing alone at the makeshift bar, I knew. This was important. He was handsome, but not in the pretty sulky way of male models. His hair was dark and flecked with gray at the temples. His face had good bones and a few character lines, a nose that was more hawk than sparrow, a wide mouth that smiled at me and showed big, strong, white teeth. He was tall, but not too tall, and looked exactly as you would want your doctor to look. Capable, calm, understanding. He left the bar and began walking toward us.

"Uh-oh," said my friend. "I'm about to lose you. That's Mitchell Sands bearing down on us and he looks like he means business. Be warned. Don't ever call him Mitch. He hates it and has been known to inflict damage on those who dare to use it. He's an actor and crazy and one of my closest friends. I met him on a wilderness survival trip, and he made damn sure I survived.''

My friend finished his whispered commentary just as Mitchell Sands arrived at my side.

''Congratulations to the survivor of law school,'' he said. ''Everything you learned on the trail with me, you can put to use in the corporate jungle. I don't believe I know this lady.''

I hadn't been called a lady in years. Bearded poets don't go in much for ladyhood these days. Coming from Mitchell on the heels of my new resolve, it sounded just fine. My friend did the introductions and tactfully disappeared. Mitchell and I were inseparable from that moment. He'd had a streak of phenomenal luck, had money in the bank, a brand-new apartment, and a good role in a to-be-filmed-in-New York movie. I told him of my idea of going back to school, probably business school because neither law nor medicine appealed to me, but I'd always been good at math although I'd tried to hide it. He thought the idea was wonderful; he thought *I* was wonderful. We left the party together. We were married three weeks later.

I discovered I had a talent for finance and an unsuspected ability to convince people to see things my way. I zipped through business school as if it were a perpetual Fourth of July picnic. Oh, it was hard work, all right. But I enjoyed every minute of it, especially the competitiveness of my fellow students. *Especially* when I bested everyone, men and women alike, and finished top of my class. But with Mitchell there to encourage me, it had been easy, a piece of cake.

And finding a job had been a piece of cake, too. Women were in, and qualified women were still pretty scarce. I took the best of the offers and settled in to prove that I was worth every cent of the staggering amount of money I was being paid. Mitchell was proud of me. My father openly bragged about me to his cronies. My mother looked a little wistful sometimes, but never mentioned grandchildren.

It was about this time that Mitchell's career took a downward turn. It wasn't noticeable at first. Only that there were longer and longer free periods between jobs. Nothing you could really put your finger on. He went to fewer and fewer auditions. His agent began not returning phone calls. He hadn't done television commercials since his early apprentice days, and how he suffered the indignity of being rejected for those.

Finally, after a six-month dry spell, he went on a raging bender with an old buddy and turned up two days later, sick, repentant, and with a temporary job filling in for a soap writer who'd wrecked himself and his car by plowing into the rear end of a disabled milk tank truck. The writer never came back. Mitchell found himself churning out low-key dialogue and fevered plots, permanently.

"It could be worse," he said. "I could have gone into the fascinating world of high finance."

"What does that mean?" I asked.

"Nothing. At least I'm still in show business."

"Which is no business."

Which is just about where things fetched up, and still are, between Mitchell and me. We have no problems about money; I make more than enough for the two of us to live well, even luxuriously. Mitchell's pittance from his soap opera jobs keeps him well supplied with the flashy clothes he's come to hanker for, and the Scotch whiskey and vitamins that get delivered by the case. I've thought about divorce and, I'm sure, so has he. But big corporations tend to be conservative and although divorce is tolerated among the underlings, none of the top men carry such a blot. I just don't know how the company would feel about me as a divorcee. It's too risky right now. Besides, I don't relish the prospect, and it's a real one, of having to pay alimony.

So on we go, Mitchell and I, keeping carefully quiet about most things, still inseparable, taking idyllic vacations in Ireland where maybe, just maybe, given half a chance, we can straighten something out.

I shifted in my chair, the volume of Keats heavy in my lap, and glanced at the clock on the mantel. Two in the morning. And still no Mitchell. I wondered if I ought to be worried. From the look of the cottage when I arrived, he was probably drunk.

That happened more and more often lately. And he would sober up with large applications of vegetable juice and vitamin pills. There was no vegetable juice in the cottage. I went to bed.

In the morning Mitchell was there, sprawled over more than half of the bed, fully clothed. He smelled of stale beer and tobacco (he didn't smoke) and something sweetish and cloying. In the clean morning light his stylish denims showed grease spots and his hair was full of small burrs. I left him there making sounds somewhere between a snore and a gurgle, and went into the other room to make coffee.

Through the window at the kitchen end of the cottage I saw that our daily help had arrived and was staring at the mountain of trash in the backyard with something approaching awe.

She came in and said, "I don't know who you're going to get to cart *that* away."

Her voice was soft and her words flavored with Ireland. She was a pretty girl with the name of Rose. It suited her fresh pink and blondness, but she was sturdy as well, strong and well-fleshed. Her rosiness could turn blowsy in just a few short years. She looked everywhere in the main room but at me.

"What do you know about this, Rose?"

"Who, me?"

"You were here yesterday, weren't you?"

"Oh, yes, Ma'am. I was here. And I fried a nice fish for his dinner. He likes fried fish."

Her unspoken criticism hung on the air between us like the leftover scent of her cooking. I should have been here frying fish for my man instead of gallivanting all over London.

"He likes nothing of the kind."

"He ate it, then."

Was she smirking? Turning away to hide the sly grin? Or was she just looking over the remaining devastation in the room and planning her day's work?

"This place'll have to be cleaned up," I told her. "It's a mess."

"Oh, yes, Ma'am," she breathed. "Leave 'em alone for a minute and they'll be creating. Pigs, they are."

Her mention of pigs reminded me of the goat that had been my welcoming committee.

"Where did the goat come from?"

"Was there a goat, too?"

Her innocence was impregnable. I didn't believe it for a minute. The coffee was ready and I poured myself a cup. A groan from the bedroom came between us. Her eyes flicked to the narrow passage and away again.

"Is he sleeping, then? I'll be quiet."

"Dead to the world. But he'll be up soon, popping vitamins and pretending nothing has happened." I decided on the direct approach. "What *has* happened, Rose?"

"Ma'am?"

"Between you and him. What's been going on?"

"Oh, Ma'am. Nothing, Ma'am. Only he had a party, don't you see."

"Yes, I can see that."

"Oh, everyone was here. It was the best party ever. Devlin the postman sang, and there was fish and sausages for all. I thought my hands was surely going to stick to the frying pan there was so much of it. And they closed the pub for three days because everyone was doing their drinking here for free. And then they decided they was going to teach him how to milk a goat because he said he didn't know how and he wanted to write something about it in a book or something that he was writing, so Fenella went and got her goat and they did, and I don't know what all else."

Rose was sweeping furiously in the middle of the room, raising more dust than she was collecting, and jabbering all the while. It was a smokescreen. She was hiding something.

"What else, Rose? where was he last night? where were you?"

"Oh, Ma'am. Home in my bed. Where else would I be?"

"And where did you get those burrs in your hair?"

Her hand flew to her golden mane tied back with a blue ribbon. And then she blushed and resumed her sweeping with greater fury. The dust cloud made her sneeze.

"You're fired, Rose." I've learned in business to be decisive.

She kept on sweeping.

"Put the broom down, Rose."

Between sneezes she was weeping.

Mitchell staggered out of the bedroom wearing nothing but his red bikini briefs. "Juice!" he howled histrionically. "Cold veggie juice for a dying man!"

"There isn't any. There's nothing to drink but coffee and something in the fridge that looks suspiciously like goat's milk."

He gagged and threw himself across the sofa at the far end of the room. "Noise," he complained. "There's too much noise. You, there, stop whatever it is you're doing and get me my vitamins. And a glass of water if there is any."

Rose galloped to his side and knelt on the gritty floor, letting her tears splash onto his bare chest. "Oh, mister," she blubbered, "tell her not to give me the sack. You promised. You said I could go back to New York with you and be your housekeeper and have a room of my own and a television and all. You said she wouldn't mind."

"Did I say that?" Mitchell's eyes rolled wildly, indicating disbelief. He really was a terrible actor.

"Oh, you know you did."

"Well, I was wrong. Now be a good girl and get me those vitamins before I perish."

Rose lumbered to her feet. she wiped her flaming face on the corner of her apron and struggled for dignity.

"That I won't," she declared. "I've been a fool before the whole village, but so have you. They ate your food and they drank your whiskey well enough, but they think you're daft and a poor excuse for a man, letting your wife run off to London like that alone. I quit. It's a shame on me to work for people like you, making such an uproar in a nice cottage like this."

She swept out the front door, kicking aside a stray stout bottle as she went. Mitchell cringed on the sofa, wrapping his arms around his head and drawing his knees up to his chest. Rose poked her head in at the window.

"I'll be sending my brother around for my money."

Then, with a sniff, she was gone.

The rest of our vacation was quiet enough. An aged crone

came in to keep the place tidy and boil strange messes for our meals. Mitchell opened his ream of paper and set up his portable typewriter in a shady spot behind the house. I took long solitary walks during which I thought a great deal, and sometimes sat on a rock by the sea and read poetry. It didn't help. My thoughts were dreary, and poets had lost their power to heal.

We came together in the evenings, speaking only of commonplace things. Mitchell never mentioned his novel, although I couldn't help but notice that the level of clean paper didn't change much from day to day. And I didn't tell him what I was thinking; he didn't need to know any of that. Yet. Neither one of us spoke of the Rose episode. We went to bed early, and slept. For the first time in years I wasn't tired when I woke up in the morning.

Soon it was all over. I wasn't sorry. Long walks and long-dead poets are all very well, but I was eager to get back to the daily fray. Then, too, all my thinking had led to a conclusion, one that I could only put into effect in New York. I wasn't going to risk divorcing Mitchell, but I wasn't going to live with him any longer either. I would find him a small inexpensive apartment, pay the rent on it for a year, and wish him well. Surely a year would be long enough for him to finish his novel, even while writing soap operas, and after that he could certainly manage on his own. It would be cheaper than paying alimony.

My raise and promotion were waiting for me as promised, with an added surprise. A big, newly decorated corner office with my name on the door. From one of its windows I could see the building where I lived, where soon I would live alone. Not a chance of my ever forgetting my address again, I thought.

But Mitchell refused to leave. I thought he would leap at the chance. He could have all the Roses and Daisies and Violets he wanted and I would never know or care.

"Why should I?" he said. "I'm really quite comfortable here. Why should I settle for some dingy box in a crummy part of town? But if it'll make you feel better, we can have separate bedrooms. I'm sure we can squeeze a divan or something into your study. Then you can take your work to bed with you."

Stalemate. I couldn't force him to leave, and I wasn't about to give up the master bedroom which I'd furnished with such loving care exactly the way I wanted it. And now he knew I'd really rather not have him around.

But still we didn't talk about it. What was there to say?

One day I came home early. This happened so rarely, it was almost unthinkable. But I'd eaten something at lunch that violently disagreed with me. It was grim being sick in the ladies' room with all the secretaries finding excuses to come in and offer sympathy. As soon as I could totter, I left them to their whispers and conjectures. One of them went so far as to suggest I might be pregnant. She'd be looking for a new job soon.

The apartment was empty, except for Hank snoozing on the sofa. I put him out on the terrace where he pressed his nose against the glass and whined for the walk he felt entitled to. I knew I should lie down, but I felt restless and angry with myself. Sickness was not part of my game plan. I'd heard enough coarse jokes about women and their frailties, and I'd sworn never to give anyone the least bit of ammunition to use against me in that way.

I roamed the apartment, looking for something to take my mind off my troubles. There was nothing in the way of light reading, daytime television (especially Mitchell's soap opera) was puerile, music, no matter how soothing, was liable to worsen the headache that had set in after the stomach had settled down. Idly I poked my head into the small room off the kitchen where Mitchell spent his evenings supposedly writing his novel.

To my great surprise a stack of typed manuscript pages lay on the table next to his typewriter. A fairly respectable stack. I picked it up and flipped through it. It was neatly typed. I glanced at the title page. It read: THE BITCH WIFE. A Novel by Mitchell Sands.

So that's the way it was, I thought. Well, we'll just see about that. I took the manuscript into the bedroom and propped myself up on two pillows and read. It was good. It was bitingly true, achingly sad, and (I almost couldn't believe it) very well-written. And while it wasn't *precisely* about me, there was enough in it to make the world wonder.

I don't think I overestimated. The book would sell. Not just sell, it would be a bestseller. Mitchell would appear on television talk shows, looking handsome and dignified, and he would talk about the book, and me. There would be a movie; I would be played, bitchily, by a big Hollywood star. Secretaries would read the paperback on the subway and whisper about me behind my back. And the Chairman of the Board of my company would say nothing. He would know and he would deal with this unwelcome notoriety, but he would say absolutely nothing at all about it to me. I couldn't let that happen.

I didn't bother to read the whole thing. I didn't have to. And there wasn't time. Mitchell would be home soon. I got up and went into the living room. Hank was still out on the terrace, howling faintly through the glass. There was an arrangement of dried grasses screening the fireplace. I moved it aside and sat down on the slate hearth. Methodically I crumpled the pages of the manuscript and tossed them into the clean mouth of the fireplace. It was a little like throwing away a part of my life that had never had a chance to happen. And, of course, I realized what I was doing to Mitchell. He would probably never recover from this. But which one of us had a better right to survive? There was no question in my mind about that.

At last all the pages had been crumpled and stuffed into the fireplace. It made quite a mound. The long-stemmed fireplace matches were kept in a decorative box on a shelf nearby. I got up, opened the box, and drew out a single match. It was about ten inches long. My mind tried to play silly games with me. If the match ignited on the first strike, I would set fire to the manuscript. If not, I wouldn't. Nonsense! First strike, or fiftieth, the manuscript would burn. Even if I had to rub two sticks together to get it started.

They were good quality, expensive matches. Flame leaped from the tip at the first scrape against the fine sandpaper on the side of the matchbox. I knelt before the fireplace and touched the flaming wand there and there and there. And once again for good measure.

It didn't take long. There was an explosion of fire that scorched my face and made me draw back in alarm. But it quickly subsided and within five minutes there was nothing left but a smoldering pile of frail ashes. Not a word, not a scrap, and not a chance that he would ever be able to reconstruct it. Not Mitchell.

I got up and poured myself two inches of Mitchell's whiskey and sat in the armchair to sip it and watch the ashes cool.

Mitchell came in about an inch later.

"You're home early," he said. "What's the occasion?"

"Nothing. I wasn't feeling well."

"What is it? Bubonic plague? Typhoid? Nothing less could topple superperson from the executive suite so early in the day."

I took another sip of Scotch. "About your book, Mitchell."

"Yes? What about it?" He was standing in the hall about to move away to the bedroom or to that awful little room behind the kitchen.

"I burned it."

"Ha-ha!"

"I really did. Look."

He came into the living room and looked at the ashes.

"Is that it?"

I nodded.

"I ought to kill you," he said, his voice low.

I nodded. Idle threats have absolutely no effect on me. In business you have to learn quickly who the real sharks are, and which big talkers you can safely ignore. Hank had begun scratching at the glass door, in a frenzy to say hello to Mitchell. I got up and crossed the wide expanse of deep-piled white carpet. When I slid the door open, Hank barreled in woofing his head off, leaping and prancing and making a fool of himself. For some reason he adored Mitchell. I went out onto the terrace to avoid having to witness the display of doggy devotion.

I wasn't prepared for the shove, but some instinct made me grip the railing just in time. My drink went sailing off into space, twenty-two floors above the sidewalk. Mitchell was right behind me with a look on his face that I had never seen before. Maybe I'd underestimated him. I twisted away from the railing and got myself on the other side of a heavy metal-framed chair. Mitchell came after me.

"You bitch," he breathed, low and angry. "You're worse than anything I ever imagined. You're not fit to live."

"Stay back," I warned him. And picked up the chair. I felt ridiculous, like one of those lion-taming acts in the circus.

He stalked me around the terrace, that look of hate and rage and desperation growing more and more intense. I thrust the chair at him a couple of times, but I was afraid he would grab its legs and wrench it away from me. And it was growing heavy. I couldn't keep it between us much longer.

Hank thought it was some kind of game. He yipped and loped in circles around us. A moment came when I knew I had to do something. The dog was between us. I was just in front of the terrace door. Mitchell had his back to the railing. I threw the chair at him. The dog leaped to intercept it. Both chair and dog hit Mitchell at the same moment. He fell backward. And over. The dog looked goofily surprised and then began running back and forth, whimpering.

I decided to take him for a walk.

I've answered all their question now. Except the ones I can't answer because I don't remember. They've taken Hank away. At first I thought they'd stopped me because I didn't clean up after him, but I guess policemen have more important things to think about. Especially in Central Park at midnight. I don't remember walking to the park, but I must have because that's where they picked me up.

I only got into the police car because I was tired and wanted to go home, but I couldn't seem to remember where that was. I wish they'd stop asking me.

Charlie's Game

•

Brian Garfield

Among Brian Garfield's many virtues as a writer is his versatility. He has written traditional, historical, and comedy/mystery Westerns, contemporary mysteries, chase novels, political thrillers, and psychological suspense novels. Many of his best books have been filmed, among them Death Wish *(1972), the film versions of which Garfield has publicly decried, and* Hopscotch *(1975), which became a highly successful Walter Matthau film coproduced by Garfield. The last-named novel was also the recipient of an MWA Edgar as best novel of its year. Perhaps Garfield's most memorable series character is fat, old, conceited, and nonviolent espionage agent Charlie Dark, the hero of "Charlie's Game" and several other stories collected in 1981 under the title* Checkpoint Charlie.

When I turned the corner I saw Leonard Ross going into Myerson's office ahead of me. By the time I reached the door I heard Ross say, "Where's Charlie?"

"Late. As usual. Shut the door."

Late. As usual. As far as I could remember—and I have phenomenal recall—there had been only one time when I had been late arriving in Myerson's office and that had been the result of a bomb scare that had grounded everything for three hours at Tempelhof. His acidulous remark had been a cheap shot. But then that was Myerson.

Ross was shutting the door in my face when I pushed in past him and kicked it closed. Ross said, "Hello, Mr. Dark."

Myerson only glanced up from the desk. Then he went on pretending to read something in a manila file folder. I said,

"Welcome back, Charlie," in an effort to prompt him, but he ignored it and I decided to play his silly game so I dropped my raincoat across a chair and squeezed into one of the tubular steel armchairs and perused the photos on the wall, waiting him out.

The room was stale with Myerson's illegal Havana smoke; it was a room that obviously was unnerving to youngsters like Leonard Ross because among Myerson's varied and indeterminate functions was that of hatchet man. Any audience with him might turn out to be one's last: fall into disfavor with him and one could have a can tied to one's tail at any time, Civil Service or no Civil Service; and as junior staff, Ross had no illusions about his right to tenure. I had none myself: I was there solely at Myerson's sufferance, but that was something else—he could fire me any time he chose to but he was never going to choose to because he needed me too much and he knew it.

His rudeness meant nothing; that was what passed for amiability with Myerson. I gave Ross a glance and switched it meaningfully toward a chair and finally Ross sat down, perching uneasily on the edge of it.

The view from Myerson's window isn't terribly impressive. An enormous parking lot and, beyond it, a hedgerow of half-wilted trees. Here and there you can see the tops of the high-rises along Langley.

Finally he closed the file and looked at me. "You're late."

"Would you care for a note from my mother explaining my tardiness?"

"Your sarcasms seldom amuse me."

"Then don't provoke them."

"You are," he said, "preposterously fat."

"And you are a master of the non sequitur."

"You disgust me, do you know that?" He turned to young Ross. "He disgusts me. Doesn't he disgust you?"

Ross made embarrassed gestures and I said, "Don't put the kid on the spot. What's on?"

Myerson wasn't in a particularly savage mood, obviously, because he gave up trying to goad me with no more prompting than that. He tapped the manila folder with a fingertip. "We've got a signal from Arbuckle."

"Where's Arbuckle?"

"East Africa. You really ought to try to keep up on the postings in your own department."

Ross explained to me, "Arbuckle's in Dar-es-Salaam."

"Thank you."

Ross's impatience burst its confines and he turned to Myerson: "What's the flap, then?"

Myerson made a face. "It distresses me, Ross, that you're the only drone in this department who doesn't realize that words like 'flap' became obsolete sometime before you were born."

I said, "If you're through amusing yourself maybe you could answer the young man's question."

Myerson squinted at me; after a moment he decided not to be affronted. "As you may know, affairs in Tanzania remain sensitive. Especially since the Uganda affair. The balance is precarious—a sort of three-sided teeter-totter: ourselves, the Soviets and the Chinese. It would require only a slight upheaval to tip the bal—"

"Can't you spare us the tiresome diplomatic summaries and get down to it?"

Myerson coolly opened the file, selected a photograph and held it up on display. "Recognize the woman?"

To Ross I suppose it was only a badly focused black-and-white of a thin woman with attractive and vaguely Oriental features, age indeterminate. But I knew her well enough. "Marie Lapautre."

"Indeed."

Ross leaned forward for a closer look. I imagine it may have been the first time he'd ever seen a likeness of the dragon lady, whose reputation in our world was something like that of John Wesley Hardin in the days of the gunslingers.

"Arbuckle reports she's been seen in the lobby of the Kilimanjaro in Dar. Buying a picture postcard," Myerson added drily.

I said, "Maybe she's on vacation. Spending some of the blood money on travel like any well-heeled tourist. She's never worked that part of the world, you know."

"Which is precisely why someone might hire her if there were a sensitive job to be done there."

"That's all we've got? Just the one sighting? No evidence of a caper in progress?"

"If we wait for evidence it could arrive in a pine box. I'd prefer not to have that sort of confirmation." He scowled toward Ross. "Fidel Castro, of course, has been trying to persuade Tanzania to join him in leading the Third World toward the Moscow sphere of influence, but up to now the Nyerere regime has maintained strict neutrality. We have every reason to wish that it continue to do so. We want the status to remain quo. That's both the official line and the under-the-counter reality."

Ross was perfectly aware of all that, I'm sure, but Myerson enjoys exposition. "The Chinese aren't as charitable as we are toward neutralists," Myerson went on, "particularly since the Russian meddlings in Angola and Ethiopia. The Chinese want to increase their influence in Africa—that's confirmed in recent signals from the Far East. Add to this background the presence of Marie Lapautre in Dar-es-Salaam and I believe we must face the likelihood of an explosive event. Possibly you can forecast the nature of it as well as I can?"

The last question was addressed to me, not Ross. I rose to meet it without much effort. "Assuming you're right, I'd buy a scenario in which Lapautre's been hired to assassinate one of the top Tanzanian officials. Not Nyerere—that would provoke chaos. But one of the others. Probably one who leans toward the Russian or Chinese line."

Ross said, "What?"

I told him, "They'd want to make the assassination look like an American plot."

Myerson said, "It wouldn't take any more than that to tilt the balance over toward the East."

"Deal and double deal," Ross said under his breath in disgust.

"It's the way the game is played," Myerson told him. "If you find it repugnant I'd suggest you look for another line of work." He turned to me: "I've booked you two on the afternoon flight by way of Zurich. The assignment is to prevent Lapautre from embarrassing us.''

''All right.'' That was the sum of my response; I didn't ask any questions. I pried myself out of the chair and reached for my coat.

Ross said, ''Wait a minute. Why not just warn the Tanzanians? Tell them what we suspect. Wouldn't that get us off the hook if anything did happen?''

''Hardly,'' Myerson said. ''It would make things worse. Don't explain it to him, Charlie—let him reason it out for himself. It should be a useful exercise for him. On your way now—you've barely got time to make your plane.''

By the time we were belted into our seats Ross thought he had it worked out. ''If we threw them a warning and then somebody got assassinated, it would look like we did it ourselves and tried to alibi it in advance. Is that what Myerson meant?''

''Go to the head of the class.'' I gave him the benediction of my saintly smile. Ross is a good kid: not stupid, merely inexperienced. He has sound instincts and good moral fiber, which is more than can be said for most of the Neanderthals in the Company. I explained, ''Things are touchy in Tanzania. There's an excess of suspicion toward *auslanders*—they've been raided and occupied by Portuguese slave traders and German soldiers and British colonialists and you can't blame them for being xenophobes. You can't tell them things for their own good. Our only option is to neutralize the dragon lady without anyone's knowing about it.''

He gave me a sidewise look. ''Can we pin down exactly what we mean by that word 'neutralize'?''

I said, ''Have you ever killed a woman?''

''No. Nor a man, for that matter.''

''Neither have I. And I intend to keep it that way.''

''You never even carry a piece, do you, Charlie.''

''No. Any fool can shoot people.''

''Then how can we do anything about it? We can't just ask her to go away. She's not the type that scares.''

''Let's just see how things size up first.'' I tipped my head back against the paper antimacassar and closed my eyes and reviewed what I knew about Marie Lapautre—fact, rumor, and legend garnered from various briefings and shoptalk along the corridors in Langely.

She had never been known to botch an assignment.

French father, Vietnamese mother. Born 1934 on a plantation west of Saigon. Served as a sniper in the Viet Minh forces at Dienbienphu. Ran with the Cong in the late 1960s with assignments ranging from commando infiltration to assassinations of village leaders and then South Vietnamese officials. Seconded to Peking in 1969 for specialized terrorist instruction. Detached from the Viet Cong, inducted into the Chinese Army and assigned to the Seventh Bureau—a rare honor. Seconded as training cadre to the Japanese Red Army, a terrorist gang. It was rumored Lapautre had planned the tactics for the bombings at Tel Aviv Airport in 1975. During the past seven or eight years Lapautre's name had cropped up at least a dozen times in reports I'd seen dealing with unsolved assassinations in Laos, Syria, Turkey, Libya, West Germany, Lebanon, and elsewhere.

Marie Lapautre's weapon was the rifle. At least seven of the unsolved assassinations had been effected with long-range fire from Kashkalnikov sniper rifles—the model known to be Lapautre's choice.

She was forty-five years old, five feet four, one hundred and five pounds, black hair and eyes, mottled burn scar on back of right hand. Spoke five languages, including English. Ate red meat barely cooked when the choice was open. She lived between jobs in a seventeenth-century villa on the Italian Riviera—a home she had bought with funds reportedly acquired from hire-contract jobs as a freelance. Five of the seven suspected assassinations with Kashkalnikovs had been bounty jobs and the other two probably had been unpaid because she still held a commission in Peking's Seventh Bureau.

We had met, twice and very briefly; both times on neutral ground—once in Singapore, once in Teheran. In Singapore it had been a diplomatic reception; the British attaché had introduced us and stood by watching with amusement while we sized each other up like rival gladiators but it had been nothing more than a few minutes of inconsequential pleasantries and then she had drifted off on the arm of a Malaysian black marketeer.

The files on her were slender and all we really knew was that she was a professional with a preference for the 7.62mm Kashkalnikov and a reputation for never missing a score. By implication I added one other thing: if Lapautre became aware of the fact that two Americans were moving in to prevent her from completing her present assignment she wouldn't hesitate to kill us—and naturally she would kill us with proficient dispatch.

The flight was interminable. I ate at least five meals. We had to change planes in Zurich and from there it was another nine hours. I noticed that Ross was having trouble keeping his eyes open by the time we checked into the New Africa Hotel.

It had been built by the Germans when Tanganyika had been one of the Kaiser's colonies and it had been rebuilt by Africans to encourage business travel; it was comfortable enough and I'd picked it mainly for the food, but it happened to be within easy walking distance of the Kilimanjaro where Lapautre had been spotted. Also, unlike the luxurious Kilimanjaro, the New Africa had a middle-class businessman's matter-of-factness and one didn't need to waste time trying to look like a tourist.

The change in time zones seemed to bewilder Ross. He stumbled groggily when we went along to the shabby export office that housed the front organization for Arbuckle's soporific East Africa Station.

A fresh breeze came off the harbor. I've always liked Dar; it's a beautiful port, ringed by palm-shaded beaches and colorful villas on the slopes. Some of the older buildings bespeak a dusty poverty, but the city is more modern and energetic than anything you'd expect to find near the equator on the shore of the Indian Ocean. There are jams of hooting traffic on the main boulevards. Businessmen in various shadings: Europeans, turbaned Arabs, madrassed Asians, black Africans in tribal costumes. Now and then a four-by-four truck growls by carrying a squad of soldiers, but the place hasn't got that air of police-state tension that makes the hairs crawl on the back of my neck in countries like Paraguay and East Germany. It occurred to me as we reached Arbuckle's office that we hadn't been accosted by a single beggar.

It was crowded in among cubbyhole curio shops selling African carvings and cloth. Arbuckle was a tall man, thin and bald and nervous; inescapably he was known in the Company as Fatty. He had one item to add to the information we'd arrived with: Lapautre was still in Dar.

"She's in room four eleven at the Kilimanjaro but she takes most of her dinners in the dining room at the New Africa. They've got better beef."

"I know."

"Yeah, you would. Watch out you don't bump into her there. She must have seen your face in dossiers."

"We've met a couple of times. But I doubt she'd know Ross by sight."

Ross was grinding knuckles into his eye sockets. "Sometimes it pays to be unimportant."

"Hang onto that thought," I told him. When we left the office I added, "You'd better go back to the room and take the cure for that jet lag."

"What about you?"

"Chores and snooping. And dinner, of course. I'll see you at breakfast. Seven o'clock."

"You going to tell me what the program is?"

"I see no point in discussing anything at all with you until you've had a night's sleep."

"Don't *you* ever sleep?"

"When I've got nothing better to do."

I watched him slouch away under the palms. Then I went about my business.

The breakfast layout was a nice array of fruits, juices, breads, cold cuts. I had heaped a plate full and begun to consume it when Ross came puffy-eyed down to the second-floor dining room and picked his way through the mangoes and sliced ham. He eats like a bird.

The room wasn't crowded; a sprinkling of businessmen and a few Americans in safari costumes that appeared to have been tailored in Hollywood. I said mildly to Ross when he sat down, "I picked the table at random," by which I meant that it probably wasn't bugged. I tasted the coffee and made a face; you'd think they could make it better—after all they grow the stuff there. I put the cup down. "All right. We've got to play her cagey and careful. If anything blows loose there won't be any cavalry to rescue us."

"Us?"

"Did you think you were here just to feed me straight lines, Ross?"

"Well, I kind of figured I was mainly here to hold your coat. On-the-job training, you know."

"It's a two-man job. Actually it's a six-man job, but the two of us have got to carry it."

"Wonderful. Should I start practicing my quick draw?"

"If you'd stop asking droll questions we'd get along a little faster."

"All right. Proceed, my general."

"First the backgrounding. We're jumping to a number of conclusions based on flimsy evidence, but it can't be helped." I enumerated them on my fingers. "We assume, one, that she's here on a job and not just to take pictures of elephants. Two, that it's a Seventh Bureau assignment. Three, that the job is to assassinate someone—after all, that's her principal occupation. Four, that the target may be a government leader here, but not Nyerere. We don't know the timetable so we have to assume, five, that it could happen at any moment. Therefore, we must act quickly. Are you with me so far?"

"So far, sure."

"We assume, six, that the local Chinese station is unaware of her mission."

"Why should we assume that?"

"Because they're bugging her room."

Ross gawked at me.

I am well past normal retirement age and I'm afraid it is not beneath me to gloat at the weakness of the younger generations. I said, "*I* didn't waste the night sleeping."

He chewed a mouthful, swallowed, squinted at me. "All

right. You went through the dragon lady's room, you found a bug. But what makes you think it's a Chinese bug?''

''I found not one bug but three. One was ours—up-to-date equipment and I checked it out with Arbuckle. Had to get him out of bed; he wasn't happy but he admitted it's our bug. The second was American-made but obsolescent. Presumably placed in the room by the Tanzanian secret service—we sold a batch of that model to them about ten years ago. The third mike was made in Sinkiang Province, one of those square little numbers they must have shown you in tech briefings. Satisfied?''

''Okay. No Soviet agent worth his vodka would stoop to using a bug of Chinese manufacture, so that leaves the Chinese. So the local Peking station is bugging her room and that means either they don't know why she's here or they don't trust her. Go on.''

''They're bugging her because she's been known to freelance. Naturally they're nervous. But you're mistaken about one thing. They definitely don't know why she's here. The Seventh Bureau never tells anyone anything. So the local station wants to find out who she's working for and who she's gunning for. The thing is, Ross, as far as the local Chinese are concerned, she could easily be down here on a job for Warsaw or East Berlin or London or Washington or some Arab oil sheikh. They just don't know, do they?''

''Go on.''

''Now the Tanzanians are bugging her as well and that means they know who she is. She's under surveillance. That means we have to act circumspectly. We can't make waves that might splash up against the presidential palace. When we leave here we leave everything exactly as we found it, all right? Now then. More assumptions. We assume, seven, that Lapautre isn't a hip-shooter. If she were she wouldn't have lasted this long. She's careful, she cases the situation before she steps into it. We can use that caution of hers. And finally, we assume, eight, that she's not very well versed in surveillance technology.'' Then I added, ''That's a crucial assumption, by the way.''

''Why? How can we assume that?''

''She's never been an intelligence gatherer. Her experience is in violence. She's a basic sort of creature—a carnivore. I don't see her as a scientific whiz. She uses an old-fashioned sniper's rifle because she's comfortable with it—she's not an experimenter. She'd know the rudiments of electronic eavesdropping, but when it comes to sophisticated devices I doubt she's got much interest. Apparently she either doesn't know her room is bugged or knows it but doesn't care. Either way it indicates the whole area is outside her field of interest. Likely there are types of equipment she doesn't even know about.''

''Like for instance?''

''Parabolic reflectors. Long-range directionals.''

''Those are hardly ultrasophisticated. They date back to World War II.''

''But not in the Indochinese jungles. They wouldn't be a part of her experience.''

''Does it matter?''

''I'm not briefing you just to listen to the sound of my dulcet baritone voice, Ross. The local Chinese station is equipped with parabolics and directionals.''

''I see.'' He said it, but he obviously didn't see. Not yet. It was getting a bit tedious leading him along by the nose, but I liked him and it might have been worse: Myerson might have sent along one of the idiot computer whiz-kids who are perfectly willing to believe the earth is flat if an IBM machine says it is.

I said, ''You're feeding your face and you look spry enough, but are you awake? You've got to memorize your lines fast and play your part perfectly the first time out.''

''What are you talking about?''

According to plan Ross made the phone call at nine in the morning from a coin box in the cable office. He held the receiver out from his ear so I could eavesdrop. A clerk answered and Ross asked to be connected to extension four eleven; it rang three times and was picked up. I remembered her voice right away: low and smoky. *''Oui?''*

''Two hundred thousand dollars, in gold, deposited to a Swiss account.'' That was the opening line because it was unlikely she'd hang up on us right away after that teaser. "Are you interested?"

"Who is this?"

"Clearly, Mademoiselle, one does not mention names on an open telephone line. I think we might arrange a meeting, however. It's an urgent matter."

Ross's palm was visibly damp against the receiver. I heard the woman's voice: "For whom are you speaking, M'sieur?"

"I represent certain principals." Because she wouldn't deal directly with anyone fool enough to act as his own front man. Ross said, "You've been waiting to hear from me, *n'est-ce-pas*?" That was for the benefit of those who were bugging her phone; he went on quickly before she could deny it: "At noon today I'll be on the beach just north of the fishing village at the head of the bay. I'll be wearing a white shirt, short sleeves; khaki trousers and white plimsolls. I'll be alone and, of course, without weapons." I saw him swallow quickly.

The line seemed dead for a while, but finally the woman spoke. "Perhaps."

Click.

"Perhaps," Ross repeated dismally, and cradled it.

Driving us north in the rent-a-car he said to me, "She didn't sound enthusiastic, did she. You think she'll come?"

"She'll come."

"What makes you think so?"

"Without phone calls like that she wouldn't be able to maintain her standard of living."

"But if she's in the middle of setting up a caper here—"

"It doesn't preclude her from discussing the next job. She'll come."

"Armed to the teeth, no doubt," Ross muttered.

"No. She's a pro. A pro never carries a gun when he's not on a job—a gun can get you into too much trouble if it's discovered. But she's probably capable of dismantling you by hand in a hundred different ways so try not to provoke her until we've sprung the trap."

"You can be incredibly comforting sometimes, you know that?"

"You're green, Ross, and you have a tendency to be flip and you'd better realize this isn't a matter of frivolous heroics. You're not without courage and it's silly to pretend otherwise. But don't treat this thing with childish bravado. There's a serious risk you may end up facedown in the surf if you don't treat the woman with all the caution in the world. You job's simple and straightforward and there's nothing funny about it—just keep her interested and steer her to the right place. And for God's sake, remember your lines."

We parked off the road and walked through the palms toward the edge of the water. The beach was a narrow white strip of perfect sand curving away in a crescent. There was hardly any surf. At the far end of the curve I saw a scatter of thatched huts and a few dilapidated old piers to which were tethered a half-dozen primitive outrigger fishing boats. It was pleasantly warm and the air was clear and dry: the East African coast has none of the muggy tropicality of the West one. Two small black children ran up and down the distant sand and their strident voices carried weakly to my ears. The half-mile of beach between was empty of visible life. A tourist-poster scene, I thought, but clearly a feeling of menace was preoccupying Ross; I had to steady him with a hand on his shoulder.

Out on the open water, beyond a few small boats floating at anchor, a pair of junks drifted south with the mild wind in their square sails. A dazzling white sport fisherman with a flying bridge rode the swells in a lazy figure-eight pattern about four hundred yards offshore; two men in floppy white hats sat in the stern chairs trolling lines. Beyond, on the horizon, a tramp prowled northward—a coaster: Tanga next, then Mombosa, so forth. And there was a faint spiral of smoke even farther out—probably the Zanzibar ferry.

I put my back to the view and spoke in a voice calculated to reach no farther than Ross's ears: "Spot them?"

Ross was searching the beach. "Not a soul. Maybe they didn't get the hint."

72

"The sport fisherman, Ross. They've got telescopes and long-range microphones focused on this beach right now and if I were facing them they'd hear every word I'm saying."

That was why we'd given it several hours' lead time after making the phone call. To give the Chinese time to get in position to monitor the meeting.

"They've taken the bait," I said. "It remains to be seen whether the dragon lady will prove equally gullible."

Ross was carrying the rifle and I crooked a finger and he gave it to me. We were still in the palms, too shadowed for the watchers on the fishing boat to get much of a look at us. I slid back into the deeper shadows and watched Ross begin to walk out along the beach, kicking sand with his toes. He had his hands in his pockets but then thought better of that and took them out again, and I applauded him for that—he was making it obvious his hands were empty.

I saw him look at his watch. It was eleven fifty-five. *Don't get too nervous, Ross.* He walked out to the middle of the crescent sand and stood there looking back inland and I had some idea what he was going through: trying to ignore the fishing boat a quarter of a mile behind him, trying to talk himself out of the acute feeling that someone's telescopic crosshairs were centered between his shoulder blades.

I watched him begin to walk around in an aimless little circle—perhaps he felt they'd have a harder time hitting a moving target. He hadn't much to worry about, actually; they had no reason to take potshots at him—they'd be curious, but not murderous—but perhaps Ross was no longer in a state of mind where logic was the ruling factor. I trusted him to do his part, though. I knew a little about him. He'd come right into the Company after college, seeking adventure and challenge, and if he'd been worried by the stink of the Company's growing notoriety he'd balanced it with a naïve notion that the Company needed people like him to keep it clean. Mainly what I knew about him was that Joe Cutter gave him very high marks and there's nobody in Langley whose judgment I'd sooner trust than Joe's. This caper should have been Joe's by rights—it was more in his line than mine, I'm more of a troubleshooter and rarely get picked for front-line counterespionage capers because I'm too visible—but Joe hates Myerson even more than I do and he'd managed to get himself posted out to the Near East away from Myerson's influence.

I heard the putt-putt of an engine and watched a little out-board come in sight around the headland and beat its way forward, its bow gently slapping the water, coming at a good clip. Ross saw it, too—looked at it, then looked away, back into the palm trees—probably wondering when the woman would show up. He hadn't yet realized she was already here. I saw him do a slow take and turn on his heel again. Then we both watched the outboard come straight onto the beach.

It was the dragon lady and she was alone at the tiller. She tipped the engine up across the transom, jumped overside and came nimbly ashore, dragging the boat up onto the sand a bit. Then she turned to look at Ross across the intervening forty yards of sand. I had a good view of her in profile. Ross was trying to meet her stare without guile. Her eyes left him after a bit and began to explore the trees. I didn't stir; I was in among a cluster of palm boles and the thing she'd spot first would be movement.

She made a thorough job of it before she turned toward Ross. She walked with lithe graceful strides: petite but there was nothing fragile about her. She wore an *ao dai*, the simple formfitting dress of Indochina; it was painted to her skin and there was no possibility she could have concealed a weapon under it. Perhaps she wore it for that reason.

Ross didn't move. He let her come to him. It was in his instructions.

I was near enough to hear them because the offshore breeze carried their voices to me.

"Well then, M'sieur."

"The money," Ross began, and then he stopped, tongue-tied.

Christ. He'd forgotten his lines.

"Oui?"

He looked away from her. Perhaps it was the glimpse of the white sport boat out there that galvanized him. I heard him speak

74

clearly and calmly: "The money's on deposit and we have the receipt and the numbered account book. If you do the job you'll be given both of them. Two hundred thousand American dollars in gold. That works out to something over a half million Swiss francs at the current rate."

She said, "I would need a bit more information than that."

"The name of the target, of course. The deadline date by which the assignment must be completed. More than that you don't need." Ross kept his face straight. I had a feeling he was feverishly rehearsing the rest of his lines.

She said, "You've left out one thing."

"I don't think so, Mlle. Lapautre."

"I must know who employs me."

"Not included in the price of your ticket, I'm afraid."

"Then we've wasted our morning, both of us."

"For two hundred thousand dollars we expected a higher class of discretion than you seem inclined to exercise." It was a line I had drilled into him and apparently he hadn't liked it— it went against his usual mode of expression—but I had insisted on the precise wording, and now she responded as I'd said she would: it was as if I'd written her dialogue as well as Ross's.

She said, "Discretion costs a little more, M'sieur, especially if it concerns those whom I might regard as my natural enemies. You *are* American."

"I am. That's not to say my principals are."

The thing is, Ross, you don't want to close the door, you want to keep her talking. String her along, whet her curiosity. She's going to insist on more information. Stall. Stretch it out. Don't give her the name of the target until she's in position.

Casually Ross put his hands in his pockets and turned away from her. I watched him stroll very slowly toward me. He didn't look back to see if she was following him. He spoke in a normal tone so that she'd have trouble hearing him against the wind if she let him get too far ahead of her. "My principals are willing to discuss the matter more directly with you if you agree to take the job on. Not a face-to-face meeting, of course, but one of them may be willing to speak to you on a safe line. Coin telephones at both ends—you know the drill."

It was working. She was trailing along, moving as casually as he was. Ross threw his head back and stared at the sky. I saw what she couldn't see—Ross wetting his lips nervously. "The target isn't a difficult one. The security measures aren't too tough."

"But he's important, isn't he? Visible. Otherwise the price would not be so high.

It was something I hadn't forecast for him and I wasn't sure Ross would know how to handle it, but he did the right thing: he made no reply at all. He just kept drifting toward the palms, off on a tangent from me now, moving in seemingly aimless half-circles. After a moment he said, "Of course, you weren't followed here." It was in the script.

"Why do you think I chose to come by open boat? No one followed me. Can you say the same?"

Position.

Ross turned and she moved alongside. She had, as I had predicted, followed his lead: it was Indochinese courtesy, inbred and unconscious—the residue of a servile upbringing.

She stood beside him now a few feet to his right; like Ross she was facing the palm trees.

Ross dropped his voice and spoke without turning his head; there was no possibility the microphones on the boat would hear him. I barely caught his words myself, and I was only about thirty feet downwind of him. "Don't speak for a moment now, Mademoiselle. Look slightly to your right—the little cluster of palm trees."

She was instantly alert and suspicious; I saw her face come around and I stirred a bit and it was enough to make her spot me. Then I leveled the rifle, aiming down the sights.

In the same guarded low voice Ross said, "It's a Mannlicher bolt action with high-speed ammunition. Hollowpoint bullets and he's an expert marksman. You'd stand no chance at all if you tried to run for it." Ross kept stepping back because I'd told him not to let her get close enough to jump him and use him for a shield. Yet he had to stay within voice range because if he lifted his tone or turned his head the fine-focus directional mike on the sport fishing boat would pick up his words immediately.

I saw her shoulders drop half an inch and felt relief. *If she doesn't break for it in the first few seconds, she won't break at all.* She's a pro and a pro doesn't fight the drop.

"You're in a box, Mlle. Lapautre. You've got one way to get out of it alive. Are you listening to me?"

"Certainly."

"Don't try to figure it out because there are parts of it you'll never know. We're playing out a charade, that's all you need to keep in mind. Play your part as required and you'll walk away alive."

"What do you want, then?"

It was evident that her cool aplomb amazed Ross, even though I'd told him to expect it.

I knew she couldn't have recognized me; most of me was behind one of the palms and all she really could see was a heavyset fellow with a rifle. Because of the angle I was hidden completely from the view of those on board the sport fishing boat. All they'd be able to tell was that Ross and Lapautre were having a conversation in tones too low for their equipment to record. They'd be frustrated and angry, but they'd hang on hoping to pick up scraps of words that they could later edit together and make some sense out of it.

Ross answered her, *sotto voce*: "I want you to obey my instructions now. In a moment I'm going to step around and face you. The man in the trees will kill you if you make any sudden move, so pay attention. . . . Now I'm going to start talking to you in a loud voice. The things I say may not make much sense to you. I don't care what you say by way of response—but say it quietly so that nobody hears your answers. And I want you to nod your head 'yes' now and then to make it look as if you're agreeing with whatever proposition I make to you. Understand?"

"No," she said, "I do not understand."

"But you'll do as I say, won't you."

"I seem to have little choice." She was looking right at me when she said that.

"That's good enough. Here we go."

Then Ross stepped off to the side and made a careful circle around her, keeping his distance, looking commendably casual. He started talking midway around: "Then we've got a deal. I'm glad you agreed to take it on."

He stopped when he was facing her from her port bow. The woman didn't speak; she only watched him. Ross enunciated clearly and I appreciated that; we both were mindful of the shotgun microphone focused on his lips from four hundred yards offshore.

"I'm glad," he said again. "You're the best in the business, I think everybody knows that."

Her lip curled ever so slightly: an expression exquisite in its subtle contempt. "And just what is it I'm supposed to have agreed to?"

Ross nodded vigorously. "Exactly. When you talk to my principals you'll recognize the Ukrainian accents immediately but I hope that won't deter you from putting your best effort into it."

"This is absurd." But she kept her voice right down. I was aiming the thing straight at her heart.

"That's right," Ross said cheerfully. "There will be no official Soviet record of the transaction. If they're accused of anything naturally they'll deny it, so you can see that it's in your own best interests to keep absolutely silent."

"This is pointless. Who can possibly benefit from this ridiculous performance?"

"I think they'll find that acceptable," Ross said. "Now then, about the target. He must be taken out within the next twelve days because that's the deadline for a particular international maneuver, the details of which needn't concern you. The target is here in Dar-es-Salaam, so you'll have plenty of time to set up the assassination. Do you recognize the name Chiang Hsien?"

She laughed then. She actually laughed. "Incredible."

Ross managed to smile. "Yes. The chief of the Chinese station in Dar. Now there's just one more detail."

"Is that all? Thank goodness for that."

Ross nodded pleasantly. "Yes, that's right. You've got to make it look as if it's the work of Americans. I'd suggest you use an American rifle. I leave the other details in your hands, but the circumstantial evidence must point to an American plot against the Chinese people's representative. You understand?''

"Is that all, then?''

"If you still want confirmation I'll arrange for a telephone contact between you and my principals. I think that covers everything, then. It's always pleasant doing business with a professional.'' With a courtly bow—he might have been Doug Fairbanks himself—Ross turned briskly on his heel and marched away toward the trees without looking back.

I watched the woman walk back to her open boat. The junks had disappeared past the point of land to the south; the outriggers were still tethered in the water by the village; the coastal steamer was plowing north, the Zanzibar ferry's smoke had disappeared—and the two white-hatted men in the stern of the sport fishing boat were packing up their rods and getting out of their swivel chairs. The dragon lady pushed her boat into the surf, climbed over the gunwale, made her way aft, and hooked the outboard engine over the transom. She yanked the cord a few times. It sputtered and roared; and she went chugging out in a wide circle toward the open water, angling to starboard to clear the headland.

When she'd gone a couple of hundred yards, Ross came though the trees beside me and said, "What happens now?''

"Watch." I smiled at him. "You did a beautiful job, you know.''

"Yeah, I know I did.''

I liked him for that. I hate false modesty.

The sport fisherman was moving, its engines whining, planing the water: collision course. Near the headland it intercepted the little open outboard boat. The woman tried to turn away, but the big white boat leaped ahead of her and skidded athwart her course.

"That skipper knows how to handle her," Ross commented without pleasure.

With no choice left, the woman allowed her boat to be drawn

alongside by a long-armed man with a boathook. One of the men in the stern—one of the two with white hats—gave her a hand aboard. She didn't put up a struggle; she was a pro. I saw them push her toward the cabin—they went below, out of sight, and then the two boats disappeared around the headland, one towing the other.

Ross and I walked back to the car; I tossed the rifle into the backseat—we'd drop it off at Arbuckle's. It wasn't loaded. If she'd called our bluff, I'd have let her run for it. (There's always another day.)

I said, "They'll milk her, of course, but they won't believe a word of it. They've got the evidence on tape and they won't buy her denials. They wouldn't believe the truth in a thousand years and it's all she's got to offer."

Ross leaned against the car, both arms against the roof, head down between his arms. "You know what they'll do to her, don't you. After they squeeze her dry."

I said, "It'll happen a long way from here and nobody will ever know about it."

"And that makes it right?"

"No. It adds another load to whatever we've already got on our consciences. If it makes you feel a little better, it's a form of justice—think of the people she's murdered. She may survive this, you know. She may come out of it alive. But if she does she'll never get another job in that line of work. Nobody'll trust her again."

"It hasn't solved a thing," he complained. He gave me a petulant little boy look. "They'll just send somebody to take her place, won't they? Next week or next month."

"Maybe they will. If they do we'll have to deal with it when it happens. You may as well get used to it, Ross—you play one game, you finish it, you add up the score and then you put the pieces back onto the board and start the next game. That's all there is to it—and that's the fun of it. As long as you stay lucky, there's always another game."

Ross stared at me. "I guess there is," he said reluctantly.

We got in the car and Ross turned the key. I smiled briefly, trying to reassure him. The starter meshed and he put it in gear.

He said with sudden savagery, "But it's not all that much fun for the losers, is it."

"That's why you should always play to win," I replied.

Ross fishtailed the car angrily out into the road.

The Curious Facts Preceding My Execution

•

Donald E. Westlake

Like Brian Garfield, Donald E. Westlake is a most versatile and award-winning writer. He has written such hilarious comic mysteries as God Save the Mark *(recipient of the 1967 Best Novel Edgar),* The Hot Rock *(1970), and* Good Behavior *(1985); private eye novels such as* The Mercenaries *(1960); tales of psychological suspense such as* 361 *(1962); political thrillers such as* Kahawa *(1982); and under his Richard Stark pseudonym, hard-boiled, violent crime novels about a thief named Parker such as* The Handle *(1966) and* Butcher's Moon *(1974). "The Curious Facts Preceding My Execution," although it first appeared under the Stark name, is a neat slice of Westlakian comedy-on-wry.*

I'm not sure when it was, exactly, that I knew I must murder Janice. Oh, I'd been thinking of it off and on for months, but I don't remember at what precise moment these idle daydreams hardened into cold and determined resolution.

Perhaps it was the day the mailman brought me the bill for a mink coat of which I had never until that moment heard. When I asked my darling if I might at least *see* this coat for which I was expected to shell out two thousand dollars, one fifth of a year's wages, she confessed prettily that she no longer had it. Shortly after its purchase, while coming home from the city after an exhausting shopping spree along Fifth Avenue, she had lost the dear thing on the train.

Or perhaps it was even earlier than that. Perhaps it was the evening I returned to our midtown apartment, wearied from my labors in the advertising vineyard, and learned that in my absence Janice had managed somehow to buy a house in Connecticut. No more were we to be pallid Manhattanites. It was the invigorating air of the ranch-style developments for us. Besides, it would improve my health—if not my disposition—for me to arise an hour earlier each morning and sprint for the railroad train.

Or perhaps it was much later, after the move from the city and after the lost mink coat and after Lord knows what else. Perhaps it was the evening when, while poring over our financial records, I discovered that in the last year we had spent more in bank fines than for electricity. When I pointed this out to Janice she replied that the fault was clearly mine, since I didn't put enough money into the account to cover the money she wanted to take out.

Or perhaps it wasn't really Janice at all, not finally. Perhaps the catalyst was Karen.

What shall I say of Karen? I had finally received the promotion which made it at least possible for me to feel optimistic about catching up with Janice's spending, and with this promotion had come my own office and my own secretary, and that secretary was Karen.

It was the old story. At home, a wife who was a constant source of frustration and annoyance. At the office, a charming and intelligent—not to say lovely—secretary, with whom one felt one could talk, with whom one could relax. I took to spending evenings in town, telling Janice I had to work late at the office while actually I was with Karen, and the inevitable happened. We fell in love.

But ours could not be a dark and furtive office romance. Karen was too honest, too gentle, too *good* for such a relationship. I knew I had to free myself of Janice and marry Karen, for the sake of everyone's happiness.

I did consider divorce, at first. There was no doubt in my mind that Janice would grant me one, since divorce is quite fashionable in our circle and Janice would wish always to be in fashion, but as I thought about it I saw that there was a problem, and the name of the problem was alimony.

I might legally disencumber myself of Janice as a wife, but it seemed clear to me that I would continue to be responsible for her support. And I understood only too well Janice's insatiable need for money. Statisticians claim that 85 percent of American expenditures are made by women, but Janice beat those statistics cold. Over the course of our marriage I would venture to say that she had, month by month, never permitted her spending of my salary to fall much below 110 percent.

It was practically impossible already for me to support both Janice and myself. Add Karen to my responsibilities, and I would be in debtor's prison within six months.

No, divorce was out, and for a while the problem seemed insoluble. But then Janice bought a speedy little foreign car—one of her few purchases I had no objection to—and I waited hopefully for her to demolish the auto and herself on the Merritt Parkway, but nothing ever came of it. Those cars are mawkishly ugly, but they are also exasperatingly safe.

Still, my mind had been turned to a perhaps more productive area of speculation. Could Janice expire? Nothing but grim Death itself, obviously, would ever stop her spending, but where were she and grim D. likely to meet?

Nowhere. Our home was brick outside, plaster and linoleum and plastic inside; not too much likelihood of a good flash fire. The trains to and from the city had their derailments and so on from time to time, but the accidents were almost invariably minor and never on Ladies' Day. The possibility of a jetliner falling out of the sky and landing on Janice was a bit too remote to be counted on. As for disease, Janice was so healthy that most doctors suspected we were Socialists.

At long last I had to accept the truth: it was up to me. If you want a thing done right—or at all—you must do it yourself.

This conviction grew in me, becoming stronger and stronger, until at last I dared broach the subject to Karen. She was, at first, shocked and appalled, but as I talked on, reasoning with her, explaining why it would never be possible for us to wed while Janice still lived, she too began to accept the inevitable.

The Curious Facts Preceding My Execution

Once accepted, the only questions left to answer were *when* and *how*. I had four types of murder from which to choose:

a) Murder made to look like an accident.
b) Murder made to look like suicide.
c) Murder made to look like natural death.
d) Murder made to look like murder.

I ruled out a) accident at once. I had daydreamed for months of possible accidents which might befall Janice, and had finally come to realize that they were all unlikely. And if they were unlikely even to me, who passionately desired that Janice should have herself an accident, how much more unlikely would they seem to the police?

As for b) suicide, there were far too many of Janice's suburban friends who would be delighted to volunteer the information that Janice was happy as a lark—and about as bright—and that she had absolutely no reason in the world to want to kill herself.

As for c) natural death, I knew far too little about medicine to want to try and outwit the coroner at his own game.

Which left d) murder. Murder, that is, made to look like murder. I planned accordingly.

My opportunity came, after a number of false starts, on a Wednesday in late March. On the Thursday and Friday of that week there was to be an important meeting in Chicago, concerning a new ad campaign for one of our most important accounts, and I was scheduled to attend. All I had to do was arrange for Karen to accompany me—an easy matter to justify—and the stage was set.

Here was the plan: I had two tickets on the three P.M. train Wednesday for Chicago, due to arrive in that city at eight-forty the following morning. (Our explanation for traveling by train rather than by plane, should we need an explanation, was that I could get some preliminary paperwork done on the train, which would have been impossible in the tubular movie houses which airplanes have lately become.) At any rate, Karen was to take this train, carrying both our tickets. We would leave the ad agency together at noon, ostensibly headed for Grand Central, lunch, and the train. But while Karen went to Grand Central, I would hurry uptown to the 125th Street station, where there was a twelve fifty-five train for my portion of Connecticut. I would arrive at my town at two-ten, wearing false mustache, horn-rimmed glasses, and the kind of hat and topcoat I never wear.

Our mortgaged paradise was a good twenty blocks from the station. I would walk this distance, shoot Janice with the .32 revolver I had picked up secondhand on the lower East Side two weeks before, ransack the house, take the five-oh-two back to the city, go to a movie, take the twelve forty-five plane for Chicago, arrive at three-forty A.M., and be at the railroad station when Karen's train pulled in at eight-forty. We would both then turn in our return-trip tickets, claiming we had decided to go back to New York by plane. This would necessitate my filling out and signing a railroad company form; an extra little bit of evidence.

It was foolproof. And after a decent period of mourning, I would marry my Karen and live happily—and solvently—ever after.

The day arrived. After breakfast I told Janice I would see her on the following Monday, and I took my suitcase with me to the office. Karen and I left at twelve, and the plan went promptly into effect. Karen took both our suitcases with her to Grand Central and I headed immediately uptown, stopping off only to buy a hat and topcoat. I caught the train at 125th Street and, in its swaying men's room, I donned the horn-rimmed glasses and the mustache.

The train arrived barely five minutes late, and I found the station virtually deserted at this time of day; even the newsstand was shut down. I saw no one I knew in the twenty-block walk to the house, striding along with the pistol an unaccustomed weight in my pocket. I arrived at the house, saw the little foreign car in the driveway, which meant Janice was at home, and let myself in the front door with my key.

Janice was seated in the living room, on the unpaid-for new sofa, reading a slick women's magazine and being instructed, no doubt, in some new way to make money disappear.

At first she didn't recognize me. Then I removed the hat and glasses and she exclaimed, "Why, Freddie! I thought you were going to Chicago!"

"And so I am," I told her. I redonned the hat and glasses, and moved over to close the picture-window drapes.

She said, "Whatever are you doing with that mustache? you look terrible with a mustache."

I turned to face her, and withdrew the pistol from my pocket. "Walk out to the kitchen, Janice," I said. I planned to make it seem as though a burglar had come in the back way, been surprised by Janice in the kitchen, and he had shot her.

She blinked at the gun, then stared wide-eyed at my face. "Freddie, what on earth—"

"Walk out to the kitchen, Janice," I repeated.

"Freddie," she said petulantly, "if this is your idea of a joke—"

"I'm not joking!" I said fiercely.

All at once her eyes lit up and she clapped her hands together childishly and she cried, "Oh, you old dear!"

"What?"

"You did get the washer-dryer after all!" And she leaped to her feet and hobble-trotted out to the kitchen, her high heels going *clack-clack* on the linoleum. Even then, in the last seconds of her life, her only thought was of adding yet another artifact to the mound of possessions she had already heaped high about her.

I followed her to the kitchen, where she was turning, puzzled, to say, "There isn't any washer-dryer—"

I shot from the hip. Naturally, I missed, and the bullet perforated a dirty pot on the stove. I abandoned the cowboy-style forthwith, aimed more carefully, and the second shot cut her down in midscream.

Three seconds of silence. They were followed by the sudden *brrriinnnggg* of the front doorbell, the sound box for which was on the kitchen wall three feet from my head.

I jumped, and then froze, not knowing what to do. My first instinct was to stay frozen and wait for whoever it was to go away. But then I remembered Janice's little car in the driveway, advertising her presence. If there were no answer to the doorbell the visitor might become alarmed, might call for help from the neighbors or the police, and I would never manage to avoid detection.

So I had to go to the door. Disguised as I was, I should be able to fool any of Janice's friends, none of whom knew me that well anyway. I would say I was the family doctor, that Janice was sick in bed and could see no one.

The bell rang again while I was still thinking, and the second burst unfroze me. Putting the gun away in my pocket, I hurried through the living room and stopped at the front door. I took a deep breath, steeled myself, and eased the door open an inch.

Peering out, I saw what was obviously a door-to-door sales-man standing on the welcome mat. He carried a tan briefcase and wore a slender gray suit, a white shirt, a blue tie, and a smile containing sixty-four gleaming teeth. He said, "*Good* afternoon, sir. Is the lady of the house at home?"

"She's sick," I said, remembering to make my voice deeper and hoarser than usual.

"Well, sir," he bubbled, "perhaps I could talk to *you* for just a moment."

"Not interested," I told him. "Sorry."

"Oh, but I'm sure you will be, sir. My company has some-thing of interest to every parent—"

"I am not a parent."

"Oh." His smile faltered, but came back redoubled. "But my company isn't of interest only to parents, of course. Briefly, I represent the *Encyclopedia Universicana*, and I'm not actually a salesman. We are making a preliminary campaign in this area—"

"I'm sorry," I said firmly. "I'm not interested."

"But you haven't heard the best part," he said urgently.

"No," I said, and slammed the door, reflecting that Janice would have bought the *Encyclopedia Universicana*, and that I had dispatched her just in time.

But I had to get on with the plan. I would now ransack the house, emptying bureau drawers onto the floor, hurling clothing around in closets, and so forth. Then, when it was time, I would leave for my train.

I turned toward the bedrooms, and the phone rang.

Once again I froze. To answer or not to answer? If I did, if I didn't—I finally decided I should, and would be again the family doctor.

I picked up the receiver, said hello, and a falsely hearty female voice chirped, "Magill Communications Survey calling. Is your television set on, sir?"

I stood there with the phone to my ear.

"Sir?"

"No," I said, and I hung up.

Doggedly, I turned again toward the bedroom, and this time I reached it. Opening a bureau drawer, I tossed its entire contents on the scatter rug. I didn't have to worry about fingerprints, of course, since my fingerprints were quite naturally all over everything. The police would simply assume that the burglar, being a professional, had known enough to wear gloves.

I was working on the third drawer, having pocketed three pairs of earrings and an old watch for realism's sake, when the doorbell rang.

I sighed, plodded wearily to the living room, and opened the door the usual inch.

A short stout woman, smiling like an idiot, said, "*Hel*-lo, there! I'm Mrs. Turner, from over on Marigold Lane? I'm selling chances for our new car raffle at the United Protestant Church."

"I don't want any raffles," I said.

"New *car* raffle," she said.

"I don't want any cars," I said. I shut the door. Then I opened it again. "I have a car," I said. And closed the door again.

On the way back to the bedroom, the echo of that conversation returned to me and it seemed to me I hadn't been very coherent. Could I be more nervous than I'd thought?

No matter. In little more than an hour I would leave here and catch the train for New York.

I lit two cigarettes, got annoyed, stubbed one out, and went back to work. I finished the bureau and the one drawer in the vanity table and was about to start on the closet when the phone rang.

I had never before realized just how shrill, just how *grating*, that telephone bell actually was. And how long each ring was. And what a little space of time there was between rings. Why, it rang three times before I so much as took a step, and it managed to get in one more jarring *dreeeeep* for good measure as I hurried down the hall to the living room.

I picked up the receiver and a male voice said in my ear, "Hello, Andy?"

"Andy?"

He said it again. "Hello, Andy?"

Something was wrong. I said, "Who?"

He said, "Andy."

I said, "Wrong number," and gently hung up.

The doorbell clanged.

I jumped, knocking the phone off its stand onto the floor. I scooped it up, fumbling, and the doorbell *spanged* again.

I raced across the room, and forgetting all caution, hurled the door open wide.

The man outside was gray-haired, portly, and quite dignified. He wore a conservative suit and carried a black briefcase. He smiled upon me and said, "Has Mr. Wheet been by yet?"

"Who?"

"Mr. Wheet," he said. "Hasn't he been here?"

"No one by that name here," I said. "Wrong number."

"Well, then," said the portly man, "I suppose I'll just have to talk to you myself." And before I knew what was going on he had slipped past me and was standing in the living room, looking around with a great display of admiration and murmuring, "Lovely, lovely. A really lovely living room."

"Now, see here—" I began.

"Sampson," said the portly man, extending a firm plump hand. "*Encyclopedia Universicana*. Little woman at home?"

"She's sick," I said, ignoring the hand. "I was just fixing some broth for her. Chicken broth. Perhaps some other—"

"I see," said the portly man. He frowned as though thinking

things over, and then smiled and said, "Well, sir, you go right ahead. That'll give me a chance to set the presentation up."

With that, he sat himself down on the sofa, right where Janice had been when I first came in. I opened my mouth, but he opened his briefcase faster, dove in, and emerged with a double handful of paper. Sheets and sheets of paper, all standard typewriter size, all gaily colored in green and blue, prominently featuring photographs of receding rows of books. SAVE! roared some of the sheets of paper, in black block print. FREE! screamed others, in red. TRIAL OFFER! shrieked still more, in rainbow hues.

Portly Mr. Sampson leaned far forward, puffing a bit, and began to arrange his papers in rows upon the rug, just in front of his pointed-toe, highly polished black shoes. "Our program," he said, smiling at me, and lowered his head to distribute more sheets of paper over the floor.

I stared at him. Not five feet from where he was sitting my late wife lay sprawled upon the kitchen floor. In the bedroom chaos was the order of the day. In just under an hour I would be leaving here to catch my train back to the city. I would leave the pistol—wiped clean—in some litter basket in town, knowing full well some enterprising soul would shortly pick it out again, and that by the time the police got hold of it, if they ever did, it would have committed any number of crimes past this current one. And then I would fly to Chicago and see Karen. Lovely Karen. Dear darling Karen.

And this miserable man was trying to sell me encyclopedias!

I opened my mouth. Quite calmly I said, "Get out."

He looked up at me, smiling quizzically. "Eh?"

"Get out," I said.

The smile flickered. "But—you haven't seen—"

"Get out!" I repeated, this time a bit louder. I pointed at the door, my forearm upsetting a table lamp. "Get out! Just—just—just get out!"

The miserable creature began to sputter: "Well, but—see here—"

"GET OUT!"

I dashed forward and grabbed all his papers, crumpling them

this way and that, gathering them in my arms, and hurried with them to the front door. In turning the knob I dropped a lot of them, but the remainder I hurled outside, and they fluttered leaflike to the lawn. I kicked at those that had fallen around my feet, and turned to glare at Mr. Sampson as he scuttled from the house. He wanted to bluster, but he was a bit too startled and afraid of me to say anything.

I slammed the door after him and took a deep breath, telling myself I must be calm. I lit a cigarette. I lit another cigarette. Irritably I stubbed the first one in a handy ashtray and lit a third. "*Tcha!*" I cried, and mashed them all out, and stormed back to the bedroom, where I tore into the closet with genuine pleasure. Once the closet was a hopeless wreck I ripped the covers from the bed and dumped the mattress on the floor. Then I stood back, breathing hard, to survey my handiwork.

And the doorbell rang.

"If that is Mr. Sampson," I muttered to myself, "by heaven I'll—"

It rang again. We had an incredibly loud doorbell in that house. Odd I'd never noticed it before.

It rang a third time as I was on my way to answer, and I almost shouted at it to shut up, but managed to bring myself under control by the time I reached the door. I even remembered to open it no more than an inch.

A tiny girl in a green uniform stood looking up at me; she bore a box of cookies.

Life, I reflected at that moment, is unkind and cruel. I said, "We already bought some, little girl," and softly closed the door.

And the telephone screamed.

I leaned against the door and let my nerves do whatever they wanted. But I knew I couldn't stay there; the phone would only make that noise again. And again. And again and again and again until finally I would have to give up and answer it. The only sensible move would be to answer it right away. Then it wouldn't make that noise any more.

A good plan. I was full of good plans. I went over and picked up the phone.

"Hiya, neighbor!" shouted a male voice in my ear. "This is Dan O'Toole, of WINK. Can you Top That Mop?"

"What?"

"This is the grand new radio game everybody's talking about, neighbor. If you can Top That—"

I suppose he kept on talking. I don't know. I hung up.

I caught myself about to light a cigarette, and made myself stop. I also forced myself to be calm, to think rationally, to consider the circumstances. The house, except for my own ragged breathing, was blessedly silent.

With waning fervor I studied once more the tableau I was leaving for the police. The dead woman in the kitchen, and the ransacked house. All that remained was to fix the back door to make it look as though the burglar had forced his way in.

It seemed as though my plan should work perfectly well. It really did seem that way.

Slowly I trudged out to the kitchen. For some reason I no longer believed in my plan, but was merely going through the motions because there was nothing else to do. All of life was involved in a great conspiracy against me, and I didn't know why. Could every day be like this in the suburbs? Was it possible that Janice's reckless spending had simply been a form of escape, a kind of sublimated satisfaction in lieu of biting people like Mr. Sampson and Top That Mop?

At the back door I paused, listening for doorbells and phone bells and church bells and jingle bells, but there was only silence. So I opened the door, and a short round woman was standing there, her finger halfway to the bell button. She was our next-door neighbor, she wore a flour-stained apron, and she had an empty cup in her other hand.

I gaped at her. She looked at me in puzzled surprise, and then her gaze moved beyond me and came to rest on something behind me, at floor level. Her eyes widened. She screamed and let go of the empty cup and went dashing away.

I went rigid. I stared at the cup, watching it in helpless fascination. It seemed to hang there in midair for the longest while, long after its owner had run completely out of sight, and then, quite slowly at first, it began to fall. It fell faster, and faster, and at long last it splattered itself with a terrible crash on the patio cement.

And when that cup splattered, so did I. I went all limp, and sat down with a thud on the kitchen floor.

And there I sat, waiting. I sat waiting for the census taker and the mailman with a Special Delivery letter, for the laundry man and the Railway Express driver, for the man from the cleaners, a horde of Boy Scouts on a paper drive, a political candidate, five wrong numbers, the paper boy, the police, the milkman, a lady collecting for a worthy charity, a call from the tax assessor's office, a young man working his way through college selling magazines . . .

The Jail

•

Jesse Hill Ford

Mainstream writer Jesse Hill Ford has more than once turned his hand to stories of crime and violence in the rural South, both under his own name and the pseudonym Jess Shelton. Deceptively simple, frightening in its implications, "The Jail" was judged the best short story of 1975 by MWA and awarded an Edgar.

How I found the car was I went with the truck looking for some plows and a harrow and a mowing machine, horse-drawn stuff we had a chance to sell to a fellow who was farming produce on shares—tomatoes, in particular. You can't cultivate tomatoes with a tractor. The sticks are too high. He had located a pair of mules. He was a Do-Right, but that is another story. A Do-Right is a member of a small religion we have in west Tennessee wherein a man pledges that he will *do right* and if a Do-Right is not lazy, he's a fair credit risk. So he needed the implements and I said I'd go look and see if I could locate them over on my grandmother's place.

I got into the truck and drove over there. It was July and I looked over her cotton and beans and saw that everything looked good. She'd built her cage-laying shed spang at the other end of the 2,000 acres instead of putting it on the main road like I advised her, and I crossed the stock gaps and the dust powdered on the hood of my green truck. I put up the windows and put the air-conditioning on and turned up the music on the country station and presently I saw the laying house and drove on back to the barn, white-painted and neat. I found the key on my ring and unlocked the doors and swung them open and saw the implements almost at once and the stalls just as they had been left, cleaned out and swept after the last mule died. It was a fine old barn and maybe I still would not have found the car except that I went walking down the hall, looking in the big old box stalls and thinking how it was when I was a boy. It was the fourth stall down and when I saw the car, red and low and foreign, with a good bit of dust on it that had filtered down from the old loft above, I took a look at the outer wallboards and could see where they had been removed in order to put the car in there. My first thought was of Sheriff, my little brother, for I well knew his love of cars. And I thought, Well, Sheriff has bought a car and for some reason stored it in here without saying a word to anybody about it. Then I stepped inside the stall and stooped down and rubbed the barn dust off the license plate. New York State, 1965—I crouched there in the silence of the barn and pondered that. I could feel my heart beating. I stood up and opened the car door on the driver's side. It sure needed greasing, for it kind of groaned—a coffin-lid groan—and I looked inside and saw that it was probably British and next saw that it was a Jaguar. You don't see a whole lot of Jaguars in west Tennessee. Fact of the business, you so rarely see one now that the interstate has been put through that there just isn't any telling *when* the *last* Jaguar came through Pinoak, Tennessee. The interstate, which cut us off the mainstream of travel between Florida and the Midwestern states, was opened in 1966.

I saw something on the steering column held by little coil springs and celluloid. I took it off the column and read the name on the New York driver's license. S. Jerome Luben, male, black hair, brown eyes, age 26, address on Riverside Drive, New York City. Nobody with a name like Luben could be mistaken for a member of the Pinoak Missionary Baptist Church. I tossed the license, celluloid, coil springs and all, onto the driver's seat and closed the door. It shut with a sound that was somehow so final I stood there another full minute at least before I could move. The dust of nine years in a mule barn was on my hands.

The year 1965 was the year Sheriff left home for the Marines. I recalled the day he left. I recalled a lot of things, including the way he kept whispering something and nodding to Henry. Henry is the nigger who has worked for my grandmother since he was a little boy: he kind of waited on Sheriff and buddied around with him since Sheriff was little.

Did I say my little brother is spoiled? Spoiled rotten. The baby in the family. My mother thought she was in the change of life and went around eight months thinking he was a tumor and probably malignant until she finally went to the doctor after she had got our family lawyer, Oman Hedgepath, to make her will, which would have left most of her estate for the support of foreign missions. Mother worried about the souls of the heathens. When Ocie Pentecost told her she was pregnant, I think she felt cheated. A month later, here came Sheriff. That is not his name, of course. His real name is Caleb Batsell Beeman Baxter. Mother had an uncle in Somerton whose name was Caleb and he got into real estate and insurance and put his signs up so they read: C. BATSELL BEEMAN FOR EVERYTHING IN REAL ESTATE AND INSURANCE NEEDS. He put that sign on every road leading in and out of town and had a fine income all his life right up to the moment he fell into the wheat bin and suffocated. Wheat is like water, you fall into it and you go under. Uncle Batsell could not swim.

Mother figured Sheriff would be a lawyer like Oman Hedgepath and have a sign on his door and a shingle hanging in the breeze on Main Street, reading: C. BATSELL B. BAXTER, which she thought would make everybody with any law business want to see her youngest son.

As for me, I was never in her mind otherwise than somebody to run everything. To gin cotton during ginning season and combine beans during bean season, to buy hay and manage for the silage and between times build rent houses and work in the store and manage the tractor-and-implement company and make private loans and buy farms and run the sawmill—or, in other words, just like my daddy always did, to run everything and see to everything and mind everything and when there was nothing else to do, to step in behind the meat counter and weigh hams.

Not Sheriff, though. Once it got through her head that he was not a tumor, she saw him in the practice of the law. Then he started to grow up and almost from the first word he spoke, it was obvious that all in the world he would ever want to do would be to be a sheriff and enforce the law. It was all that he spoke about, and because he was a baby, we gave him toy guns and little uniforms and hats and badges. He went around dressed like that and went to school that way. What else would we call him but Sheriff? Everybody in Sligo County thought he was cute as a bug, and during the strawberry festival every year we'd build him a float in the shape of a sheriff's patrol car with little wheels on it and the aerial and all and Sheriff would ride in it, with Henry and a couple of others pulling him in the children's parade. Time and again he won first or got an honorable mention from the judges who come each year from Memphis to judge the parade and the beauty contest.

Then he got to high school and we gave him an automobile and Grandmother gave him police lights for the top of it and my father bought him a siren from Sears. I got him a real badge from a pawnshop in Memphis. It saved us from having to wonder what to do for him when it came Christmas.

If something happened in Pinoak, we had Sheriff as our private police force to investigate things and make arrests and take people over to Somerton to the jail. Nothing official, understand, but a convenience in a small place like Pinoak, where you don't have a police force.

Sheriff, for the most part, confined himself to stopping out-of-state cars if they were speeding or if they looked suspicious. He'd pull them over, get out, walk up to the driver's side and tip his hat. He was young and blond and blue-eyed and had such an innocent face. Yet behind it there was always something that made folks do exactly what he told them to do. Show their driver's license, open their trunk lid, even open their suitcases. He confiscated ever so much liquor and beer, but never went so far as to actually arrest anybody . . . that I ever knew anything about.

He seemed happy and he seemed contented. When he asked if he could have a jail, my father consulted highway patrol. They advised against it. The law in Tennessee did not, they said, let folks operate private jails. That could cause problems, they said. Otherwise, as long as Sheriff never arrested anybody or gave a ticket or fined anybody, he could pretty well do as he pleased, for he was a deterrent to speeders. Pinoak got known far and wide as a speed trap. Back before they opened the interstate, the out-of-state traffic would drive through Pinoak so slow you could walk alongside it the whole two blocks. They'd come at a crawl sometimes, with Sheriff so close behind in his cruiser he was all but bumper to bumper, and Sheriff just daring them to make a wrong move or do anything sudden or reckless.

More than anything else, he liked to stop a car with a New York tag, for when this happened, like as not he'd get a loud-mouth who would start to complain and bitch and raise his voice and Sheriff would end up practically taking the fellow's car apart in front of his eyes. New York drivers were a challenge to Sheriff. Looking at that red car gave me a chill in spite of the heat.

I went outside and stood just beyond the white-painted doors of the mule barn. I could see the cage-laying house and hear the hens and could smell that special odor of hen shit and cracked eggs and ground feed. I saw that Henry's truck was there, so I went down to the packing room and found him. He had collected the eggs and had them in the tank with the vibrator that washed them and he was grading them and putting them in big square cartons of fifty. The cracked ones he broke all the way and put the yolks and whites into big pickle jars to be hauled to the poor farm and to the Somerton jail, because the old and the poor and the prisoners are just as well fed on cracked eggs as on whole ones and cracked eggs come a whole lot cheaper; besides, otherwise we'd have to feed the cracked ones to the hogs. Henry never looked up and the vibrator hummed and the water danced the hen shit off the eggs and the smell of spoiled eggs was in the room. The floor was a little wet. A black-and-white cat was asleep on the sofa Henry had made for himself by welding legs onto a truck seat taken from a wreck.

"S. Jerome Luben," I said. "That mean anything to you?"

He froze, egg in hand, just that quick.

"S. Jerome Luben," I said again.

He dropped the egg and it broke on the wet concrete between his black, down-at-heel shoes.

"Is he dead?" I asked.

Henry reached into the tank for another egg, got one, and then cut off the vibrator. He wiped the egg carefully on the corner of his apron. Flies were worrying about the floor, lighting at the edges of the egg he had dropped.

"Naw, sah, he ain't dead. Leastways he wasn't dead this morning."

"This morning? You saw S. Jerome Luben this morning?"

"Yes, sah. He looked OK to me." Instead of looking at me, he looked at the egg in his hand and pushed with his thumbnail at what might have been a speck on its white, curving surface. "How come you to know about him, sah?"

"I just saw his car."

"Little red automobile."

"Did you knock the wall loose?"

"I prised some of the boards loose. It wouldn't go in if I didn't prise some boards off. But now I nailed 'em back."

"Nine years ago."

"Something lack that," he said, still examining the egg. "It had to be after Christmas, wadn't it?"

"How would I know?" I said.

"It was after Christmas of sixty-five, I b'lieve it was," he said. He never looked blacker. I began to feel something between my shoulder blades in the middle of my back, a cold sensation. He was so utterly still. "Yes, sah. Sixty-five," he said.

"What happened?"

He was quiet a moment. "I tole 'em it was bound to cause trouble."

"Who—told who?"

"Your grandmother, Miss Mettie Bell. And him—Sheriff. He got on her about wanting her to give him a jail—"

"A what?"

"Jail. Tole her wouldn't nothing else make him happy that Christmas if he didn't git him a jail. Jest a teeny little jail. Two cells, he tole her. That's all he wanted Santy to bring him and what if he went away to—where was it he went?"

"Vietnam."

"Nam, that's it. What if he went there and got kilt and hadn't never had him the pleasure of a jail of his own? He started on her in the summertime in weather about like this and she sent to Birmingham for the contractor and they come and built it and she handed him the keys on Christmas Eve. I was standing in the kitchen next to the sink when she handed them keys to him and made him promise he wouldn't abuse his privilege and wouldn't make no trouble and wouldn't tell nobody local from around here anything about it. She tole me I'd have to feed anybody he locked up and keep the jail swept and mopped and cleaned good. She wadn't going to endure with no dirty jail, she said. So I promised and Sheriff, he promised, too.''

I sat down on the sofa. The cat raised her head and gave me a green stare. Then, closing her eyes again, she laid her head back down. I heard the vibrator come on.

"S. Jerome Luben," I said. "Is he in the jail?"

"He was this morning when I carried him his breakfast."

"Where the hell is this jail?"

I no sooner asked than something dawned on me. It was like looking at the flat surface of a pool. You can look ever so long at the surface and you will see only the reflection of the sky and the trees, but then, sometimes very suddenly, you'll see below it—you'll see a fish or a turtle.

It had to be the poison house. We bought farm poisons in such quantities, all the new poisons and defoliants, the sprays and powders for controlling everything from the boll weevil to the cabbage butterfly, plus all the weed killers. I recalled drawing the check to the Birmingham contractor and wondering why Grandmother got somebody from Alabama instead of a Somerton builder, but it was Grandmother's money and if she wanted the poison house set off in a field on the backside of nowhere, then it was fine with me, because the poisons always gave me a headache when I had to be around them. I never went to the poison house, not I or my father or any white man. It gives you a headache, a poison room does. They say the stuff can collect in your system and shorten your life. So, for nine years, I'd been looking at a goddamned jail and had never known what it was. I had never before wondered why Grandmother would put up a two-story poison house and have a Birmingham contractor build it. Hell, *I* could have built the thing. Only when you are busy as I am all the time, with one season falling on you before the last one is over—starting with cabbage and strawberries and rolling right on through corn and soybeans and cotton and wheat and winter pasture and back to cabbage and strawberries again—you are so goddamned relieved when anybody will take even a little something off your back you never wonder about it and you get so you never ask questions. Nine years can flit past you like a moth in the dark. You never give it a second thought.

"Henry?"

"Sah?"

"Cut that goddamned thing off and come with me." I stood up, feeling light-headed.

"Cut it *off?*"

"You heard me."

"But I got to grade these eggs—"

"Who feeds him his dinner?"

"Sah?"

"S. Jerome Luben."

He cut off the vibrator, wiped his hands and reached beneath his apron and hauled out his watch. He looked at it and then shucked off the apron and threw it onto the truck-seat sofa before sticking the watch back into the pocket of his gray work trousers.

"No need you to go," he said. He started out and would have gotten in his truck as though to close the matter between us once and for all. I give him credit. He was letting me have my chance to stay out of it.

"Get in my truck, Henry."

He froze again. "You don't have to go," he said.

"My truck."

He gave a sigh and turned then and went slowly to my truck and climbed into the passenger seat and slammed the door. I climbed in beside him and started the engine and felt the air conditioner take hold and start to cool me. It was the first I knew that I was sweating so heavily; it was cold sweat and dried beneath my shirt and left me clammy.

I pulled the gearshift down into drive and accelerated out

through the gate, over the stock gap and into the dusty single lane that spun between the pastures, deep and green on both sides of us. Next came cotton acreage, then a bean field with corn standing far down beyond it toward the bottoms, and beyond the corn the groves of virgin cypress timber far down in the flat distance like the faraway rim of the world, as though beyond that contained edge of green there would be nothing else, just blue space and stars. West Tennessee gives that feeling and if you grow up with it, it never leaves you. It's big and lonely and a million miles from nowhere—that's the feeling. I turned through the gate and the tires slapped on the iron pipes spanning the stock gap and the poison house was straight ahead. I pulled around behind it. Sheriff's car was there, parked ramrod straight on the neat gravel apron. On the side of its white front door was a seal and above the seal the word SHERIFF in dark gold, and below the seal in neat black lettering: OFFICIAL BUSINESS ONLY.

The sawed-off shotgun was racked forward against the dashboard and the two-way radio that he always left on was talking to itself when I opened my door, cut the engine and climbed down.

Henry didn't move.

"Get out," I said and slammed my door. He opened his door and climbed down.

"No need you to git mixed into this mess, Mr. Jim," he said, giving me another chance.

The radio in Sheriff's cruiser muttered something, asked something, answered itself.

"Follow me," I said and headed for the door. It was a glassed aluminum storm door and before I opened it, I saw the desk and Sheriff propped up behind it, reading a *True Detective* or some such magazine. His hat was on the costumer in the corner. When I went in, grateful because the building was air-conditioned, he didn't stir. Maybe he thinks it's Henry, or maybe he just doesn't care, I told myself.

Henry was behind me. The door clicked shut. Sheriff liked his thumb and turned a page. His blue gaze passed over me as though I didn't exist. He looked almost the same as he had looked the day he left for the Marines, the same tan, the same blond crewcut, the same innocent baby face. Then he saw me. The swivel desk chair creaked and he came forward until his elbows were on the desk. Then I smelled it. Henry had gone by me now into what I saw was a kitchen adjoining the office. I smelled rancid food and unwashed despair and tired mattresses and stale cigarettes—I smelled the smell of every jail in the South, from Miami to Corinth, from Memphis to Biloxi to Charleston to Birmingham—I smelled them all and every little town between. Finally, it is the smell of human fear, the scent of the caged human animal—nine years of that, one year stacked on top of the last, palpable as dust.

"Nice place," I said.

Sheriff looked at me, not sure yet what I knew. Give him credit, he's cool, I thought: my blood, my kin, my flesh. And I had as much hand in spoiling him rotten as anybody. Maybe that's what they teach you at the University of Mississippi, where I played and raised hell for four years before the army got me. They teach you how to come home and continue to spoil the little brother in the family by letting him do what he damn well pleases. Every family needs one at least with no responsibility at all to burden him. Here sat ours.

"You never seen it before?" Sheriff said. He hollered at Henry: "What you doing in there?"

"Fixin' his dinner, scramblin' his eggs." Henry turned and stood in the kitchen door, holding a pickle jar. I could see the yolks and the whites. So they fed him cracked eggs, the same as any other prisoner in Sligo County. Henry stood patiently. He was looking down at the jar. In the opposite hand he held the lid.

"Fixin' whose dinner?" Sheriff said.

"His—upstairs," said Henry. He didn't look up and his voice was low, a sunken, below-surface sound.

"What the hell you talking about?" said Sheriff.

"He knows," Henry said in the same sunken voice.

"I found the car," I said.

"Oh," said Sheriff.

"The red car and a driver's license and a name."

"Well, now you know about him," Sheriff said. "Figured

you or Dad, one was bound to come to the poison house some-day. I'd say it was my office and you'd go away and not worry. How come you to find the car, Jim?''

"Just unlucky. A Do-Right wants some old tools and machinery—''

"I told Henry I'd bust his ass if he ever let it out. Didn't I tell you I'd bust your ass, Henry?''

"Yes, sah. Want me to feed him? It's time.''

"Goddamn it,'' Sheriff said. "Goddamn it.''

"Just answer me one question,'' I said. I heard eggs hit the hot skillet.

"Shoot.''

"Why would you lock a man up and keep him locked up nine years?''

"You mean Jerome? Why would I keep him so long? It's a fair question. I never intended to leave him in here longer than just overnight to teach him a lesson. He passed through Pinoak that night doing above ninety. I risked my life and never caught him until the son of a bitch was nearly to McKay—lights and siren and giving my car a fit. Goddamn him. He could have been the death of us both. See?'' He looked at me with that blue stare of innocence and passed his fingers over the crown of his close-cropped hair. "And he swore at me.''

"So you locked him up for nine years. You buried him alive because he cussed you and he was from New York. Do you know how long they'll keep you in prison for this? Did it ever dawn on you?''

"I know all about it,'' he said.

"God help us,'' I said. "God *help* us—Henry's in it. I'm in it!''

"Look—go upstairs and talk to him. Please? Go up and let Jerome explain how it happened. He understands it and—'' He stopped talking and stood up and took some keys off his belt and went to the steel security door and unlocked and opened it. I climbed the concrete stairs with Sheriff behind me.

There was a hallway at the top with a cell on either side of it and two windows and a toilet and lavatory in each cell. The cell on the right was open and had bookshelves on every wall to the ceiling. The cell on the left was closed. I saw the prisoner, a slender, black-haired man wearing blue jeans and loafers and a T-shirt. He was clean-shaven and his hair was cropped close to his head like Sheriff's and he was working at a typewriter. A book lay open beside him on the desk.

"What's for lunch?" he said. Then he saw me and pushed his chair back. On the cell floor lay the rug that used to be in my grandmother's parlor, a pattern of roses. "Who's this, Sheriff?"

"It's Jim."

"What a surprise. I'm Jerome Luben." He came to the cell door, swung it open and put out his hand to me. We shook hands. "So what brings you here?"

"He found your car," said Sheriff. "And Henry told him."

"You just now found out? Told anybody?" He was handsome in a Jewish way and looked none the worse for wear. There was premature gray at his temples, just a touch.

"Not yet I haven't told anybody," I said.

Luben looked at Sheriff. "Why don't you leave us alone for a few minutes? Tell Henry to hold my lunch. Need to explain things to Jim, don't I?"

Sheriff nodded and turned and went back down the stairs. I heard the security door clank shut.

"We can sit in here, if you like," said Luben, leading the way into the cell on the right. "My library," he said.

I recognized two of Grandmother's parlor chairs and one of her floor lamps.

"You upset, Jim?"

"A little," I said.

"Don't be upset. Because what happened couldn't happen again in a thousand—a million—years. I'm not angry, you see that, don't you?"

"Yes," I said. "But what the hell happened? This is the ruination of my family—the end."

"It's not the end. Listen to me. It's back in 1965, I'm fresh out of Columbia Law School. I'm driving like a bat out of hell, with no respect for anything—asking for it. I've got long hair and a beard and I'm smoking grass and everybody who thinks the war in Vietnam is right is a pissant in my book, shit beneath my feet. Get the picture? I'm bigger and richer and smarter than the world, the entire fucking—pardon me—world. I know Southerners do not use those words."

"Not often, no," I said.

"So your brother stops me. Polite? A complete gentleman. I tell him to eat shit. I hit him. I spit on him. I'm begging him to lock me up so I can be some kind of goddamned martyr and get my ass in jail and my name in the papers and on television and go home to New York and be a fucking hero. Now, understand, my *father* has washed his hands of me three years earlier and put my money in a trust that keeps my checking account overflowing. I mean, he's rich and my mother was rich and she's dead and I've told him what a capitalist pig he is and he hopes to God he will *never* see me again. I'm scorching the highway in the backward, backwoods, medieval South, and who stops me? Your brother."

"Lord have mercy," I whispered.

"He brings me here. He and Henry have to carry me bodily. I'm not cooperating. Then I blew it all to hell."

"How?"

"I demanded my phone call."

"Phone call?"

"Phone call. My lousy phone call. And Sheriff had to tell me there isn't a phone. I said what kind of fucking jail was it with no phone? I said did he realize what was going to happen to him if I didn't get my phone call? Did he know that he had arrested a lawyer—a member of the New York bar, an officer of the court, a graduate of Columbia and much else? Did he know how fucking rich I was? Because I was going to make a career out of him. I had nothing else to do. I was going to make him and Henry and anybody else responsible for building a jail and leaving a phone out of it suffer until they'd wish they had never been born! *Oy!*"

I began to see. I began to see it all. He went on. He was smiling now, that was the wonder of it:

"And he finally had to tell me that his grandmother had built the jail and he wasn't really a sheriff, not even a deputy. I had rolled a joint and was blowing smoke at him and getting high and I told him as soon as he let me out, I'd see his grandmother in prison, and himself, and poor old black-ass Henry. And that did it. He was due to go to the Marines. He had already enlisted. He went away and left Henry to feed me."

I didn't want to let myself think what I was thinking. In the chambers of my mind's memory, I saw the red Jaguar in the mule barn. I heard the door chunk shut; I felt all the finality of our family's situation. Coming down to it, I saw that it was me or S. Jerome Luben.

Luben was saying, "I'm sure Sheriff will keep his word, in which event I'll be free next October. Not that I will leave." He frowned. "I find this hard to believe. I therefore know how difficult it may be for you to believe."

"Believe what, Mr. Luben?"

"That I'm finally rehabilitated. That I love the United States of America, that I'd go to war for my country if asked to serve. That I'd even volunteer. Inward things—I'm clean, I'm thinking straight. He'll unlock the door in October, you'll see."

I knew I'd have to kill him. I felt my heart stagger. He must have seen a change in my face. He looked at me quietly.

"After you're free, what will you do?" I asked. We'd bury him and the automobile. The easiest way would be to poison him, to let him die quietly in his sleep, and just as he had been carried into Sheriff's prison—unresisting but not cooperating—so would he be carried out of it and put deep in the ground. It was the only way.

Luben smiled. "Are you ready for this? I like your brother."

My look must have asked him who he was trying to bullshit, because he drew a breath, smiled again and went on talking. All the pressures of New York and the world outside and his troubles with his father and the other members of his family, the drug scene, the antiwar movement, the hippie underground, he was saying, all that passed away once he was locked up here, apparently for life. "All that shit, all those pressures were suddenly gone. I say *suddenly* like it happened overnight, when, of course, it didn't. I was maybe four years getting anywhere with myself, trying to bribe Henry to let me escape, screaming at night. Then I decided to cut my hair and get rid of the beard. Sheriff had already told me I could have anything I wanted within reason, as long as I bought it with my own money. These books, this library, the typewriter—I've got nearly every worthwhile book there is on penology. What started as a lot of shouting back and forth between Sheriff and me became long, leisurely conversations. He taught me how to play dominoes. I used to enter chess tournaments in my other life. Sheriff taught me dominoes—a simple game but really full of genuine American integrity. When I got tired of dominoes, he went home and got his Monopoly set. It was his kindness and his honesty and, at some point, it came to me that I liked him. I saw at last that there had been no forfeiture of equity on his part. You follow me?''

''I'm not sure,'' I said.

''All I'm saying is that I did wrong. He arrested me and when I threatened him like I did, in effect I locked the door on myself. Now, after ten years, almost, you see the result. You see what I've become.''

''Which is what?'' I asked. I got the feeling you have when a salesman goes too fast and gets close to selling you a bill of goods. In a desperate way, I wanted to believe there wouldn't be any need to kill him. The thing about him was that he was so goddamned nice and likable and, what's more, his voice and his accent reminded me of Sheriff's voice, just a touch, or maybe an echo, but it got to me where I lived. Yet I knew it couldn't be possible that he was really one of us. He was a New York Jew and a lawyer and he had to hate us. He was dangerous as a rattlesnake. ''What are you now?'' I asked.

''A model prisoner, a rehabilitated man. This is a copy of an essay for *The American Journal of Penology*,'' he said, opening the top drawer of a little olive-green filing cabinet. ''Wrote it in my spare time,'' he said, laughing a quiet little laugh at his own joke.

I looked at the title page. ''Some Problems of Local Authorities in Administering Small-Community Jails and Lockups'' and, under it, ''By Solomon Jerome Luben, B.A., LL.B.'' ''Well, nice, real nice,'' I said. My hand was trembling.

109

"That's nothing. Take a look at these." And he grabbed a long tube of rolled-up papers from the top of the nearest bookshelf and started unrolling it on the library table.

Seeing the back of his neck, I thought maybe it would be better just to shoot him when he wasn't looking. If I knew Henry and Sheriff, they'd leave that part up to me.

"Don't you want to see this?" he asked.

"All right." And I moved in beside him and looked.

"Front elevation," he said. "Innovative design, eh? Wait till you see the modern features!"

All I saw was a long building.

"I'm financing the whole thing. We break ground in October, when I walk out of here. The end of the medieval monstrosity that has been the bane of every small community in the South." He peeled the top sheet aside. "Of course, there'll be a wall. Now, this is your floor plan, your maximum-security block. Dining hall is here. Exercise yard. Library, of course. Kitchen. Sheriff and I have been two years planning this little jewel. Like it?"

I stood dumbfounded. Again he said his fortune was sufficient to see the place built and maintained. He, S. Jerome Luben, would be the administrator. Sheriff would provide the prisoners, of course. Henry might need help in the kitchen, with so many additional mouths to feed. "We'll have to cross that bridge when we get to it." A dreamy look came into his eyes. Small-town mayors and city officials would be brought here, in greatest secrecy, of course, he said. It was his plan to see what he called "Sheriff's great idea" applied all over the South, for openers. "Ultimately, of course, it will sweep the globe. Once they see how it cuts all the red tape. No criminal lawyers getting some bastard, some baby raper, some fiend out just because his confession got the case thrown out of court. No trial, no court. Just the jail to end all jails, with an indeterminate sentence for everybody. No mail, no phone calls. Just . . ." And he snapped his fingers.

"Where would you plan to build it?" I asked.

"Why, here, right here! Can you imagine a better location for the first one?" He peeled the next sheet away. "These are below ground—solitary-confinement cells, soundproof, totally dark. I tell you, Jim, when Sheriff and I get through with this thing, it's really going to be something! *Oy!*"

I couldn't think what to say. I couldn't think, period.

"What a plan, what a beautiful fucking plan," Jerome Luben was whispering.

The steel door opened and clanged below. Footsteps on the stairs; it was Henry—bringing the eggs.

The Arrow of God

•

Leslie Charteris

Leslie Charteris has been chronicling the escapades of that rogue among rogues, Simon Templar, better known as the Saint, since 1928. To date there have been close to fifty books in the Templar saga, as well as hundreds of films, radio plays, and TV shows in the United States and in England. Especially noteworthy among the Saint novels and collections of shorter works are The Last Hero *(1930),* The Brighter Buccaneer *(1933),* The Saint in New York *(1935),* The Happy Highwayman *(1939), and* The Saint on the Spanish Main *(1955). Our intrepid hero is at his most urbane in "The Arrow of God," in which he solves a baffling—and seemingly impossible—beachfront murder in Nassau.*

One of Simon Templar's stock criticisms of the classic type of detective story is that the victim of the murder, the reluctant sparkplug of all the entertaining mystery and strife, is usually a mere nonentity who wanders vaguely though the first few pages with the sole purpose of becoming a convenient body in the library by the end of Chapter One. But what his own feelings and problems may have been, the personality which has to provide so many people with adequate motives for desiring him to drop dead, is largely a matter of hearsay, retrospectively brought out in the conventional process of drawing attention to one suspect after another.

"You could almost," Simon has said, "call him a *corpus derelicti.* . . . Actually, the physical murder should only be the midpoint of the story: the things that led up to it are at least as interesting as the mechanical solution of who done it. . . . Per-

112

sonally, I've killed very few people that I didn't know plenty about first."

Coming from a man who is generally regarded as almost a detective-story character himself, this comment is at least worth recording for reference; but it certainly did not apply to the shuffling-off of Mr. Floyd Vosper, which caused a brief commotion on the island of New Providence in the early spring of that year.

2

Why Simon Templar should have been in Nassau (which, for the benefit of the untraveled, is the city of New Providence, which is an island in the Bahamas) at the time is one of those questions which always arise in stories about him, and which can only be answered by repeating that he liked to travel and was just as likely to show up there as in Nova Zembla or Namaqualand. As for why he should have been invited to the house of Mrs. Herbert H. Wexall, that is another irrelevancy which is hardly covered by the fact that he could just as well have shown up at the house of Joe Wallenski (of the arsonist Wallenskis) or the White House—he had friends in many places, legitimate and otherwise. But Mrs. Wexall had some international renown as a lion hunter, even if her stalking had been confined to the variety which roars loudest in plush drawing rooms; and it was not to be expected that the advent of such a creature as Simon Templar would have escaped the attention of her salon safari.

Thus one noontime Simon found himself strolling up the driveway and into what little was left of the life of Floyd Vosper. Naturally he did not know this at the time; nor did he know Floyd Vosper, except by name. In this he was no different from at least fifty million other people in that hemisphere; for Floyd Vosper was not only one of the most widely syndicated pundits of the day, but his books (*Feet of Clay*; *As I Saw Them*; and *The Twenty Worst Men in the World*) had all been the selections of one book club or another and still sold by the million in reprints. For Mr. Vosper specialized in the ever-popular sport of shattering reputations. In his journalistic years he had met, and apparently had unique opportunities to study, practically every great name in the national and international scene, and could unerringly remember everything in their biographies that they would prefer forgotten, and could impale and epitomize all their weaknesses with devastatingly pinpoint precision, leaving them naked and squirming on the operating table of his vocabulary. But what this merciless professional iconoclast was like as a person, Simon had never heard or bothered much to wonder about.

So the first impression that Vosper made on him was a voice, a still unidentified voice, a dry and deliberate and peculiarly needling voice, which came from behind a bank of riotous hibiscus and oleander.

"My dear Janet," it said, "you must not let your innocent admiration for Reggie's bulging biceps color your estimate of his perspicacity in world affairs. The title of All-American, I hate to disillusion you, has no reference to statesmanship."

There was a rather strained laugh that must have come from Reggie, and a girl's clear young voice said: "That isn't fair, Mr. Vosper. Reggie doesn't pretend to be a genius, but he's bright enough to have a wonderful job waiting for him on Wall Street."

"I don't doubt that he will make an excellent contact man for the more stupid clients," conceded the voice with the measured nasal gripe. "And I'm sure that his education can cope with the simple arithmetic of the Stock Exchange, just as I'm sure it can grasp the basic figures of your father's Dun and Bradstreet. This should not dazzle you with his brilliance, any more than it should make you believe that you have some spiritual fascination that lured him to your feet."

At this point Simon rounded a curve in the driveway and caught his first sight of the speakers, all of whom looked at him with reserved curiosity and two-thirds of them with a certain hint of relief.

There was no difficulty in assigning them to their lines—the young red-headed giant with the pleasantly rugged face and the slim pretty blonde girl, who sat at a wrought-iron table on the terrace in front of the house with a broken deck of cards in front of them, which established an interrupted game of gin rummy, and the thin stringy man reclining in a long cane chair with a cigarette-holder in one hand and a highball glass in the other.

Simon smiled and said: "Hello. This is Mrs. Wexall's house, is it?"

The girl said "Yes," and he said: "My name's Templar, and I was invited here."

The girl jumped up and said: "Oh, yes. Lucy told me. I'm her sister, Janet Blaise. This is my fiancé, Reg Herrick. And Mr. Vosper."

Simon shook hands with the two men, and Janet said: "I think Lucy's on the beach. I'll take you around."

Vosper unwound his bony length from the long chair, looking like a slightly dissolute and acidulated mahatma in his white shorts and burnt chocolate tan.

"Let me do it," he said. "I'm sure you two ingenues would rather be alone together. And I need another drink."

He led the way, not into the house but around it, by a flagged path which struck off to the side and meandered through a bower of scarlet poinciana. A breeze rustled in the leaves and mixed flower scents with the sweetness of the sea. Vosper smoothed down his sparse gray hair; and Simon was aware that the man's beady eyes and sharp thin nose were cocked toward him with brash speculation, as if he were already measuring another target for his tongue.

"Templar," he said. "Of course, you must be the Saint—the fellow they call the Robin Hood of modern crime."

"I see you read the right papers," said the Saint pleasantly.

"I read all the papers," Vosper said, "in order to keep in touch with the vagaries of vulgar taste. I've often wondered why the Robin Hood legend should have so much romantic appeal. Robin Hood, as I understand it, was a bandit who indulged in some well-publicized charity—but not, as I recall, at the expense of his own stomach. A good many unscrupulous promoters have also become generous—and with as much shrewd publicity—when their ill-gotten gains exceeded their personal spending capacity, but I don't remember that they succeeded in being glamorized for it."

"There may be some difference," Simon suggested, "in who was robbed to provide the surplus spoils."

"Then," Vosper said challengingly, "you consider yourself an infallible judge of who should be penalized and who should be rewarded."

"Oh, no," said the Saint modestly. "Not at all. No more, I'm sure, than you would call yourself the infallible judge of all the people that you dissect so definitively in print."

He felt the other's probing glance stab at him suspiciously and almost with puzzled incredulity, as if Vosper couldn't quite accept the idea that anyone had actually dared to cross swords with him, and moreover might have scored at least even on the riposte—or if it had happened at all, that it had been anything but a semantic accident. But the Saint's easily inscrutable poise gave no clue to the answer at all; and before anything further could develop there was a paragraphic distraction.

This took the form of a man seated on top of a truncated column, which for reasons best known to the architect had been incorporated into the design of a wall which curved out from the house to encircle a portion of the shore like a possessive arm. The man had long curly hair that fell onto his shoulders, which with his delicate ascetic features would have made him look more like a woman if it had not been complemented with an equally curly and silken beard. He sat cross-legged and upright, his hands folded symmetrically in his lap, staring straight out into the blue sky a little above the horizon, so motionless and almost rigid that he might easily have been taken for a tinted statue except for the fluttering of the long flowing white robe he wore.

After rolling with the first reasonable shock of the apparition, Simon would have passed on politely without comment, but the opportunity was irresistible for Vosper to display his virtuosity again, and perhaps also to recover from his momentary confusion.

"That fugitive from a Turkish bath," Vosper said, in the manner of a tired guide to a geek show, "calls himself Astron. He's a nature boy from the Dardanelles who just concluded a very successful season in Hollywood. He wears a beard to cover a receding chin, and long hair to cover a hole in the head. He purifies his soul with a diet of boiled grass and prune juice. Whenever this diet lets him off the pot, he meditates. After he was brought to the attention of the Western world by some engineers of the Anglo-Mongolian Oil Company, whom he cures of stomach ulcers by persuading them not to spike their ration of sacramental wine with rubbing alcohol, he began to meditate about the evils of earthly riches.''

"Another member of our club?" Simon prompted innocuously.

"Astron maintains," Vosper said, leaning against the pillar and giving out as oracularly as if the object of his dissertation were not sitting on it at all, "that the only way for the holders of worldly wealth to purify themselves is to get rid of as much of it as they can spare. Being himself so pure that it hurts, he is unselfishly ready to become the custodian of as much corrupting cabbage as they would like to get rid of. Of course, he would have no part of it himself, but he will take the responsibility of parking it in a shrine in the Sea of Marmora, which he plans to build as soon as there is enough kraut in the kitty."

The figure on the column finally moved. Without any waste motion, it simply expanded its crossed legs like a lazy tongs until it towered at its full height over them.

"You have heard the blasphemer," it said. "But I say to you that his words are dust in the wind, as he himself is dust among the stars that I see."

"I'm a blasphemer," Vosper repeated to the Saint, with a sort of derisive pride combined with the ponderous bonhomie of a vaudeville old-timer in a routine with a talking dog. He looked back up at the figure of the white-robed mystic towering above him, and said: "So if you have this direct pipeline to the Almighty, why don't you strike me dead?"

"Life and death are not in my hands," Astron said, in a calm and confident voice. "Death can only come from the hands of the Giver of all Life. In His own good time He will strike you down, and the arrow of God will silence your mockeries. This I have seen in the stars."

"Quaint, isn't he?" Vosper said, and opened the gate between the wall and the beach.

Beyond the wall a few steps led down to a kind of Grecian courtyard open on the seaward side, where the paving merged directly into the white sand of the beach. The courtyard was furnished with gaily colored lounging chairs and a well-stocked pushcart bar, to which Vosper immediately directed himself.

"You have visitors, Lucy," he said, without letting it interfere with the important work of reviving his highball.

Out on the sand, on a towel spread under an enormous beach umbrella, Mrs. Herbert Wexall rolled over and said: "Oh, Mr. Templar."

Simon went over and shook hands with her as she stood up. It was hard to think of her as Janet Blaise's sister, for there were at least twenty years between them and hardly any physical resemblances. She was a big woman with an open homely face and patchily sun-bleached hair and a sloppy figure, but she made a virtue of those disadvantages by the cheerfulness with which she ignored them. She was what is rather inadequately known as "a person," which means that she had the personality to dispense with appearances and the money to back it up.

"Good to see you," she said, and turned to the man who had been sitting beside her, as he struggled to his feet. "Do you know Arthur Gresson?"

Mr. Gresson was a full head shorter than the Saint's six foot two, but he weighed a good deal more. Unlike anyone else that Simon had encountered on the premises so far, his skin looked as if it was unaccustomed to exposure. His round body and his round balding brow, under a liberal sheen of oil, had the hot rosy blush that the kiss of the sun evokes in virgin epidermis.

"Glad to meet you, Mr. Templar." His hand was soft and earnestly adhesive.

"I expect you'd like a drink," Lucy Wexall said. "Let's keep Floyd working."

They joined Vosper at the bar wagon, and after he had started to work on the orders, she turned back to the Saint and said: "After this formal service just make yourself at home. I'm so glad you could come."

"I'm sure Mr. Templar will be happy," Vosper said. "He's a man of the world like I am. We enjoy Lucy's food and liquor, and in the return we give her the pleasure of hitting the society columns with our names. A perfectly businesslike exchange."

"That's progress for you," Lucy Wexall said breezily. "In the old days I'd have had a court jester. Now all I get is a professional stinker."

"That's no way to refer to Arthur," Vosper said, handing Simon a long cold glass. "For your information, Templar, Mr. Gresson—Mr. Arthur *Granville* Gresson—is a promoter. He has a long history of selling phony oil stock behind him. He is just about to take Herb Wexall for another sucker; but since Herb married Lucy he can afford it. Unless you're sure you can take Janet away from Reggie, I advise you not to listen to him."

Arthur Gresson's elbow nudged Simon's ribs.

"What a character!" he said, almost proudly.

"I only give out with facts," Vosper said. "My advice to you, Templar, is, never be an elephant. Resist all inducements. Because when you reach back into that memory, you will only be laughed at, and the people who should thank you will call you a stinker."

Gresson giggled, deep from his round pink stomach.

"Would you like to get in a swim before lunch?" Lucy Wexall said. "Floyd, show him where he can change."

"A pleasure," Vosper said. "And probably a legitimate part of the bargain."

He thoughtfully refilled his glass before he steered Simon by way of the verandah into the beachward side of the house, and into a bedroom. He sat on the bed and watched unblinkingly while Simon stripped down and pulled on the trunks he had brought with him.

"It must be nice to have the Body Beautiful," he observed. "Of course, in your business it almost ranks with plant and machinery, doesn't it?"

The Saint's blue eyes twinkled.

"The main difference," he agreed goodhumoredly, "is that if I get a screw loose it may not be so noticeable."

As they were starting back through the living room, a small

birdlike man in a dark and (for the setting outside the broad picture window) incongruous business suit bustled in by another door. He had the bright baggy eyes behind rimless glasses, the slack but fleshless jowls, and the wide tight mouth which may not be common to all laywers, bankers, and business executives, but which is certainly found in very few other vocations; and he was followed by a statuesque brunette whose severe tailoring failed to disguise an outstanding combination of curves, who carried a notebook and a sheaf of papers.

"Herb!" Vosper said. "I want you to meet Lucy's latest addition to the menagerie which already contains Astron and me—Mr. Simon Templar, known as the Saint. Templar—your host, Mr. Wexall."

"Pleased to meet you," said Herbert Wexall, shaking hands briskly.

"And this is Pauline Stone," Vosper went on, indicating the nubile brunette. "The tired business man's consolation. Whatever Lucy can't supply, she can."

"How do you do," said the girl stoically.

Her dark eyes lingered momentarily on the Saint's torso, and he noticed that her mouth was very full and soft.

"Going for a swim?" Wexall said, as if he had heard nothing. "Good. Then I'll see you at lunch, in a few minutes."

He trotted busily on his way, and Vosper ushered the Saint to the beach by another flight of steps that led directly down from the verandah. The house commanded a small half-moon bay, and both ends of the crescent of sand were naturally guarded by abrupt rises of jagged coral rock.

"Herbert is the living example of how really stupid a successful businessman can be," Vosper said tirelessly. "He was just an officeboy of some kind in the Blaise outfit when he got smart enough to woo and win the boss's daughter. And from that flying start, he was clever enough to really pay his way by making Blaise Industries twice as big as even the old man himself had been able to do. And yet he's dumb enough to think that Lucy won't catch on to the extracurricular functions of that busty secretary sooner or later—or that when she does he won't be out on a cold doorstep in the rain. . . . No, I'm not going in. I'll hold your drink for you."

Simon ran down into the surf and churned seaward for a couple of hundred yards, then turned over and paddled lazily back, coordinating his impressions with idle amusement. The balmy water was still refreshing after the heat of the morning, and when he came out the breeze had become brisk enough to give him the luxury of a fleeting shiver as the wetness started to evaporate from his tanned skin.

He crossed the sand to the Greek patio, where Floyd Vosper was on duty again at the bar in a strategic position to keep his own needs supplied with a minimum of effort. Discreet servants were setting up a buffet table. Janet Blaise and Reg Herrick had transferred their gin rummy game and were playing at a table right under the column where Astron had resumed his seat and his cataleptic meditations—a weird juxtaposition of which the three members all seemed equally unconscious.

Simon took Lucy Wexall a martini and said with another glance at the tableau: "Where did you find him?"

"The people who brought him to California sent him to me when he had to leave the States. They gave me such a good time when I was out there, I couldn't refuse to do something for them. He's writing a book, you know, and of course he can't go back to that dreadful place he came from wherever it is, before he has a chance to finish it in reasonable comfort."

Simon avoided discussing this assumption, but he said: "What's it like, having a resident prophet in the house?"

"He's very interesting. And quite as drastic as Floyd, in his own way, in summing up people. You ought to talk to him."

Arthur Gresson came over with an hors d'oeuvre plate of smoked salmon and stuffed eggs from the buffet. He said: "Anyone you meet at Lucy's is interesting, Mr. Templar. But if you don't mind my saying so, you have it all over the rest of 'em. Who'd ever think we'd find the Saint looking for crime in the Bahamas?"

"I hope no one will think I'm looking for crime," Simon said deprecatingly, "anymore than I take it for granted that you're looking for oil."

"That's where you'd be wrong," Gresson said. "As a matter of fact, I am."

The Saint raised an eyebrow.

"Well, I can always learn something. I'd never heard of oil in the Bahamas."

"I'm not a bit surprised. But you will, Mr. Templar, you will." Gresson sat down, pillowing his round stomach on his thighs. "Just think for a moment about some of the places you have heard of, where there is certainly oil. Let me mention them in a certain order. Mexico, Texas, Louisiana, and the recent strike in the Florida Everglades. We might even include Venezuela in the south. Does that suggest anything to you?"

"Hm-mm," said the Saint thoughtfully.

"A pattern," Gresson said. "A vast central pool of oil somewhere under the Gulf of Mexico, with oil wells dipping into it from the edges of the bowl, where the geological strata have also been forced up. Now think of the islands of the Caribbean as the eastern edge of the same bowl. Why not?"

"It's a hell of an interesting theory," said the Saint.

"Mr. Wexall thinks so too, and I hope he's going into partnership with me."

"Herbert can afford it," intruded the metallic sneering voice of Floyd Vosper. "But before you decide to buy in, Templar, you'd better check with New York about the time when Mr. Gresson thought he could dig gold in the Catskills."

"Shut up, Floyd," said Mrs. Wexall, "and get me another martini."

Arthur Granville Gresson chuckled in his paunch like a happy Buddha.

"What a guy!" he said. "What a ribber. And he gets everyone mad. He kills me!"

Herbert Wexall came down from the verandah and beamed around. As a sort of tacit announcement that he had put aside his work for the day, he had changed into a sport shirt on which various exotic animals were depicted wandering through an idealized jungle, but he retained his business trousers and business shoes and business face.

122

"Well," he said, inspecting the buffet and addressing the world at large. "Let's come and get it whenever we're hungry."

As if a spell had been snapped, Astron removed himself from the contemplation of the infinite, descended from his pillar, and began to help himself to cottage cheese and caviar on a foundation of lettuce leaves.

Simon drifted in the same direction, and found Pauline Stone beside him, saying: "What do you feel like, Mr. Templar?"

Her indication of having come off duty was a good deal more radical than her employer's. In fact, the bathing suit which she had changed into seemed to be based more on the French minimums of the period than on any British tradition. There was no doubt that she filled it opulently; and her question amplified its suggestiveness with undertones which the Saint felt it wiser not to challenge at that moment.

"There's so much to drool over," he said, referring studiously to the buffet table. "But that green turtle aspic looks pretty good to me."

She stayed with him when he carried his plate to a table as thoughtfully diametric as possible from the berth chosen by Floyd Vosper, even though Astron had already settled there in temporary solitude. They were promptly joined by Reg Herrick and Janet Blaise, and slipped at once into an easy exchange of banalities.

But even then it was impossible to escape Vosper's tongue. It was not many minutes before his saw-edged voice whined across the patio above the general level of harmless chatter:

"When are you going to tell the Saint's fortune, Astron? That ought to be worth hearing."

There was a slightly embarrassed lull, and then everyone went on talking again; but Astron looked at the Saint with a gentle smile and said quietly: "You are a seeker after truth, Mr. Templar, as I am. But when instead of truth you find falsehood, you will destroy it with a sword. I only say 'This is falsehood, and God will destroy it. Do not come too close, lest you be destroyed with it.' "

"Okay," Herrick growled, just as quietly. "But if you're talking about Vosper, it's about time someone destroyed it."

"Sometimes," Astron said, "God places His arrow in the hand of a man."

For a few moments that seemed unconscionably long nobody said anything; and then before the silence spread beyond their small group the Saint said casually: "Talking of arrows—I hear that the sport this season is to go hunting sharks with a bow and arrow."

Herrick nodded with a healthy grin.

"It's a lot of fun. Would you like to try it?"

"Reggie's terrific," Janet Blaise said. "He shoots like a regular Howard Hill, but of course he uses a bow that nobody else can pull."

"I'd like to try," said the Saint, and the conversation slid harmlessly along the tangent he had provided.

After lunch everyone went back to the beach, with the exception of Astron, who retired to put his morning's meditations on paper. Chatter surrendered to an afternoon torpor which even subdued Vosper.

An indefinite while later, Herrick aroused with a yell and plunged roaring into the sea, followed by Janet Blaise. They were followed by others, including the Saint. An interlude of aquatic brawling developed somehow into a pick-up game of touch football on the beach, which was delightfully confused by recurrent arguments about who was supposed to be on which of the unequal sides. This boisterous nonsense churned up so much sand for the still-freshening breeze to spray over Floyd Vosper, who by that time had drunk enough to be trying to sleep under the big beach umbrella, that the misanthropic oracle finally got back on his feet.

"Perhaps," he said witheringly, "I had better get out of the way of you perennial juveniles before you convert me into a dune."

He stalked off along the beach and lay down again about a hundred yards away. Simon noticed him still there, flat on his face and presumably unconscious, when the game eventually broke up through a confused water-polo phase to leave everyone gasping and laughing and dripping on the patio with no immediate resurge of inspiration. It was the last time he saw the unpopular Mr. Vosper alive.

"Well," Arthur Gresson observed, mopping his short round body with a towel, "at least one of us seems to have enough sense to know when to lie down."

"And to choose the only partner who'd do it with him," Pauline added vaguely.

Herbert Wexall glanced along the beach in the direction that they both referred to, then glanced for further inspiration at the waterproof watch he was still wearing.

"It's almost cocktail time," he said. "How about it, anyone?"

His wife shivered, and said: "I'm starting to freeze my tail off. It's going to blow like a son-of-a-gun any minute. Let's all go in and get some clothes on first—then we'll be set for the evening. You'll stay for supper of course, Mr. Templar?"

"I hadn't planned to make a day of it," Simon protested diffidently, and was promptly overwhelmed from all quarters.

He found his way back to the room where he had left his clothes without the benefit of Floyd Vosper's chatty courier service, and made leisured and satisfactory use of the freshwater shower and monogrammed towels. Even so, when he sauntered back into the living room, he almost had the feeling of being lost in a strange and empty house, for all the varied individuals who had peopled the stage so vividly and vigorously a short time before had vanished into other and unknown seclusions and had not yet returned.

He lighted a cigarette and strolled idly toward the picture window that overlooked the verandah and the sea. Everything around his solitude was so still, excepting the subsonic suggestion of distant movements within the house, that he was tempted to walk on tiptoe; and yet outside the broad pane of plate glass the fronds of coconut palms were fluttering in a thin febrile frenzy, and there were lacings of white cream on the incredible jade of the short waves simmering on the beach.

He noticed, first, in what should have been a lazily sensual survey of the panorama, that the big beach umbrella was no longer where he had first seen it, down to his right outside the pseudo-Grecian patio. He saw, as his eye wandered on, that it had been moved a hundred yards or so to his left—in fact, to the very place where Floyd Vosper was still lying. It occurred to him first that Vosper must have moved it himself, except that no shade was needed in the brief and darkening twilight. After that he noticed that Vosper seemed to have turned over on his back; and then at last as the Saint focused his eyes he saw with a weird thrill that the shaft of the umbrella stood straight up out of the left side of Vosper's scrawny brown chest, not in the sand beside him at all, but like a gigantic pin that had impaled a strange and inelegant insect—or, in a fantastic phrase that was not Simon's at all, like the arrow of God.

3

Major Rupert Fanshire, the senior Superintendent of Police, which made him third in the local hierarchy after the Commissioner and Deputy Commissioner, paid tribute to the importance of the case by taking personal charge of it. He was a slight pinkish blond man with rather large and very bright blue eyes and such a discreetly modulated voice that it commanded rapt attention through the basic effort of trying to hear what it was saying. He sat at an ordinary writing desk in the living room, with a Bahamian sergeant standing stiffly beside him, and contrived to turn the whole room into an office in which seven previously happy-go-lucky adults wriggled like guilty schoolchildren whose teacher has been found libelously caricatured on their blackboard.

He said, with wholly impersonal conciseness: "Of course, you all know by now that Mr. Vosper was found on the beach with the steel spike of an umbrella through his chest. My job is to find out how it happened. So to start with, if anyone did it to him, the topography suggests that that person came from, or through, this house. I've heard all your statements, and all they seem to amount to is that each of you was going about his own business at the time when this might have happened."

"All I know," Herbert Wexall said, "is that I was in my

study, reading and signing the letters that I dictated this morning.''

"And I was getting dressed," said his wife.

"So was I," said Janet Blaise.

"I guess I was in the shower," said Reginald Herrick.

"I was having a bubble bath," said Pauline Stone.

"I was still working," said Astron. "This morning I started a new chapter of my book—in my mind, you understand. I do not write by putting everything on paper. For me it is necessary to meditate, to feel, to open floodgates in my mind, so that I can receive the wisdom that comes from beyond the—"

"Quite," Major Fanshire assented politely. "The point is that none of you have alibis, if you need them. You were all going about your own business, in your own rooms. Mr. Templar was changing in the late Mr Vosper's room—"

"I wasn't here," Arthur Gresson said recklessly. "I drove back to my own place—I'm staying at the Fort Montague Beach Hotel. I wanted a clean shirt. I drove back there, and when I came back here all this had happened."

"There's not much difference," Major Fanshire said. "Dr. Horan tells me we couldn't establish the time of death within an hour or two, anyway. . . . So the next thing we come to is the question of motive. Did anyone here," Fanshire said almost innocently, "have any really serious trouble with Mr. Vosper?"

There was an uncomfortable silence, which the Saint finally broke by saying: "I'm on the outside here, so I'll take the rap. I'll answer for everyone."

The Superintendent cocked his bright eyes.

"Very well, sir. What would you say?"

"My answer," said the Saint, "is—everybody."

There was another silence, but a very different one, in which it seemed, surprisingly, as if all of them relaxed as unanimously as they had stiffened before. And yet, in its own way, this relaxation was as self-conscious and uncomfortable as the preceding tension had been. Only the Saint, who had every attitude of the completely careless onlooker, and Major Fanshire, whose deferential patience was impregnably correct, seemed immune to the interplay of hidden strains.

"Would you care to go any further?" Fanshire asked.

"Certainly," said the Saint. "I'll go anywhere. I can say what I like, and I don't have to care whether anyone is on speaking terms with me tomorrow. I'll go on record with my opinion that the late Mr. Vosper was one of the most unpleasant characters I've ever met. I'll make the statement, if it isn't already general knowledge, that he made a specialty of needling everyone he spoke to or about. He goaded everyone with nasty little things that he knew, or thought he knew, about them. I wouldn't blame anyone here for wanting, at least theoretically, to kill him."

"I'm not exactly concerned with your interpretation of blame," Fanshire said detachedly. "But if you have any facts, I'd like to hear them."

"I have no facts," said the Saint coolly. "I only know that in the few hours I've been here, Vosper made statements to me, a stranger, about everyone here, any one of which could be called fighting words."

"You will have to be more specific," Fanshire said.

"Okay," said the Saint. "I apologize in advance to anyone it hurts. Remember, I'm only repeating the kind of thing that made Vosper a good murder candidate. . . . I am now specific. In my hearing, he called Reg Herrick a dumb athlete who was trying to marry Janet Blaise for her money. He suggested that Janet was a stupid juvenile for taking him seriously. He called Astron a commercial charlatan. He implied that Lucy Wexall was a dope and a snob. He inferred that Herb Wexall had more use for his secretary's sex than for her stenography, and he thought out loud that Pauline was amenable. He called Mr. Gresson a crook to his face."

"And during all this," Fanshire said, with an offensiveness that had to be heard to be believed, "he said nothing about you?"

"He did indeed," said the Saint. "He analyzed me, more or less, as a flamboyant phony."

"And you didn't object to that?"

"I hardly could," Simon replied blandly, "After I'd hinted to him that I thought he was even phonier."

128

It was a line on which a stage audience could have tittered, but the tensions of the moment let it sink with a slow thud.

Fanshire drew down his upper lip with one forefinger and nibbled it inscrutably.

"I expect this bores you as much as it does me, but this is the job I'm paid for. I've got to say that all of you had the opportunity, and from what Mr. Templar says you could all have had some sort of motive. Well, now I've got to look into what you might call the problem of physical possibility."

Simon Templar lighted a cigarette. It was the only movement that anyone made, and after that he was the most intent listener of them all as Fanshire went on: "Dr. Horan says, and I must say I agree with him, that to drive that umbrella shaft clean through a man's chest must have taken quite exceptional strength. It seems to be something that no woman, and probably no ordinary man, could have done."

His pale bright eyes came to rest on Herrick as he finished speaking, and the Saint found his own eyes following others in the same direction.

The picture formed in his mind, the young giant towering over a prostrate Vosper, the umbrella raised in his mighty arms like a fantastic spear and the setting sun flaming on his red head, like an avenging angel, and the thrust downward with all the power of those herculean shoulders . . . and then, as Herrick's face began to flush under the awareness of so many stares, Janet Blaise suddenly cried out: "No! No—it couldn't have been Reggie!"

Fanshire's gaze transferred itself to her curiously, and she said in a stammering rush: "You see, it's silly, but we didn't quite tell the truth, I mean about being in our own rooms. As a matter of fact, Reggie was in my room most of the time. We were—talking."

The Superintendent cleared his throat and continued to gaze at her stolidly for a while. He didn't make any comment. But presently he looked at the Saint in the same dispassionately thoughtful way that he had first looked at Herrick.

Simon said calmly: "Yes, I was just wondering myself

whether I could have done it. And I had a rather interesting thought."

"Yes, Mr. Templar?"

"Certainly it must take quite a lot of strength to drive a spike through a man's chest with one blow. But now remember that this wasn't just a spike, or a spear. It had an enormous great umbrella on top of it. Now think what would happen if you were stabbing down with a thing like that?"

"Well, what would happen?"

"The umbrella would be like a parachute. It would be like a sort of sky anchor holding the shaft back. The air resistance would be so great that I'm wondering how anyone, even a very strong man, could get much momentum into the thrust. And the more force he put into it, the more likely he'd be to lift himself off the ground, rather than drive the spike down."

Fanshire digested this, blinking, and took his full time to do it.

"That certainly is a thought," he admitted. "But damn it," he exploded, "we know it was done. So it must have been possible."

"There's something entirely backward about that logic," said the Saint. "Suppose we say, if it was impossible, maybe it wasn't done."

"Now you're being a little ridiculous," Fanshire snapped. "We saw—"

"We saw a man with the sharp iron-tipped shaft of a beach umbrella through his chest. We jumped to the natural conclusion that somebody stuck it into him like a sword. And that may be just what a clever murderer meant us to think."

Then it was Arthur Gresson who shattered the fragile silence by leaping out of his chair like a bouncing ball.

"I've got it!" he yelped. "Believe me, everybody, I've got it! This'll kill you!"

"I hope not," Major Fanshire said dryly. "But what is it?"

"Listen," Gresson said. "I knew something rang a bell somewhere, but I couldn't place it. Now it all comes back to me. This is something I only heard at the hotel the other day, but some of you must have heard it before. It happened about a year ago, when Gregory Peck was visiting here. He stayed at the same hotel where I am, and one afternoon he was on the beach, and the wind came up, just like it did today, and it picked up one of those beach umbrellas and carried it right to where he was lying, and the point just grazed his ribs and gave him a nasty gash, but what the people who saw it happen were saying was that if it'd been just a few inches the other way, it could have gone smack into his heart, and you'd've had a film star killed in the most sensational way that ever was. Didn't you ever hear about that, Major?"

"Now you mention it," Fanshire said slowly, "I think I did hear something about it."

"Well," Gresson said, *"what if it happened again this afternoon, to someone who wasn't as lucky as Peck?"*

There was another of those electric silences of assimilation, out of which Lucy Wexall said: "Yes, I heard about that." And Janet said: "Remember, I told you about it! I was visiting some friends at the hotel that day, and I didn't see it happen, but I was there for the commotion."

Gresson spread out his arms, his round face gleaming with excitement and perspiration.

"That's got to be it!" he said. "You remember how Vosper was lying under the umbrella outside the patio when we started playing touch football, and he got sore because we were kicking sand over him, and he went off to the other end of the beach? But he didn't take the umbrella with him. The wind did that, after we all went off to change. And this time it didn't miss!"

Suddenly Astron stood up beside him; but where Gresson had risen like a jumping bean, this was like the growth and unfolding of a tree.

"I have heard many words," Astron said, in his firm gentle voice, "but now at last I think I am hearing truth. No man struck the blasphemer down. The arrow of God smote him, in his wickedness and his pride, as it was written long ago in the stars."

"You can say that again," Gresson proclaimed triumphantly. "He sure had it coming."

Again the Saint drew at his cigarette and created his own

vision behind half-closed eyes. He saw the huge umbrella plucked from the sand by the invisible fingers of the wind, picked up and hurled spinning along the deserted twilight beach, its great mushroom spread of gaudy canvas no longer a drag now but a sail for the wind to get behind, the whole thing transformed into a huge unearthly dart flung with literally superhuman power, the arrow of God indeed. A fantastic, an almost unimaginable solution; and yet it did not have to be imagined because there were witnesses that it had actually almost happened once before. . . .

Fanshire was saying: "By Jove, that's the best suggestion I've heard yet—without any religious implication, of course. It sounds as if it could be the right answer!"

Simon's eyes opened on him fully for an instant, almost pityingly, and then closed completely as the true and right and complete answer rolled through the Saint's mind like a long peaceful wave.

"I have one question to ask," said the Saint.

"What's that?" Fanshire said, too politely to be irritable, yet with a trace of impatience, as if he hated the inconvenience of even defending such a divinely tailored theory.

"Does anyone here have a gun?" asked the Saint.

There was an almost audible creaking of knitted brows, and Fanshire said: "Really, Mr. Templar, I don't quite follow you."

"I only asked," said the Saint imperturbably, "if anyone here had a gun. I'd sort of like to know the answer before I explain why."

"I have a revolver," Wexall said with some perplexity. "What about it?"

"Could we see it, please?" said the Saint.

"I'll get it," said Pauline Stone.

She got up and left the room.

"You know I have a gun, Fanshire," Wexall said. "You gave me my permit. But I don't see—"

"Neither do I," Fanshire said.

The Saint said nothing. He devoted himself to his cigarette, with impregnable detachment, until the voluptuous secretary came back. Then he put out the cigarette and extended his hand.

Pauline looked at Wexall, hesitantly, and at Fanshire. The Superintendent nodded a sort of grudging acquiescence. Simon took the gun and broke it expertly.

"A Colt .38 Detective Special," he said. "Unloaded." He sniffed the barrel. "But fired quite recently," he said, and handed the gun to Fanshire.

"I used it myself this morning," Lucy Wexall said cheerfully. "Janet and Reg and I were shooting at the Portuguese men-of-war. There were quite a lot of them around before the breeze came up."

"I wondered what the noise was," Wexall said vaguely.

"I was coming up the drive when I heard it first," Gresson said, "and I thought the next war had started."

"This is all very int'resting," Fanshire said, removing the revolver barrel from the proximity of his nostrils with a trace of exasperation, "but I don't see what it has to do with the case. Nobody has been shot—"

"Major Fanshire," said the Saint quietly, "may I have a word with you, outside? And will you keep that gun in your pocket so that at least we can hope there will be no more shooting?"

The Superintendent stared at him for several seconds, and at last unwillingly got up.

"Very well, Mr. Templar." He stuffed the revolver into the side pocket of his rumpled white jacket, and glanced back at his impassive chocolate sentinel. "Sergeant, see that nobody leaves here, will you?"

He followed Simon out on to the verandah and said almost peremptorily: "Come on now, what's this all about?"

It was so much like a flash of a faraway Scotland Yard Inspector that the Saint had to control a smile. But he took Fanshire's arm and led him persuasively down the front steps to the beach. Off to their left a tiny red glowworm blinked low down under the silver stars.

"You still have somebody watching the place where the body was found," Simon said.

"Of course," Fanshire grumbled. "As a matter of routine. But the sand's much too soft to show any footprints, and—"

"Will you walk over there with me?"

Fanshire sighed briefly, and trudged beside him. His polite-
ness was dogged but unfailing. He was a type that had been
schooled from adolescence never to give up, even to the ultimate
in ennui. In the interests of total fairness, he would be game to
the last yawn.

He did go so far as to say: "I don't know what you're getting
at, but why *couldn't* it have been an accident?"

"I never heard a better theory in my life," said the Saint
equably, "with one insuperable flaw."

"What's that?"

"Only," said the Saint, very gently, "that the wind wasn't
blowing the right way."

Major Fanshire kept his face straight ahead to the wind and
said nothing more after that until they reached the glowworm
that they were making for and it became a cigarette-end that a
constable dropped as he came to attention.

The place where Floyd Vosper had been lying was marked
off in a square of tape, but there was nothing out of the ordinary
about it except some small stains that showed almost black under
the flashlight which the constable produced.

"May I mess up the scene a bit?" Simon asked.

"I don't see why not," Fanshire said doubtfully. "It doesn't
show anything, really."

Simon went down on his knees and began to dig with his
hands, around and under the place where the stains were. Minutes later he stood up, with sand trickling through his fingers,
and showed Fanshire the mushroomed scrap of metal that he
had found.

"A .38 bullet," Fanshire said, and whistled.

"And I think you'll be able to prove it was fired from the gun
you have in your pocket," said the Saint. "Also you'd better
have a sack of sand picked up from where I was digging. I think
a laboratory examination will find that it also contains fragments
of bone and human flesh."

"You'll have to explain this to me," Fanshire said quite hum-
bly.

Simon dusted his hands and lighted a cigarette.

"Vosper was lying on his face when I last saw him," he said,

134

"and I think he was as much passed out as sleeping. With the wind and the surf and the soft sand, it was easy for the murderer to creep up on him and shoot him in the back where he lay. But the murderer didn't want you looking for guns and comparing bullets. The umbrella was the inspiration. I don't have to remind you that the exit hole of a bullet is much larger than the entrance. By turning Vosper's body over, the murderer found a hole in his chest that it can't have been too difficult to force the umbrella shaft through—obliterating the original wound and confusing everybody in one simple operation."

"Let's get back to the house," said the Superintendent abruptly.

After a while, as they walked, Fanshire said: "It's going to feel awfully funny, having to arrest Herbert Wexall."

"Good God!" said the Saint, in honest astonishment. "You weren't thinking of doing that?"

Fanshire stopped and blinked at him under the still distant light of the uncurtained windows.

"Why not?"

"Did Herbert seem at all guilty when he admitted he had a gun? Did he seem at all uncomfortable—I don't mean just puzzled, like you were—about having it produced? Was he ready with the explanation of why it still smelled of being fired?"

"But if anyone else used Wexall's gun," Fanshire pondered laboriously, "why should they go to such lengths to make it look as if no gun was used at all, when Wexall would obviously have been suspected?"

"Because it was somebody who didn't want Wexall to take the rap," said the Saint. "Because Wexall is the goose who could still lay golden eggs—but he wouldn't do much laying on the end of a rope, or whatever you do to murderers here."

The Superintendent pulled out a handkerchief and wiped his face.

"My God," he said, "you mean you think Lucy—"

"I think we have to go all the way back to the prime question of motive," said the Saint. "Floyd Vosper was a nasty man who made dirty cracks about everyone here. But his cracks were dirtiest because he always had a wickedly good idea what he was talking about. Nevertheless, very few people become murderers because of a dirty crack. Very few people except me kill other people on points of principle. Vosper called us all variously dupes, phonies, cheaters, and fools. But since he had roughly the same description for all of us, we could all laugh it off. There was only one person about whom he made the unforgivable accusation. . . . Now shall we rejoin the mob?''

"You'd better do this your own way," Fanshire muttered.

Simon Templar took him up the steps to the verandah and back through the french doors into the living room, where all eyes turned to them in a deathly silence.

"A parrafin test will prove who fired that revolver in the last twenty-four hours, aside from those who have already admitted it," Simon said, as if there had been no interruption. "And you'll remember, I'm sure, who supplied that very handy theory about the arrow of God."

"Astron!" Fanshire gasped.

"Oh, no," said the Saint, a little tiredly. "He only said that God sometimes places His arrow in the hands of a man. And I feel quite sure that a wire to New York will establish that there is actually a criminal file under the name of Granville, with fingerprints and photos that should match Mr. Gresson's—as Vosper's fatally elephantine memory remembered. . . . That was the one crack he shouldn't have made, because it was the only one that was more than gossip or shrewd insult, the only one that could be easily proved, and the only one that had a chance of upsetting an operation which was all set—if you'll excuse the phrase—to make a big killing."

Major Fanshire fingered his upper lip.

"I don't know," he began; and then, as Arthur Granville Gresson began to rise like a floating balloon from his chair, and the ebony-faced sergeant moved to intercept him like a well-disciplined automaton, he knew.

Dagger

•

John Jakes

John Jakes's bestselling Kent Family Chronicles, *and equally bestselling* North-South Trilogy, *are historical novels at their finest. His crime fiction—of which he wrote much in the early years of his career—has the same compelling and suspenseful qualities. His mystery novels, written under his own name and such pseudonyms as Alan Payne and Jay Scotland, include:* The Devil Has Four Faces *(1958),* The Imposter *(1959),* Johnny Havoc *(1960), and* Making It Big *(1968). "Dagger" is the realistic tale of the members of a jazz combo, a woman confined to a wheelchair, a Nazi SS dagger—and sudden death.*

They had been three inseparable comrades, drawn together by their work—Jimmy Ridgely, the trumpeter; Len Hunt, the piano player; and Laurie. Lovely Laurie, who sang, and lifted them from a low-class outfit to a small group with something of a style. They had drunk many beers together, told many jokes together, sipped many cups of coffee together in the cold early morning hours when the rest of the people in town were asleep. And now their world had been torn apart, and only two of them were left.

Lieutenant Stagg sat behind the desk, a thick-jawed man who needed a shave. His hands juggled the Nazi SS dagger. Behind him, rain slanted down the glass, the chilling rain of the predawn hours.

"This *is* your knife, isn't it?" Stagg said heavily to Len Hunt.

Hunt was seated on the other side of the desk, a slender, slightly stoop-shouldered man with unruly straw-colored hair. His eyes were bleary. They had dragged him out of bed and

137

down here to police headquarters to tell him that Jimmy Ridgely had been murdered and that he was the boy tagged with doing the job.

Hunt's voice was raw-edged. "I told you," he said, "that it was mine. I got it in Berlin, during the war. I keep it in my dressing room. It's kind of a good luck charm. Everybody knew I had it." His voice grew heavy with the repetition of the words.

Inside, his stomach churned. He glanced quickly at Laurie, sitting on a bench along the wall. She was bundled into a woolly green coat, and her hair was tangled, and she wore no makeup. Her blue-gray eyes were rimmed with red, but she was lovely. Still lovely. He looked quickly away.

Stagg threw down the dagger. "You people make me tired. Hunt, we know damned well how you felt about Miss Connors here. We talked to your manager."

Wolf? Sure, Len thought, Ted Wolf would know. Aging gray-haired Ted. He knew. So did everybody else. But that didn't make him guilty, just feeling the way he did.

One of the detectives leaning against the wall scraped a match loudly and lit a cigarette. Stagg sighed heavily. "Hunt, were you in love with Miss Connors?"

Len wound his fingers together and stared at them. Why didn't it work out, like a piece on the piano? Clearly, logically, the chords in proper sequence. No, it was jumbled, tangled in a mass of feelings and half-thoughts.

"I want the truth," Stagg rumbled. "Were you in love with Miss Connors?"

"Yes," Len said quietly. He did not look at Laurie. "I still am."

Stagg picked up the dagger again and leaned back. "That's what I thought." He turned toward Laurie. "Miss Connors, you're a very attractive girl. I've learned from Mr. Wolf that most every man that came into the club . . . well . . . fell for you. But you and Hunt here were the closest people to Jimmy Ridgely. That's why we tagged Hunt."

Len glanced at Laurie again. Her head was bowed. He got angry then, and jerked to his feet, facing the big detective. "You haven't got a bit of evidence."

"I've got a motive," Stagg said. "Jealousy. Ridgely and Miss Connors were to be married Saturday. You were jealous. It was evident to everybody at the club, Hunt. To *everybody*, get me? The way you mooned around. All right, you got sore. After the last show, you and Ridgely and some of the others shot craps with Ted Wolf until almost four. And then you got Ridgely to come to your dressing room. That's where we found him. With the SS dagger . . . yours . . . stuck in his chest. The scrubwoman put in the call." The words carried a note of finality.

"Damn it," Len shouted, "I went right home after the crap game. I didn't see Jimmy. He walked off. He was acting funny, so I let him go."

Stagg picked up a pencil. "Did he lose much in the crap game?"

"He won three bucks."

"Oh." The detective's face sagged and he put the pencil down. "Just checking."

"Damn it . . ." Len said loudly again.

"Easy, buddy," the detective against the wall said. "Don't talk like that around here."

Len let the breath rip in and out of his chest. He heard Laurie sobbing quietly. Sure, it broke him up when Jimmy announced their wedding. So what? He loved her too much to try and mess things up for her. And now this cop. . . .

Suddenly, his breathing quieted. A loose grin appeared on his face. He was waking up now, throwing off some of the warm daze of sleepiness. He was beginning to pick up the loose ends, with which they wanted to hang him so methodically.

"You got anything more to say?" Stagg asked.

"Yes, I have," Len said. "I went back to my hotel right after the crap game with Wolf. I got my key from the night clerk." He jabbed a finger at Stagg. "Check him. I hit the sack and your boys woke me up, just about a quarter of six. Check it, and find out how right you are."

Stagg shook his head. "The clerk probably wouldn't remember exactly when it was. You could have killed Ridgely and grabbed a cab back to the hotel. Besides, Wolf told us he saw you leaving with Jimmy Ridgely. You walked out of the bar together, when the crap game broke up. There was time.''

"Wolf's a liar!'' Len said sharply.

"We'll decide that. He's coming in to sign a statement this morning. We've already contacted him by phone.''

"He had too much to drink,'' Len said. "He was drinking a lot.''

"Look,'' Stagg said harshly, "quit playing games with us.''

Len breathed deeply. Far, far down in his stomach was a core of cold, terrible fear. Here was the deadly question. He felt sweat bead his palms as he stared at Stagg. Laurie's rhythmic sobs counterpointed with the lonely tap of the rain on the window. Outside, the sky was growing faintly gray.

"Tell me something,'' Len said quietly. "Whose prints were on the knife. Mine?''

Stagg looked quickly at the cold gray blade of the dagger lying on the desk blotter. "There weren't any prints.'' Len felt a quick surge of inward triumph. "But you could have used gloves,'' he added hastily.

Len started to button up his topcoat. The detective against the wall straightened up and stuck one hand in his pocket, his eyes gleaming warily.

"I'm getting out of here,'' Len said, staring straight at Stagg. "I'm taking Miss Connors with me. And until you get some kind of evidence that sticks, don't try to tag me with killing Jimmy.''

Stagg juggled the knife and slammed it down on the desk abruptly. "All right. But I'm warning you, Hunt. Don't make a move out of this town. Around here, when somebody dies, we look for motives. You're it this time. So we'll keep working on it until we find some evidence like you want. And then we *will* make it stick!''

His words were threatening, but Len saw the slump of his shoulders beneath the faded blue suit. He was a tired man, tired as Len himself, and in almost the same position, except for the fact that he had already established Len as the killer in his own mind. Both of them were looking for the hand that had pushed the knife into Ridgely's chest. But Stagg would try to make Len's hand fit the dagger.

Len walked quickly over to Laurie and touched her shoulder. She nodded without glancing up. The detective who had leaned against the wall followed them without making any pretense of hiding. They walked out of the station and Len turned up his collar against the chill rain.

Across the street was an all-night restaurant. They went in, ordered coffee, and sank down in a corner booth. The detective yawned as he relaxed on a stool near the juke box.

Laurie's spoon rattled against the cup. "Len . . ." she said quietly. It was the first word she had uttered since Len had walked into the police station nearly an hour before.

Len reached out hesitantly and put his hand over hers. "No, honey. It wasn't me."

"I . . . I . . . didn't realize . . . until that policeman asked you . . . how you felt . . ." She took a quick drink of the coffee, still not looking at him.

"Let's not talk about that now." His voice went lower. "Jimmy's dead, and somebody killed him."

Her eyes came up slowly, round blue-gray pits of loneliness. "Who?"

Len shook his head. "I don't know. But I know I don't want to get stuck with it. And right now, I'm scared. Scared they'll make it stick somehow. Stagg looks like a one-track man. He can't be thrown off, unless we turn up the real guy."

She smiled, briefly and bitterly, and stirred her coffee again in an aimless way. Her eyes wandered to the rain-spattered window. "Out there, someplace. But who is he?"

The detective shoved a nickel in the juke box, and in a moment the music poured out of the speaker. The detective hunched over his coffee and grinned sourly at them. Len listened, his insides knotted up. Laurie was listening, too, and she started to cry once more.

It was one of their few records. Laurie sang, and Jimmy's trumpet came out high and shrill and sweet, ripping up and up, translating the words that Laurie sang into emotions of brass, making them live. *With a Song In My Heart.* That was all that was left, Len thought hatefully. A few grooves in a couple of dozen records, and some memories in the minds of a handful of people. Oh, he wasn't a great horn man. Others had been better, others would be a lot better after him. But they had been three, Len and Laurie and Jimmy, and somebody pushed the SS dagger into Jimmy's chest and stopped the sound of that horn. It meant something when you knew the guy.

"I've got an idea," Len said hesitantly, as if he wasn't sure.

Laurie took a handkerchief from her purse and wiped at her face. "What . . . what is it?"

"Wolf." Len pronounced the word softly. "His name cropped up quite a lot in what Lieutenant Stagg said. Wolf told them I was in love with you. Wolf said Jimmy and I left the crap game together. He's too damned eager to volunteer information."

"Why would he want to kill Jimmy, Len? He managed the band, and it would hurt him to lose him. Jimmy had his own reputation, at least around here."

Len shook his head. Nothing was straight in his mind. Only a suspicion. "No reasons, honey. Just wild ideas, right now. But if Stagg works on his wild idea, I damned well better work on mine. And fast." He patted her arm. "You need sleep."

She nodded. "I'm kind of dead all over, Len. I can't feel anything."

"It'll take a while for the shock to wear off. Come on. I'll take you home."

He payed the bill and hailed a cab out on the street. Traffic was beginning to move, and although the rain still slashed down, the sky had grown considerably lighter. Len stifled a yawn as he climbed in after Laurie. He was tired, but he knew he wouldn't get any sleep for a long time yet. He couldn't afford it.

A squad car pulled away from the front of police headquarters and started out after them. Len turned around with a disgusted sigh. Laurie leaned against the side of the cab and closed her eyes.

Len sat staring out into the rain, watching the ribbons of water obscure the buildings. *Wolf.* He kept hearing that name. *Wolf.*

He kept seeing the face, fiftyish, balding, bag-cheeked, somehow worried and pressed all the time. *Wolf*. Managing the outfit. *Wolf*, rolling the dice in the after-hour sessions, rolling them like his life depended on it, rolling them like a fanatic pleading to a strange god.

He was the only other person that even approached the edges of the picture. Barring, of course, somebody around the club that nobody ever noticed. If that was it, then Len knew he didn't have a chance. The cell would be waiting for him; Stagg would see to that.

But if Wolf fitted in somewhere . . . but damn it, where? Nervously, Len lit a cigarette. They were nearing Laurie's apartment, one of a series of brownstone walkups. Quickly, Len thought the thing over. He had to follow it up, while the idea was fresh.

What motive would Wolf have? Did he love Laurie, too, as Len did? Had it become twisted in him, making him take the dagger from Len's dressing table? No. Len stared hard at the glowing orange end of the cigarette. It didn't fit. Ted Wolf was a businessman. He had no personal connections with anyone in the outfit. Strictly percentage. Irritatingly, Len knew he was right, but he couldn't remember why. Something didn't click into place.

The feeling of certainty vanished before the lack of evidence. Maybe Wolf *did* have some emotional connection with them. Maybe it was hidden down deep in his brain, festering, swelling, with none of them knowing about it. Maybe . . . *maybe* . . . Len ground the cigarette out on the floor. Too damned much depended on *maybe*.

The cab pulled to a stop before one of the brownstones. "Here you are, mister," the cabbie said.

Len told him to wait and walked up to the door of Laurie's apartment on the second floor. Her eyes still held their dazed, unbelieving look. Len took the key from her trembling hand and opened the door.

"Promise me you'll get some sleep," he said quietly.

She nodded wearily.

"I'll let you know if anything breaks." He glanced away

quickly. Even now, he couldn't help seeing how beautiful she was. And somehow, he hated himself for it. He patted her shoulder again and stalked off down the hall. He heard the door shut behind him as he headed down the stairs.

The cabbie took him back to his apartment. The police car stayed right behind them, and parked across the street from the hotel. Len mixed himself a drink and went to the window, staring down at the car. The symbol, he thought. They're after me, and they'll get me, just by dogging me, unless I do something.

He swallowed the drink hastily and felt it jolt into his stomach. He looked at his watch. Quarter after seven. Well, he couldn't see Wolf for a while yet.

As he stood under the shower, letting the icy points of water dig into his skin and restore it to life, he kept thinking back over the whole thing. What was it he wanted to remember? What part of the thing made him so sure Wolf could not have killed out of jealousy? Somehow, this unseen factor ruled out the one alternative and brought in another. But it was one of those things heard once that sinks to the bottom of the mind and lies there, growing sluggish from disuse. If only he *would* remember. . . .

He sighed loudly and stepped out of the shower. The thick towel felt good on his back. He decided to give himself a couple of hours. It would come to him. Things like that always did. Names he couldn't remember at the moment, no matter how he tried, always came, in time.

Another drink made him warmer, but he stopped at two. He had to keep his mind clear and alert. He dressed in a better suit and walked two blocks to a drugstore, where he had bacon, eggs and toast. His body had thrown off its tiredness. He knew that he would be exhausted tomorrow, but now he felt normally awake and perceptive.

The detective got back into his squad car when Len found a cab and started out to see Ted Wolf. The squad car stayed behind the cab all the way.

Ted Wolf lived in a not-quite-exclusive apartment hotel near the river. The detective posted himself at the curb as Len stepped into the vestibule and pressed the buzzer. A moment later, he heard a voice over the speaking tube.

"Who is it, please?"

His breath cut off short. That was it! The voice belonged to a woman. *Ted Wolf's wife!*

"It's Len Hunt, about Jimmy Ridgely."

There was a gasp. "Oh." The door clicked abruptly and Len jerked it open. The elevator rose to the fifth floor with horrible slowness. Down the hall, a door stood open, and beyond the door sat Mrs. Wolf in her wheelchair.

Len walked in and closed the door. Mrs. Wolf started to speak, but instead she pressed a white handkerchief to her mouth and doubled over, coughing wetly. The handkerchief showed faint reddish stains that had not come out in laundering. Only one kind of person coughed like that. Len felt his stomach quiver. Somewhere, a connection. . . .

"I'm sorry, Mr. Hunt," Mrs. Wolf said, wheeling herself into the living room. She was a thin gray-haired woman whose skin had somehow taken on that same dead grayish color. Len stood awkwardly until she asked him to sit down. He did not want to look at her, because he could see that she had once been a beautiful woman, until paralysis and tuberculosis had torn the beauty away.

"I'm sorry," she said again. "We heard about the death last night. The police called. Ted left about half an hour ago. He was going to police headquarters, and then to pick up our tickets."

Tickets. . . . the word stung Len's mind. Now he remembered part of it. It was a subject seldom mentioned by anyone, least of all by Wolf himself. He had heard it at the club, how Wolf was devoted to this pale trembling frame of a woman. How she was slowly dying, how he cared for her, tried to prolong her life, took her to doctors, spent money . . . devotion . . . fanatical devotion. And tickets . . .

"Were you leaving town, Mrs. Wolf?" Len asked carefully. If only she was innocent of everything, if there *was* really something there.

"We are going to Arizona next week." She smiled wanly.

"The doctor said it was imperative that we stay there for six months. But I'm afraid we couldn't get the money together, Mr. Hunt. So we're only going for one month. This climate is bad for me . . . I . . ." She stammered and bent her shoulders again, the cough wracking her. Flecks of red stained the handkerchief, and her hands fluttered wildly to conceal them. "Is there anything I could help you with?"

"No, I'll have to see Ted. Would . . . would it be all right if I waited for him?"

"Certainly. He promised to be back by nine-thirty, if you don't mind waiting that long."

"No," Len said, trying to keep the terrible eagerness out of his voice, "I don't mind . . ."

"You can wait in Ted's study if you like. I . . ." She touched her hair self-consciously. "I'm going to see what I can do about making myself look a little nicer. It's awfully early in the morning, you know." She laughed feebly at her own little joke.

"Thank you," Len said. He walked toward the study.

"Well . . ." Mrs. Wolf said awkwardly, "I hope you'll be comfortable. Make yourself at home." She wheeled herself off down the hall.

Len stepped quickly into the study, his head whipping from side to side, taking in everything. Money. *Money. Not enough money.* Of course not. The club was small, the band smaller. Not big time. Not the big money. Not enough for so many medical expenses. Where was it to come from, the money that Ted Wolf had needed so desperately and then failed to get? Wolf wanted to keep his wife alive for a few more months. *Money* . . . it tied up somewhere . . .

Tensely, Len listened. The rain hit the windows of the study, and far down the hall, Len heard a radio being switched on. He crossed quickly to the desk and began sliding the drawers open noiselessly. In the bottom drawer was a cheap gray tin box, locked.

His hands trembling, his stomach cold with anticipation, Len dragged out his apartment key and started to jimmy the box. Such a flimsy box, really. But how much deception would there be between a man and his invalid wife? She probably would never suspect him of anything, probably never ask or meddle into any of his affairs.

Len cursed quietly and twisted the key. The tin rasped as the lock snapped and broke. Len's breath came heavily. He made himself put the key back in his pocket before he opened the box lid. What would be in it? Something? Or nothing?

He sat back in the chair, took another deep breath, and listened. The radio still played. Water gurgled in a bathroom. Len reached out and opened the box and looked inside. His breath cut off as he let the three pieces of paper flutter to the desk.

He looked at the first piece of paper.

IOU to Ted Wolf, $3,500.

He licked his lips and looked at the next slip.

IOU to Ted Wolf, $2,800.

The third IOU was for $4,100.

All three were signed in a scrawl that Len knew all too well. *Jimmy Ridgely.*

Calmly now, Len put the IOU's into his coat pocket, closed the box, and replaced it in the drawer. He walked to the window and lit a cigarette, staring down at the rain-swept street five stories below. Now all he had to do was wait. Ted would be home by nine-thirty.

The manager of the band closed the door at eleven minutes after nine. Len rose from his chair. Wolf saw him through the open study door and started to speak, but Len motioned for him to be quiet. Wolf walked into the study. Len saw that the face of the man was gray, almost like his wife's, and that the flesh sagged even more than usual.

"Len . . ." Wolf said. "What's all the secrecy?"

"Were you down at police headquarters just now?" Len said.

"Why . . . why, yes . . ." Wolf laughed sheepishly and fumbled for a cigarette.

"Giving them a statement to make them surer than ever that I killed Jimmy?"

"Len, what's gotten into you . . ."

Len took the IOU's from his pocket and held them up. "This."

Wolf drew the unlighted cigarette from his lips. His eyes, circled with puffy pads of flesh, grew smaller. "What are you trying to say, Len? Spill it, before I get sore."

"I'm saying that maybe you killed Jimmy Ridgely. I'm saying that I'm almost certain you did."

"You're insane . . ." Wolf began.

Len shook his head. Beyond Wolf, Mrs. Wolf had wheeled herself into the doorway. The words of greeting froze on her lips when she heard Len speak, and she sat there, a loose vacant expression of horror on her face as she listened. Wolf himself did not see her behind him.

"It's a wild hunch," Len said. "It's been a wild hunch all along, but I stuck to it, because otherwise they'll get *me* for it. See my reason?"

Wolf stuck the cigarette back in his mouth and lit it. His eyes shone brightly, a little wildly, in the glow of the match. "Let's hear what you've got to say."

"You got your crap game going at the club after hours, only this wasn't one of the regular ones. This one was private. You were looking for a sucker and Jimmy was it. You needed money, money to take your wife to Arizona and keep her alive. Jimmy lost to you; he lost a lot. These IOU's show that. But I figure you picked a wrong guy in Jimmy, because he couldn't pay off. Last night, you collared him after the game . . ." Len grinned sourly. "After he won three bucks."

"Go on," Wolf said, his voice deadly soft.

"I'm not saying you planned it. Maybe you had too much to drink and you and Jimmy were in my dressing room. Afterward, you saw a good chance to implicate me. You wiped the prints off the knife. Or maybe you took the knife ahead of time. Anyway, you told Jimmy to pay off and he told you no dice. You lost your head, Wolf, and pushed my knife into his heart. Right into his heart, Wolf." Len's voice rose. He stepped quickly forward and grabbed the man's coat. His voice grew savage. *"Isn't that right?"*

Snarling, Wolf jerked away. His hand flashed toward the desk, closing on a dull-edged letter opener.

"You got it right, Len," Wolf whispered. "I got sore and he

went into your dressing room. He left his coat there. I got sore and the knife was on the table . . . but you can see why I did it . . . I needed the money . . . he wouldn't pay me . . . he couldn't . . . you see . . ."

Len reached for the phone. "Tell the police."

"No!" With an agonized shriek, Wolf rushed forward and jabbed the letter opener at Len. Len dodged, striking out with his fists. They whirled around and Len felt the opener tear the flesh of his cheek. He pushed at Wolf and the man stumbled backward, his arms swinging wildly, off balance.

Len tried to grab him, then. But he hurled on, striking the window. He shrieked and flapped his arms and rolled slowly backward over the sill amid a tinkling sound of breaking glass. The rain whipped in through the window. Len choked and looked away. It was five stories down.

Then he remembered Mrs. Wolf. She sat in her wheelchair, her head cocked ridiculously to one side, a pitiful smile on her lips. She was sick now, sicker than she had ever been before. "I loved him so," she murmured. "I loved him so . . ."

Len put his arms around her. In a couple of minutes, she began to cry, slow, agonized sobs that mingled with her coughing. She slumped over in the wheelchair. Len walked wearily to the desk. He picked the IOU's up from the floor, stuck them in his pocket, and picked up the telephone.

"Police headquarters," he said.

Lieutenant Stagg was not happy about it. But the testimony of Mrs. Wolf established with certainty that Ted Wolf had admitted the murder of Jimmy Ridgely. When Len walked out of police headquarters at five that evening, he was cleared. The detective followed him to the door. Len looked back. The man lit a cigarette and did not move off the steps.

He walked all the way back to his apartment. The club would be closed for a few days, thank God.

Laurie answered the phone when he called.

"I found the right one," he said.

"Who was it Len?"

"Ted Wolf."

"Wolf? Why . . . ?"

He shook his head, not thinking that she could not see him. "I'm tired. I'm going to bed. I can tell you at dinner tomorrow night, if that's all right."

"I'll be here," she said.

Len put down the phone. His eyelids felt heavy and his body ached from nervous strain. It was all over. Laurie, lovely Laurie. And Jimmy, dead. No marriage for them. Death. Sorrow. But there was time, he thought. Time ahead. Plenty of time for them, now that she knew, now that Jimmy's killer was dead.

Len walked over to his phonograph. From the rack, he pulled out three records. Their discs. With *A Song In My Heart*. One by one, he broke them and threw the pieces into the wastebasket. And then he went to bed.

Skin Deep

•

Sara Paretsky

V.I. "Vic" Warshawski, Sara Paretsky's Chicago-based sleuth, has received considerable acclaim as the toughest of the new breed of female private eye. Such novels as Deadlock *(1984),* Killing Orders *(1985), and* Bitter Medicine *(1987) amply attest to V. I.'s investigative skills and to her creator's ability to tell a fast-moving, intricately plotted, and richly characterized story. In "Skin Deep," detective and writer probe the not very beautiful goings-on behind the quest for perfect beauty in a Chicago skin-care salon.*

1

The warning bell clangs angrily and the submarine dives sharply. Everyone to battle stations. The Nazis pursuing closely, the bell keeps up its insistent clamor, loud, urgent, filling my head. My hands are wet: I can't remember what my job is in this cramped, tiny boat. If only someone would turn off the alarm bell. I fumble with some switches, pick up an intercom. The noise mercifully stops.

"Vic! Vic, is that you?"

"What?"

"I know it's late. I'm sorry to call so late, but I just got home from work. It's Sal, Sal Barthele."

"Oh, Sal. Sure." I looked at the orange clock readout. It was four-thirty. Sal owns the Golden Glow, a bar in the south Loop I patronize.

"It's my sister, Vic. They've arrested her. She didn't do it. I know she didn't do it."

151

"Of course not, Sal—Didn't do what?"

"They're trying to frame her. Maybe the manager . . . I don't know."

I swung my legs over the side of the bed. "Where are you?"

She was at her mother's house, 95th and Vincennes. Her sister had been arrested three hours earlier. They needed a lawyer, a good lawyer. And they needed a detective, a good detective. Whatever my fee was, she wanted me to know they could pay my fee.

"I'm sure you can pay the fee, but I don't know what you want me to do," I said as patiently as I could.

"She—they think she murdered that man. She didn't even know him. She was just giving him a facial. And he dies on her."

"Sal, give me your mother's address. I'll be there in forty minutes."

The little house on Vincennes was filled with neighbors and relatives murmuring encouragement to Mrs. Barthele. Sal is very black, and statuesque. Close to six feet tall, with a majestic carriage, she can break up a crowd in her bar with a look and a gesture. Mrs. Barthele was slight, frail, and light-skinned. It was hard to picture her as Sal's mother.

Sal dispersed the gathering with characteristic firmness, telling the group that I was here to save Evangeline and that I needed to see her mother alone.

Mrs. Barthele sniffed over every sentence. "Why did they do that to my baby?" she demanded of me. "You know the police, you know their ways. Why did they come and take my baby, who never did a wrong thing in her life?"

As a white woman, I could be expected to understand the machinations of the white man's law. And to share responsibility for it. After more of this meandering, Sal took the narrative firmly in hand.

Evangeline worked at La Cygnette, a high-prestige beauty salon on North Michigan. In addition to providing facials and their own brand-name cosmetics at an exorbitant cost, they massaged the bodies and feet of their wealthy clients, stuffed them into steam cabinets, ran them through a Bataan-inspired exercise routine, and fed them herbal teas. Signor Giuseppe would style their hair for an additional charge.

Evangeline gave facials. The previous day she had one client booked after lunch, a Mr. Darnell.

"Men go there a lot?" I interrupted.

Sal made a face. "That's what I asked Evangeline. I guess it's part of being a Yuppie—go spend a lot of money getting cream rubbed into your face."

Anyway, Darnell was to have had his hair styled before his facial, but the hairdresser fell behind schedule and asked Evangeline to do the guy's face first.

Sal struggled to describe how a La Cygnette facial worked—neither of us had ever checked out her sister's job. You sit in something like a dentist's chair, lean back, relax—you're naked from the waist up, lying under a big down comforter. The facial expert—cosmetician was Evangeline's official title—puts cream on your hands and sticks them into little electrically-heated mitts, so your hands are out of commission if you need to protect yourself. Then she puts stuff on your face, covers your eyes with heavy pads, and goes away for twenty minutes while the face goo sinks into your hidden pores.

Apparently while this Darnell lay back deeply relaxed, someone had rubbed some kind of poison into his skin. "When Evangeline came back in to clean his face, he was sick—heaving, throwing up, it was awful. She screamed for help and started trying to clean his face—it was terrible, he kept vomiting on her. They took him to the hospital, but he died around ten tonight.

"They came to get Baby at midnight—you've got to help her, V. I.—even if the guy tried something on her, she never did a thing like that—she'd haul off and slug him, maybe, but rubbing poison into his face? You go help her."

2

Evangeline Barthele was a younger, darker edition of her mother. At most times, she probably had Sal's energy—sparks of it flared now and then during our talk—but a night in the holding cells had worn her down.

I brought a clean suit and makeup for her; justice may be blind but her administrators aren't. We talked while she changed.

"This Darnell—you sure of the name?—had he ever been to the salon before?"

She shook her head. "I never saw him. And I don't think the other girls knew him either. You know, if a client's a good tipper or a bad one they'll comment on it, be glad or whatever that he's come in. Nobody said anything about this man."

"Where did he live?"

She shook her head. "I never talked to the guy, V. I."

"What about the PestFree?" I'd read the arrest report and talked briefly to an old friend in the M.E.'s office. To keep roaches and other vermin out of their posh Michigan Avenue offices, La Cygnette used a potent product containing a wonder chemical called chorpyrifos. My informant had been awe-struck—"Only an operation that didn't know shit about chemicals would leave chorpyrifos lying around. It's got a toxicity rating of five—it gets you through the skin—you only need a couple of tablespoons to kill a big man if you know where to put it."

Whoever killed Darnell had either known a lot of chemistry or been lucky—into his nostrils and mouth, with some rubbed into the face for good measure, the pesticide had made him convulsive so quickly that even if he knew who killed him he'd have been unable to talk, or even reason.

Evangeline said she knew where the poison was kept—everyone who worked there knew, knew it was lethal and not to touch it, but it was easy to get at. Just in a little supply room that wasn't kept locked.

"So why you? They have to have more of a reason than just that you were there."

She shrugged bitterly. "I'm the only black professional at La Cygnette—the other blacks working there sweep rooms and haul trash. I'm trying hard not to be paranoid, but I gotta wonder."

She insisted Darnell hadn't made a pass at her, or done anything to provoke an attack—she hadn't hurt the guy. As for anyone else who might have had opportunity, salon employees were always passing through the halls, going in and out of the little cubicles where they treated clients—she'd seen any number of people, all with legitimate business in the halls, but she hadn't seen anyone emerging from the room where Darnell was sitting.

When we finally got to bond court later that morning, I tried to argue circumstantial evidence—any of La Cygnette's fifty or so employees could have committed the crime, since all had access and no one had motive. The prosecutor hit me with a very unpleasant surprise: the police had uncovered evidence linking my client to the dead man. He was a furniture buyer from Kansas City who came to Chicago six times a year, and the doorman and the maids at his hotel had identified Evangeline without any trouble as the woman who accompanied him on his visits.

Bail was denied. I had a furious talk with Evangeline in one of the interrogation rooms before she went back to the holding cells.

"Why the hell didn't you tell me? I walked into the courtroom and got blindsided."

"They're lying," she insisted.

"Three people identified you. If you don't start with the truth right now, you're going to have to find a new lawyer and a new detective. Your mother may not understand, but for sure Sal will."

"You can't tell my mother. You can't tell Sal!"

"I'm going to have to give them some reason for dropping your case, and knowing Sal it's going to have to be the truth."

For the first time she looked really upset. "You're my lawyer. You should believe my story before you believe a bunch of strangers you never saw before."

"I'm telling you, Evangeline, I'm going to drop your case. I can't represent you when I know you're lying. If you killed Darnell we can work out a defense. Or if you didn't kill him and knew him we can work something out, and I can try to find the real killer. But when I know you've been seen with the guy any number of times, I can't go into court telling people you never met him before."

Tears appeared on the ends of her lashes. "The whole reason I didn't say anything was so Mama wouldn't know. If I tell you the truth, you've got to promise me you aren't running back to Vincennes Avenue talking to her."

I agreed. Whatever the story was, I couldn't believe Mrs. Barthele hadn't heard hundreds like it before. But we each make our own separate peace with our mothers.

Evangeline met Darnell at a party two years earlier. She liked him, he liked her—not the romance of the century, but they enjoyed spending time together. She'd gone on a two-week trip to Europe with him last year, telling her mother she was going with a girlfriend.

"First of all, she has very strict morals. No sex outside marriage. I'm thirty, mind you, but that doesn't count with her. Second, he's white, and she'd murder me. She really would. I think that's why I never fell in love with him—if we wanted to get married I'd never be able to explain it to Mama."

This latest trip to Chicago, Darnell thought it would be fun to see what Evangeline did for a living, so he booked an appointment at La Cygnette. She hadn't told anyone there she knew him. And when she found him sick and dying, she'd panicked and lied.

"And if you tell my mother of this, V. I.—I'll put a curse on you. My father was from Haiti and he knew a lot of good ones."

"I won't tell your mother. But unless they nuked Lebanon this morning or murdered the mayor, you're going to get a lot of lines in the paper. It's bound to be in print."

She wept at that, wringing her hands. So after watching her go off with the sheriff's deputies, I called Murray Ryerson at the *Herald-Star* to plead with him not to put Evangeline's liaison in the paper. "If you do she'll wither your testicles. Honest."

"I don't know, Vic. You know the *Sun-Times* is bound to have some kind of screamer headline like DEAD MAN FOUND IN FACE-LICKING SEX ORGY. I can't sit on a story like this when all the other papers are running it."

I knew he was right, so I didn't push my case very hard.

He surprised me by saying, "Tell you what: you find the real killer before my deadline for tomorrow's morning edition and

I'll keep your client's personal life out of it. The sex scoop came in too late for today's paper. The *Trib* prints on our schedule and they don't have it, and the *Sun-Times* runs older, slower presses, so they have to print earlier."

I reckoned I had about eighteen hours. Sherlock Holmes had solved tougher problems in less time.

3

Roland Darnell had been the chief buyer of living-room furnishings for Alexander Dumas, a high-class Kansas City department store. He used to own his own furniture store in the nearby town of Lawrence, but lost both it and his wife when he was arrested for drug smuggling ten years earlier. Because of some confusion about his guilt—he claimed his partner, who disappeared the night he was arrested, was really responsible—he'd only served two years. When he got out, he moved to Kansas City to start a new life.

I learned this much from my friends at the Chicago police. At least, my acquaintances. I wondered how much of the story Evangeline had known. Or her mother. If her mother didn't want her child having a white lover, how about a white ex-con, ex-(presumably) drug-smuggling lover?

I sat biting my knuckles for a minute. It was eleven now. Say they started printing the morning edition at two the next morning, I'd have to have my story by one at the latest. I could follow one line, and one line only—I couldn't afford to speculate about Mrs. Barthele—and anyway, doing so would only get me killed. By Sal. So I looked up the area code for Lawrence, Kansas, and found their daily newspaper.

The *Lawrence Daily Journal-World* had set up a special number for handling press inquiries. A friendly woman with a strong drawl told me Darnell's age (forty-four); place of birth (Eudora, Kansas); ex-wife's name (Ronna Perkins); and ex-partner's name (John Crenshaw). Ronna Perkins was living elsewhere in the country and the *Journal-World* was protecting her privacy. John Crenshaw had disappeared when the police arrested Darnell.

Crenshaw had done an army stint in Southeast Asia in the late sixties. Since much of the bamboo furniture the store specialized in came from the Far East, some people speculated that Crenshaw had set up the smuggling route when he was out there in the service. Especially since Kansas City immigration officials discovered heroin in the hollow tubes making up chair backs. If Darnell knew anything about the smuggling, he had never revealed it.

"That's all we know here, honey. Of course, you could come on down and try to talk to some people. And we can wire you photos if you want."

I thanked her politely—my paper didn't run too many photographs. Or even have wire equipment to accept them. A pity—I could have used a look at Crenshaw and Ronna Perkins.

La Cygnette was on an upper floor of one of the new marble skyscrapers at the top end of the Magnificent Mile. Tall, white doors opened onto a hushed waiting room reminiscent of a high-class funeral parlor. The undertaker, a middle-aged, highly made-up woman seated at a table that was supposed to be French provincial, smiled at me condescendingly.

"What can we do for you?"

"I'd like to see Angela Carlson. I'm a detective."

She looked nervously at two clients seated in a far corner. I lowered my voice. "I've come about the murder."

"But—but they made an arrest."

I smiled enigmatically. At least I hoped it looked enigmatic. "The police never close the door on all options until after the trial." If she knew anything about the police she'd know that was a lie—once they've made an arrest you have to get a presidential order to get them to look at new evidence.

The undertaker nodded nervously and called Angela Carlson in a whisper on the house phone. Evangeline had given me the names of the key players at La Cygnette; Carlson was the manager.

She met me in the doorway leading from the reception area into the main body of the salon. We walked on thick, silver pile through a white maze with little doors opening onto it. Every now and then we'd pass a white-coated attendant who gave the manager a subdued hello. When we went by a door with a police order slapped to it, Carlson winced nervously.

"When can we take that off? Everybody's on edge and that sealed door doesn't help. Our bookings are down as it is."

"I'm not on the evidence team, Ms. Carlson. You'll have to ask the lieutenant in charge when they've got what they need."

I poked into a neighboring cubicle. It contained a large white dentist's chair and a tray covered with crimson pots and bottles, all with the cutaway swans that were the salon's trademark. While the manager fidgeted angrily I looked into a tiny closet where clients changed—it held a tiny sink and a few coat hangers.

Finally she burst out, "Didn't your people get enough of this yesterday? Don't you read your own reports?"

"I like to form my own impressions, Ms. Carlson. Sorry to have to take your time, but the sooner we get everything cleared up, the faster your customers will forget this ugly episode."

She sighed audibly and led me on angry heels to her office, although the thick carpeting took the intended ferocity out of her stride. The office was another of the small treatment rooms with a desk and a menacing phone console. Photographs of a youthful Mme. de Leon, founder of La Cygnette, covered the walls.

Ms. Carlson looked through a stack of pink phone messages. "I have an incredibly busy schedule, Officer. So if you could get to the point. . . ."

"I want to talk to everyone with whom Darnell had an appointment yesterday. Also the receptionist on duty. And before I do that I want to see their personnel files."

"Really! All these people were interviewed yesterday." Her eyes narrowed suddenly. "Are you really with the police? You're not, are you. You're a reporter. I want you out of here now. Or I'll call the real police."

I took my license photostat from my wallet. "I'm a detective. That's what I told your receptionist. I've been retained by the Barthele family. Ms. Barthele is not the murderer and I want to find out who the real culprit is as fast as possible."

She didn't bother to look at the license. "I can barely tolerate answering police questions. I'm certainly not letting some snoop for hire take up my time. The police have made an arrest on extremely good evidence. I suppose you think you can drum up a fee by getting Evangeline's family excited about her innocence, but you'll have to look elsewhere for your money."

I tried an appeal to her compassionate side, using half-forgotten arguments from my court appearances as a public defender. (Outstanding employee, widowed mother, sole support, intense family pride, no prior arrests, no motive.) No sale.

"Ms. Carlson, you the owner or the manager here?"

"Why do you want to know?"

"Just curious about your stake in the success of the place and your responsibility for decisions. It's like this: you've got a lot of foreigners working here. The immigration people will want to come by and check out their papers.

"You've got lots and lots of tiny little rooms. Are they sprinklered? Do you have emergency exits? The fire department can make a decision on that.

"And how come your only black professional employee was just arrested and you're not moving an inch to help her out? There are lots of lawyers around who'd be glad to look at a discrimination suit against La Cygnette.

"Now if we could clear up Evangeline's involvement fast, we could avoid having all these regulatory people trampling around upsetting your staff and your customers. How about it?"

She sat in indecisive rage for several minutes: how much authority did I have, really? Could I offset the munificent fees the salon and the building owners paid to various public officials just to avoid such investigations? Should she call headquarters for instruction? Or her lawyer? She finally decided that even if I didn't have a lot of power I could be enough of a nuisance to affect business. Her expression compounded of rage and defeat, she gave me the files I wanted.

Darnell had been scheduled with a masseuse, the hair expert Signor Giuseppe, and with Evangeline. I read their personnel files, along with that of the receptionist who had welcomed him to La Cygnette, to see if any of them might have hailed from Kansas City or had any unusual traits, such as an arrest record for heroin smuggling. The files were very sparce. Signor Giuseppe Fruttero hailed from Milan. He had no next-of-kin to be notified in the event of an accident. Not even a good friend. Bruna, the masseuse, was Lithuanian, unmarried, living with her mother. Other than the fact that the receptionist had been born as Jean Evans in Hammond but referred to herself as Monique from New Orleans, I saw no evidence of any kind of cover-up.

Angela Carlson denied knowing either Ronna Perkins or John Crenshaw or having any employees by either of those names. She had never been near Lawrence herself. She grew up in Evansville, Indiana, came to Chicago to be a model in 1978, couldn't cut it, and got into the beauty business. Angrily she gave me the names of her parents in Evansville and summoned the receptionist.

Monique was clearly close to sixty, much too old to be Roland Darnell's ex-wife. Nor had she heard of Ronna or Crenshaw.

"How many people knew that Darnell was going to be in the salon yesterday?"

"Nobody knew." She laughed nervously. "I mean, of course, *I* knew—I made the appointment with him. And Signor Giuseppe knew when I gave him his schedule yesterday. And Bruna, the masseuse, of course, and Evangeline."

"Well, who else could have seen their schedules?"

She thought frantically, her heavily mascaraed eyes rolling in agitation. With another nervous giggle she finally said, "I suppose anyone could have known. I mean, the other cosmeticians and the makeup artists all come out for their appointments at the same time. I mean, if anyone was curious they could have looked at the other people's lists."

Carlson was frowning. So was I. "I'm trying to find a woman who'd be forty now, who doesn't talk much about her past. She's been divorced and she won't have been in the business long. Any candidates?"

Carlson did another mental search, then went to the file cabinets. Her mood was shifting from anger to curiosity and she flipped through the files quickly, pulling five in the end.

"How long has Signor Giuseppe been here?"

"When we opened our Chicago branch in 1980 he came to

us from Miranda's—I guess he'd been there for two years. He says he came to the States from Milan in 1970.''

"He a citizen? Has he got a green card?"

"Oh, yes. His papers are in good shape. We are very careful about that at La Cygnette." My earlier remark about the immigration department had clearly stung. "And now I really need to get back to my own business. You can look at those files in one of the consulting rooms—Monique, find one that won't be used today."

It didn't take me long to scan the five files, all uninformative. Before returning them to Monique I wandered on through the back of the salon. In the rear a small staircase led to an upper story. At the top was another narrow hall lined with small offices and storerooms. A large mirrored room at the back filled with hanging plants and bright lights housed Signor Giuseppe. A dark-haired man with a pointed beard and a bright smile, he was ministering gaily to a thin, middle-aged woman, talking and laughing while he deftly teased her hair into loose curls.

He looked at me in the mirror when I entered. "You are here for the hair, Signora? You have the appointment?"

"No, Signor Giuseppe. Sono qui perchè la sua fama se è sparsa di fronte a lei. Milano è una bella città, non è vero?"

He stopped his work for a moment and held up a deprecating hand. "Signora, it is my policy to speak only English in my adopted country."

"Una vera stupida e ignorante usanza io direi." I beamed sympathetically and sat down on a high stool next to an empty customer chair. There were seats for two clients. Since Signor Giuseppe reigned alone, I pictured him spinning at high speed between customers, snipping here, pinning there.

"Signora, if you do not have the appointment, will you please leave? Signora Dotson here, she does not prefer the audience."

"Sorry, Mrs. Dotson," I said to the lady's chin. "I'm a detective. I need to talk to Signor Giuseppe, but I'll wait."

I strolled back down the hall and entertained myself by going into one of the storerooms and opening little pots of La Cygnette creams and rubbing them into my skin. I looked in a mirror and could already see an improvement. If I got Evangeline sprung maybe she'd treat me to a facial.

Signor Giuseppe appeared with a plastically groomed Mrs. Dotson. He had shed his barber's costume and was dressed for the street. I followed them down the stairs. When we got to the bottom I said, "In case you're thinking of going back to Milan—or even to Kansas—I have a few questions."

Mrs. Dotson clung to the hairdresser, ready to protect him.

"I need to speak to him alone, Mrs. Dotson. I have to talk to him about bamboo."

"I'll get Miss Carlson, Signor Giuseppe," his guardian offered.

"No, no, Signora. I will deal with this crazed woman myself. A million thanks. *Grazie, grazie.*"

"Remember, no Italian in your adopted America," I reminded him nastily.

Mrs. Dotson looked at us uncertainly.

"I think you should get Ms. Carlson," I said. "Also a police escort. Fast."

She made up her mind to do something, whether to get help or flee I wasn't sure, but she scurried down the corridor. As soon as she had disappeared, he took me by the arm and led me into one of the consulting rooms.

"Now, who are you and what is this?" His accent had improved substantially.

"I'm V. I. Warshawski. Roland Darnell told me you were quite an expert on fitting drugs into bamboo furniture."

I wasn't quite prepared for the speed of his attack. His hands were around my throat. He was squeezing and spots began dancing in front of me. I didn't try to fight his arms, just kicked sharply at his shin, following with my knee to his stomach. The pressure at my neck eased. I turned in a half circle and jammed my left elbow into his rib cage. He let go.

I backed to the door, keeping my arms up in front of my face and backed into Angela Carlson.

"What on earth are you doing with Signor Giuseppe?" she asked.

"Talking to him about furniture." I was out of breath. "Get the police and don't let him leave the salon."

A small crowd of white-coated cosmeticians had come to the door of the tiny treatment room. I said to them, "This isn't Giuseppe Fruttero. It's John Crenshaw. If you don't believe me, try speaking Italian to him—he doesn't understand it. He's probably never been to Milan. But he's certainly been to Thailand, and he knows an awful lot about heroin."

4

Sal handed me the bottle of Black Label. "It's yours, Vic. Kill it tonight or save it for some other time. How did you know he was Roland Darnell's ex-partner?"

"I didn't. At least not when I went to La Cygnette. I just knew it had to be someone in the salon who killed him, and it was most likely someone who knew him in Kansas. And that meant either Darnell's ex-wife or his partner. And Giuseppe was the only man on the professional staff. And then I saw he didn't know Italian—after praising Milan and telling him he was stupid in the same tone of voice and getting no response it made me wonder."

"We owe you a lot, Vic. The police would never have dug down to find that. You gotta thank the lady, Mama."

Mrs. Barthele grudgingly gave me her thin hand. "But how come those police said Evangeline knew that Darnell man? My baby wouldn't know some convict, some drug smuggler."

"He wasn't a drug smuggler, Mama. It was his partner. The police have proved all that now. Roland Darnell never did anything wrong." Evangeline, chic in red with long earrings that bounced as she spoke, made the point hotly.

Sal gave her sister a measuring look. "All I can say, Evangeline, is it's a good thing you never had to put your hand on a Bible in court about Mr. Darnell."

I hastily poured a drink and changed the subject.

Buried Treasure

·

John Lutz

*John Lutz is one of today's most respected writers of the crimi-
nous short story. He has won both of the field's top short fiction
awards: a PWA Shamus in 1984 for "What You Don't Know
Can Hurt You," and an MWA Edgar in 1986 for "Ride the
Lightning." Both of these stories feature his St. Louis private
detective Alo Nudger, as do such first-rate novels as* Nightlines
(1984) and Dancer's Debt *(1988). A long-overdue collection of
Lutz's best short stories,* Better Mousetraps, *also appeared in
1988. "Buried Treasure," a poignant nonseries tale about "the
past that lives within the memories of others," is vintage Lutz
and thus very good indeed.*

What is it that fascinates us about the past that lives within the
memories of others, yet is only wistful words, dry pages, and
film to ourselves? Is it that we can't fully conceive of such a
hazy yet achingly familiar world existing prior to our own? Or
that we can?

I wondered about that as I signed the closing papers on our
new-old home in Jade Point, Missouri. Jade Point was a small
town, but within commuting distance of Saint Louis, and the
house was a three-story Victorian monstrosity nearly a hundred
years old. Exactly what Effie, my wife, had always wanted to
own and renovate. I'd just received a substantial sum from the
sale of my advertising agency back East; I could afford, barely,
to be indulgent.

We'd bought the house from the estate of an old woman named
Beatrice Logan, the last of a proud local family. As soon as we'd
moved into the high-ceilinged deteriorated monster, my wife

began to show me what she called the house's "buried treasure." I admit to being impressed. There were corners and alcoves in that house that probably hadn't been looked into in years. Effie came up with rare cut glass, solid brass fixtures buried beneath layers of faded paint, intricately scrolled woodwork now impossibly expensive to duplicate. But the most unexpected thing we found was the box in the basement.

It was a gray metal box, not large or exceptionally heavy, but obviously containing something that didn't rattle when shook.

"See if you can get it open, Warren," Effie said. "Anything might be inside."

I went to my toolbox and got a hammer. One sharp blow, and the box's steel lid sprang open.

Letters. Various papers. Curled and yellowed about the edges. Most of the postmarks were dated in the midthirties, the letters addressed to someone named Leonard Carvell. Effie and I read a few of the letters there at the base of the cellar steps. They were personal, at the time not very interesting, with frequent references to someone named Floyd. The handwriting was poor, with many misspelled words and malapropisms, and there was a curious, almost guarded obliqueness to the phrasing.

"These stamps might be worth something," Effie said.

"I think what I'd better do," I told her, replacing the letters and closing the metal lid, "is ask around and see if anyone knows the family. This Leonard Carvell might still be alive or have some survivors who'd want this box."

Effie agreed to the reasonableness of that idea, and the next day I drove in to Jade Point's tiny shopping area and asked in the A&P store and at the post office if anyone had heard of Leonard Carvell or his family. No one had. And no one had in the Drop-In Tavern next to the barber shop, though I sensed a surprised kind of reticence in some of the old-timers bent over the checkerboard near the end of the long mahogany bar.

"What now?" Effie asked, when I'd returned and stretched out on the antique sofa she'd bought to match the decor of the living room.

"We'll put a classified ad in the Saint Louis papers," I said, shading the light from my eyes with my forearm. Some of the letters in the box had a Saint Louis postmark and were signed simply "Eddie." Strangely, none of the envelopes in the box had a return address.

"You word the ad and I'll phone it in for Sunday," Effie said, continuing to apply paint stripper to the curved oak banister.

The box's contents were probably worthless, of only personal interest, but we felt obligated.

For over a week there was no reply to our ad in the Saint Louis *Post Dispatch*, and I'd almost forgotten about the metal box, when late Tuesday morning the doorbell rang.

Effie was out combing the antique shops in nearby Greenville, so I answered the door to find an old man standing on the wooden porch, smiling nervously, wiping perspiration from his cheeks and forehead with a folded white handkerchief. "Did you place the ad about the Leonard Carvell letters?" he asked in a hesitant but hopeful voice.

I told him I had, told him my name was Warren Aikin, and invited him inside, out of the heat. He was a stooped man, probably in his early seventies, but still taller than my own six feet. His clothes were threadbare but once expensive, and he still moved well. He looked anxiously around as he entered and sat down in the wing chair near the cold fireplace. There was something fearless and rather desperate in his faded gray eyes. I waited for him to introduce himself. He didn't.

"I'd like to obtain those letters," he said gently.

"Are you a member of the Carvell family?"

He almost glared at me despite no alteration of his parchmentlike features. "No, I'm not that."

I suspected then he might be an antique dealer or stamp collector trying to make a fast dollar or a valuable find. "Are you a dealer of some sort?" I asked.

He shook his head, saw that I didn't believe him, and said succinctly, "No."

"Then what claim have you to the letters?" I asked.

He wasn't a fool. "I could tell you, Mr. Aikin, but would you believe me?"

"Frankly, not unequivocally. I suspected my ad might attract some antique buffs or dealers, and to be honest with you, I had in mind only turning the box over to a family member. I'm no expert, but it seems to me there isn't any monetary worth there."

The old man seemed to think over what I'd said. He knew that whatever farfetched tale I heard, I would be skeptical and that I'd require some proof of any claim to Carvell family membership.

"I'll pay you a thousand dollars for the box and its contents," he said calmly.

I was stunned enough to have to sit down. "You know something I don't," I said.

"Do you accept?"

If the old man was willing to pay that much money for the contents of the box, they must be worth something to the Carvell family—if there was any family remaining. I would be selling someone's personal effects, and I began to wonder if that was even legal. I could just see some distraught Carvell materializing in a week or a month to sue me on some charge I couldn't imagine.

"I can't," I said. "I'm sure that eventually some member of the Carvell family will claim the box."

The old man nodded with an odd little smile. "Someone will," he said, and stood, nodded good-bye, and left.

I sat a while wondering who he was. For that matter, did *he* know? There was that cast to his eyes, and his strange manner, that suggested someone living in his own world, almost to the point of mental aberration. He had to be crazy to offer a thousand dollars for a batch of old letters and papers.

On the other hand, I'd have been crazy not to take a closer look at the contents of the metal box. I locked the front door and went down into the cellar.

Five minutes later, I had the box's contents spread over the dining room table. Mostly old letters; a guarantee on a wristwatch dated January 1934; a dozen blank title forms for automobiles licensed in the state of Illinois; even a yellowed operating manual for a vacuum cleaner. I began to read the letters, this time all of them, and thoroughly.

Buried Treasure

It didn't take long for me to discover that Leonard Carvell was also known as Blackie Carvell, and apparently had been an infamous Depression-era gangster. I was fascinated to conclude that the Floyd referred to in many of the letters was Charles "Pretty Boy" Floyd, the notorious bank robber and killer, who had hidden out in a Missouri roadhouse for many months and had even become an accepted part of the community. There was also, folded with a letter in a large envelope, a map of the state of Florida, and stapled to it a detailed map of a small area near central Florida. I held the penciled letter to the light streaming through the curtained windows and read,

> *Eddie,*
> *Keep the two pieces in seperate places. Betty L. is fine and will be ready to travel soon. See you in Chi. or St. Lu.*
>
> *Blackie*

I saw that the letter, addressed to a Mr. Eddie Pepp at a number on Oakland Avenue in Saint Louis, was stamped but not postmarked. It had never been mailed.

My curiosity was aroused. When Effie came home I told her something of what had happened and that I was going to drive into Saint Louis tomorrow. She said fine, she was going to Vandalia to see about a brass hall tree for the foyer. She also asked me who the old man was she kept seeing near the house. I told her I had a pretty good idea, but by then she was busy measuring the foyer.

It was easy to find Oakland Avenue in Saint Louis. It was an east-west avenue that ran past a sporting arena, office buildings, a TV station, and to the west some older apartment buildings and a hospital. I estimated that an office building sat at the former site of Carvell's letter to Eddie Pepp.

After parking my car in the lot of a small restaurant on a side street, I walked across the heat-scoured cement, went inside, and asked for a hamburger and information. I found that, in the thirties, the address on Oakland Avenue had been that of a large amusement park. Not an unreasonable hideout for a Depression-era desperado.

When I was finished with the greasy hamburger and a cup of coffee, I drove from the restaurant to the downtown library. I asked the librarian for microfilmed copies of the midthirties Saint Louis papers. Then I sat at one of the microfilm viewers and began to read.

It wasn't hard to piece together the violent career of Leonard "Blackie" Carvell. He'd appeared in the news first in June of 1932 as a murder suspect, avoided trial in that case, but not for the September 1932 slaying of a tavern owner during a holdup. He was sentenced to life imprisonment in the state penitentiary but escaped en route. In 1933 he went on a bank-robbing spree along with two partners, Vern Molako and Eddie Pepp. Molako was killed by police in a small Arkansas town in late 1933, but Pepp continued his partnership with Carvell for the next four years. They robbed several more banks and were suspects in a kidnapping case and a bombing.

In June of 1937 Carvell was shot to death after a Union, Missouri, bank robbery, surprised by federal agents in a farmhouse outside of Jade Point, Missouri. The June 14, 1937 paper contained a death photo of a lean-faced man with a shock of unruly dark hair. The paper also revealed that the thirty thousand dollars stolen in that robbery, which was committed by two armed men, hadn't been recovered.

I scanned the papers for the next several months of that year. I could find no record of the money's having been found.

When I got back to Jade Point late that afternoon, I kissed Effie hello and made directly for the desk where I'd placed the steel box. I got out the letter to Eddie Pepp and the Florida maps and examined them again.

The larger map was an old Florida roadmap with a red-penciled route to a town called Oleana; the smaller map was a carefully inked, detailed drawing of what looked to be three roads that formed an obtuse triangle, a number of small squares that no doubt designated houses, and smaller circles and odd shapes within the triangle. There was no scale and no revealing marks or lettering on the map. In the upper-left corner of the paper on which the smaller map was drawn, outside the lined boundaries of the map, was a small scrawled five-pointed star.

None of it meant anything to me.

But when I started to return the letter and maps to the envelope, something hindered me. I looked inside the envelope and found another sheet of folded paper, exactly like the sheet on which the smaller map was drawn. The sheet of paper was blank but for a scrawled star in one corner and an X to the right of center. The star was a replica of the one in the upper-left corner of the map paper.

It wasn't long before I caught on. I pressed the map against the inside of a window pane so the light shone through it, then placed the blank paper against it so the stars matched. That rested the X at a spot near the center of the triangle formed by the roads. I held the papers there and used a pin to pierce the center of the X and mark the map beneath.

I knew then that what I had in my hand might be a genuine treasure map, worth thirty thousand dollars. And I could figure out who the old man must have been, and why he kept up his constant watch on the house.

"Effie!" I shouted. "I'm going to Florida!"

She listened to what I had to say and told me I was crazy.

But I went.

Oleana was a small town off Highway 24 with a population of 2,966. I pulled my rental car into the lot of the Oleana Drowsy-Stop Motel and went into the office to register.

Darkness was falling, so after settling into my room, I had dinner at the motel restaurant. Then I went back to my room and tried to make time pass by watching a string of television shows.

The next morning, after a virtually sleepless night, I got in the car and followed Carvell's map to where the roads formed— or used to form—a triangle. The area had become part of central Florida's pattern of progress.

The three roads were still there, but one of them was now a four-lane highway. I was in orange-grove country. The medium-size, almost uniformly shaped dark-green trees dotted with bright orange stretched nearly from horizon to horizon. Letting the car roll uphill at idle speed, I reached a relatively high spot and parked to survey the area of the small map.

Most of the houses on the map were gone, but I was excited to see in the approximate spot of the map's X a large and unusual rock formation whose shape matched precisely the shape of one of the figures on the map. The neat rows of orange trees had parted widely there to miss it and I also saw what appeared to be a thick tree trunk. I checked the map and found a circle drawn to designate a tree exactly where the stump rose angled from the ground. Even from where I sat it was simple to make out the area of the map's X, near the tapered end of the rock formation.

I'd had the foresight to bring a spade in the car's trunk, and I parked on the road shoulder and walked with the spade toward the rock formation. There was no one around; the nearest building was over a quarter of a mile away and appeared deserted. The only sound among the brightly sunlit orange trees was the occasional whir of unseen traffic on the nearby four-lane highway. I determined what I thought was the exact spot of the X and plunged the shovel into the soft, powdery earth to mark it. Then I rolled up my sleeves and began to dig.

Within ten minutes, I struck what appeared to be a pipe jutting upward to ground level. At first I thought it might be an irrigation pipe, but I saw that it was rusted and the end was stuffed with dirt. I began to dig harder.

What I discovered after an hour's hard digging was the lid of a rotted wooden box approximately two by five feet. From each end of the box a rusted pipe jutted toward the earth's surface; perhaps markers. There was a hasp and padlock on the box's lid, but rust and time had worked their deterioration and I easily sprung the black-pitted hasp from the moldering wood with one stroke of the shovel.

Grinning inanely, still struggling for breath, I bent and flung open the box's rotted lid.

There was no money in the box—it contained the bones of a child.

I felt my face contort stiffly as I drew back, scrambling up the sloping sandy side of the hole I'd dug. Standing numbly at the edge of the hole, I found that I couldn't avert my gaze from the horror.

Alongside the head of the skeleton were the moldering remains of what looked like a small battery-operated pump. I knew then that the two pieces were for air, and that the child had been buried alive. Near the colorless tattered clothing that still clung to the bones were a tarnished heart-shaped locket and some crumpled papers.

The sound behind me made me wheel so suddenly that I almost slipped and fell back into the hole I'd dug.

The old man I had talked to in Jade Point was standing there, pointing an ancient long-barreled revolver in my direction. But he was gazing past me, into the hole.

"You trailed me all the way down here. . . ." I said unbelievingly.

"I had to." The light of unreason I'd noticed in his eyes shone brighter now than before. On each side of his drawn lips the sagging flesh of his cheeks was twitching.

A car door slammed, and we both turned toward the sound.

"He followed me. . . ." I heard the old man say in a soft, tragic voice touched with fear.

A plain white sedan was parked nearby, and a short gray-haired man was striding toward us with a shotgun slung beneath his right arm. He was absurdly paunchy, walking with much effort, his legs pumping with rubbery uncertainty on the powdery earth.

I turned and found that the old man was gone. Then I saw him beyond the orange trees, hobbling with fear-born speed toward where his car must have been parked.

The dumpy gray-haired man had walked up beside me, and we both stood and watched the old man disappear beyond the trees.

"No point chasing him now," the man said, as we heard the racing whine of a car engine. There was a hint of strained control in his voice.

Dazed by the unfolding of events, I looked at the man. He was in his late sixties, with an open, deeply etched face and vivid blue eyes that had seen too much too long, eyes that contained a deep-set desperation.

"Sheriff Seth Davis," he said by way of introduction, "Oleana County. Who are you?"

I told him in a stammering voice. "What . . . what is all this?" I asked.

"It's the remains of the Bosner girl," he said. "Six-year-old Sissy Bosner was kidnapped from her wealthy family in Miami in 1937 and held for a hundred thousand dollars ransom. It was never paid. Two men named Carvell and Pepp were suspected, but nothing was ever proved for lack of evidence."

"Carvell and Pepp . . ." I said. "My God, they buried her alive, let her . . ." I turned and gazed at the spot where the old man had disappeared beyond the orange-dotted trees, driven by decades-old fear and guilt.

"You let me know where you're staying, Mr. Aikin, and go on back there. I'll need you later for a statement."

I nodded, gave him the information he requested, and drove back to the motel, trying not to think about the terror that must have passed through a six-year-old mind, buried alive in darkness, with each breath a searing agony. Whatever compassion I might have had for Eddie Pepp disappeared.

I expected Sheriff Davis to appear at my Oleana motel that afternoon, but he didn't. And he didn't show up that evening. Or the next morning.

In the motel restaurant, as I read the morning paper, I understood why.

Thick black lettering low on the front page told me that Owen Bosner, aged, wealthy, one-time king of the Florida citrus processing industry, had hanged himself in an Orlando hotel. Mr. Bosner had become almost a total recluse after personal tragedy in the midthirties. After his six-year-old daughter Sibyl Ann "Sissy" Bosner was kidnapped, Owen Bosner decided that the kidnappers were bluffing and refused to pay the demanded ransom. Though Depression-era gangsters Edward Pepp and Leonard "Blackie" Carvell were suspected of the crime, charges were never brought because Sissy Bosner was never found and had supposedly been seen alive and well on a Chicago street corner by a distant relative. Only that reported sighting by what seemed to be a reliable witness prevented kidnapping and murder charges.

Intimates of Owen Bosner said that he was haunted by his decision for the rest of his life, living in seclusion and employing a full-time staff to scour daily copies of virtually every newspaper in the country for some clue to his lost daughter's fate. This quest apparently came to dominate his life and in his mind became the sole reason for his existence.

But what interested me most was the photograph of Owen Bosner, taken in 1976, a melancholy likeness marked by the tragic uncertainty and guilt that must have dogged him into the waning hours of his life.

Bosner and I had met at my house in Jade Point, Missouri. I knew he had found the truth he had so long feared and sought, that had been his obsession.

I used the telephone then to try to make connections with Sheriff Davis of Oleana County. There was no Sheriff Davis, I was informed. There was not even an Oleana County.

Immediately I left the motel and drove along sun-washed highways back to the orange grove where I had unearthed Sissy Bosner's remains. A heavy, guilty regret settled over me. My classified ad in the newspaper had set turning old and inexorable wheels.

I stood amid the wind-rustled orange trees with a lump in my throat. The hole had been refilled, the loose earth neatly leveled.

There was no statute of limitations on murder, but "Sheriff" Eddie Pepp was no longer worried. It must have been Carvell who had buried Sissy Bosner alive, then for some reason, probably unexpected sudden pressure from the law, had been forced to flee abruptly from the state, and was the only one who knew her whereabouts. Pepp was to have handled things in Florida, including the collection of the ransom and release of Sissy Bosner. Both Pepp and Carvell were wanted in several states, so the Saint Louis address had been a mail drop, a forwarding service, so they couldn't be traced through the mails. Through it, Pepp was supposed to learn where Sissy Bosner was concealed.

But Pepp, waiting in Florida while Sissy Bosner waited underground for endless days and nights with only so much food, water, and sanity, never learned where Sissy was hidden. Because Blackie Carvell, apparently the lodger and secret lover of Beatrice Logan in the house I would later buy, had been killed in Jade Point by federal agents before he mailed Pepp the map and letter. The old-timers at the Drop-In Tavern in Jade Point had been reticent with me, a newcomer in town, because they wanted to protect the reputation of the recently deceased Logan woman.

Owen Bosner's maniacal determination to find his daughter had received a great deal of publicity, and he had the vast resources to indulge in such a search. Pepp, who never before had killed, could only protect himself from a murder charge by staying in Florida and observing Bosner, and moving in whatever fast and deadly fashion was necessary to reclaim and better conceal Sissy Bosner's body if ever it was located. It was easy to imagine any man in such circumstances becoming paranoid.

So through the years Pepp must have watched the reclusive and obsessive Owen Bosner ever more warily, as the part of central Florida where he knew the body must be became heavily developed with industry, highways, and tourist attractions, increasing daily the chances that someone would uncover Sissy Bosner's remains and thus prove that she had been kidnapped and murdered in Florida and never seen in Chicago.

Owen Bosner's obsession had created and nourished Eddie Pepp's. The two men were bound together in a pattern of apprehension. And as each of them aged, their obsessions became the mainsprings of their otherwise empty lives, the very purpose of those lives. All of the passing years had strengthened rather than diminished this strange adversity that had developed into need. Probably Pepp even had paid off one of Bosner's employees to keep him posted if Bosner interrupted his reclusiveness to travel.

Pepp must have followed Bosner to Saint Louis, then back to Florida even as Bosner followed me. Then he cleverly passed himself off as a sheriff when Bosner saw him and ran from him. How both men must have doubted and suffered through the years! One from the fear of a murder charge, the other from the guilt of not having paid a long-ago ransom. And both from the slow, insidious cancer of obsession.

But now it was ended. Pepp had reburied the incriminating, pathetic bones where he could be sure they wouldn't be discovered, in their final resting place, this time leaving no map except within the darkening confines of his own fear-wasted mind. And with them he had buried his reason for living.

Even in the blasting sunlight, I shivered sadly as I walked back to my car.

I hoped Eddie Pepp had treated the buried treasure gently. And that now it would be part of an undisturbed past, alive only in faded photographs and yellowed newspapers.

The Candy Skull

•

Ray Bradbury

Although he is best known as a writer of literary, fantasy, and science fiction, and as a poet, Ray Bradbury has published numerous mystery/suspense stories during his forty-year career. And his most recent novel, Death is a Lonely Business *(1985), is a nostalgic mystery whose protagonist is a 1940s pulp writer. Bradbury's own forties crime stories appeared in such pulps as* Detective Tales, New Detective, *and* Dime Mystery *(where the excursion into terror that follows was first published in 1948). The best of these pulp criminous tales were collected in 1984 under the title,* A Memory of Murder.

In the morning light, shadows of the children ran and ran across the pink and blue tiles of the plaza, while on the bronze bench Old Tomás sat, very withered, very indignant, waving his scarred hands at them. One small Mexican boy held a cape and wooden sword; another enacted the part of the enraged bull.

"No, No!" cried Old Tomás. "No, this way, and this!" He rose suddenly and stood to show the boys how to make a veronica, *so*! And another, *so*! "You see! With the body *this* way, see?"

The small boys ran, dodged, squealed.

Later they came and said, "Show us your scars, old one."

And Old Tomás pulled out his handwoven shirt to bare his right hip, once more to show them where the bull had gored thirty years ago. The boys touched the scar. "How long since you fought the bulls, old one?"

"Before your mothers were born," he replied.

A young Spanish woman crossed the plaza tiles. She wore a

178

tailored gray gabardine suit; her hair was black and shining. Her head was high. She did not look at Tomás as she passed and went up the steps into the tourist hotel.

Tomás watched her all of the way. He saw how her ankles took the clear morning light. He saw how her dark shining hair was. His eyes followed. His tongue moved on his lip, ever so little.

On the second-floor balcony of the hotel a moment later a young pink, blond man suddenly appeared. Old Tomás narrowed his vision, his eyes tight, his mouth pressed shut. The young pink man on the balcony looking down. The clean, loud, American tourist who had driven into town last week. Old Tomás looked up at the clean man on the balcony. And when the clean tourist American turned and went back into his room, Tomás spat upon the pink and blue tiles and would no longer play with the children at their game.

Roby Cibber awakened this morning with a feeling as if something had happened. He couldn't tell exactly what or how or why, but something out of the ordinary had occurred during the night. He sat up and hung his legs over the edge of the bed and looked down at his feet for a long time. Then he remembered where he was.

He was in Guanajuato, Mexico, he was a writer, and tonight was the Day of the Dead ceremony. He was in a little room on the second floor of a hotel, a room with wide windows and a balcony that overlooked the plaza where the children ran and yelled each morning. He heard them shouting now. And this was Mexico's Death Day. There was a smell of death all through Mexico you never got away from, no matter how far you went. No matter what you said or did, not even if you laughed or drank, did you ever get away from death in Mexico. No car went fast enough, no drink was strong enough.

He looked over at the lamp table in the dim light and he did not recoil. With only a dull movement of his heart in his chest, he saw the white object that lay upon the table.

A small white sugar-candy skull.

It was the kind of skull they eat on *el Día de Muerte*—the Day of Death. It was made of white sugar and it would crumple if you held it tightly. It had sockets and teeth and it glinted like a hard-packed snowball.

It had his name on it.

Roby.

Scrawled across the top in a thin pink candy rope—his name.

Roby.

The skull hadn't been there when he'd gone to sleep last night. It was there now.

The room was cold. He got up and threw back the vast wooden doors over the windows that shut out the night air.

He caught a glimpse of himself, blond and pink faced, in the wall mirror as he stepped out on the balcony to take the sun and breathe the good air. He did not look back at the skull on the table. He didn't want to look at it. He looked instead, from the balcony, upon the small green plaza below with the rococo bronze bandstand and the trees clipped into round green drums and the tiles laid blue and pink on the walk where people strolled arm in arm on Thursdays and Sundays with the music hammering and crashing out into the silent Mexican sky.

There was no music now. Children ran on the tiles. Old Tomás sat on a bronze bench, instructing them on something or other.

Roby Cibber went back into his room. He touched his face. He needed a shave. It was good, feeling the warm, early-morning sunlight. It was nice living and moving about. His stomach was sickish—too much tequila last night with Celia Diaz. His throat was sore—too much singing.

Someone rapped on the door. He started, laughed at himself, opened the door.

"*Buenos días, señor.*"

The little cleaning woman stood in the hall. Would it be possible that he was ready for breakfast? The ham and eggs were awaiting him and she would clean his room and set it right for him if he so wished—was this possible?

This was possible. He then turned and caused her to follow him in to the table, where he pointed at the small sugar-candy skull. He spoke to her in Spanish. Did she know where this came from? Had she seen anyone enter his rooms during the night?

She looked at the skull and laughed. Death is a good thing in Mexico; it is a thing to talk of at dinner, at breakfast, with or without a drink, with or without a smile. No, señor, she gave him to understand, she had seen no one enter or leave his room. Was not the sugar skull fine? Such good lettering of the señor's name!

Yes, he had to admit, the lettering was fine.

He went down to breakfast unshaved.

As always, there was ham and eggs. The Mexican people, once they have happened on a good food, he thought, flay the thing to distraction. Ham and eggs every morning now for two weeks. Since arriving in Guanajuato, bearing his typewriter, it had been the same thing each morning at nine. He stared at his plate, gently grieved.

Celia Diaz came across the dining room, smiling. She wore a tailored gray gabardine suit, and her hair was black and shining.

He rose to let her into her place, and they said their good-mornings. "It's a nice morning," she said. "A very nice morning."

"Yes," he said.

She had dark hair, a great lot of it, and dark eyes, large and inquiring and gentle, and full lips, and she did not look as a woman looks getting up in the morning. She was an anachronism. She looked as if it were eight o'clock, the core of the evening, everything at its highest point, everything fresh and delightful. He looked at her. He didn't look away.

"You were tired," she said quietly.

"I *am*," he said. "I came to Mexico a tired man, I live in Mexico a tired man, and I shall leave Mexico a tired man. It is a continuous state, having nothing to do with wine, women, or guitars. Nor is it the altitude, which frequently causes me to have hot and cold flashes in the middle of the afternoon. No, it is none of these."

"Perhaps I know what it is," she said, not flickering her steady gaze that was always on him.

"You couldn't possibly know," he said.

"But I *do*."

"No, no. You'd never guess." He shook his head.

"I know Americans—they are always afraid of the same thing in Mexico. They always look over their shoulders in fear, they do not sleep, they digest poorly. They laugh and say it is the change in climate. It is not," she said. "I know what it is."

He put down his fork. "What, then, is it?"

"Death," she said.

The sunlight fell through the wide French window and touched upon half her face and illumined all the silverware and blazed upon the painted wooden bowls hung from the walls.

She placed a small candy skull on the table.

"I stopped at your room just now," she said. "The cleaning woman was there. I saw this on your table."

He looked at the skull.

"You're afraid," she said.

The lettering was very exquisite, very fine.

"Yes," he said at last, settling back in his chair. "I'm afraid."

They had coffee to finish up the breakfast. Then they went out into the green *zócalo*. They passed Old Tomás, who sat on the bronze bench. "Señorita, señor," he said.

"Tomás," they said, walking on, glancing at him briefly. The children came to play with Old Tomás after they had walked by, with capes and wooden swords.

Celia and Roby sat on a bronze bench and had cigarettes, one after the other.

"Who would want to hurt you?" she asked.

"I don't know." He flung down a used match. "Dammit, I don't know anyone in Mexico!"

"Why did you come to Mexico?"

"To write. And there was that friend of mine, Douglas McClure."

"Yes, I knew him. He was here in Guanajuato last year. He left suddenly one night. I never saw him again. I was surprised. He never wrote me."

182

"Or me. His last letter was from here, last September. Then he went up in thin air. Never heard from him again. I know what you're thinking—I'm one of those half-cocked adventurers looking for trouble. Frankly, I'm selfish as hell. I came down to collect material for my novel. On the side, I'm looking for McClure. He wrote about you, Celia, in three of his letters. That's why I thought you might be able to help me."

"I am not much good." She lifted her hands. "One week he was here, the next gone. He was very nice. We talked much and had many dinners together. When he vanished, I said to myself, ah, these Americans. I did not worry. Did you look for him in Acapulco?" She smiled shyly.

"Acapulco! That's all I hear. Everyone tells me, 'Go to Acapulco!' That's where all the people go who vanish. I went. I didn't see any beachcomber that looked like Douglas McClure. Anyway, he was in this town last of all. His letters about you were very flattering, Celia. I thought, well, maybe this Celia Diaz has a Spanish sweetheart who got jealous of Douglas and killed him."

"That is all very flattering and romantic, but hardly true," she said. "I am the modern Mexican woman. I am disliked by my people, I walk alone, I do not follow the customs. But I am no one's woman yet. There was no jealous sweetheart to hurt your friend. Tell me of this sugar skull you found in your room."

"I'm warm," he said. "I must be close to Douglas. Some nights I almost feel how close he is to me. I expect to run into him at the Thursday night band concert, or in a bar. Whoever left this sugar skull in my room was pretty silly. If they think they can scare me off, they're wrong. I'm scared, but I won't go away. The sugar skull is a mistake. It only confirms my suspicions. They should have let matters stand, not bothered me. Maybe I am close to Douglas, but maybe I would have missed the next clue, missed Douglas, and gone back to the United States next week."

"Maybe you *can't* miss the next clue," Celia replied, logically. "Maybe they knew your next move was so obvious you couldn't miss your friend. Therefore they warned you before you made the move. Not a very pleasant warning. What *is* your next move?''

"I don't know."

"But they know. It's not something you'd have to do today, but something you'd have to do before you finally left town next week. What would that be, Señor Roby? What would you do in the next week, what would you see that you have not already seen?''

He had the answer.

She saw that he had the answer and she put out her hand swiftly to gentle him. He drew deeply on his cigarette and flickered his eyes and his breath came in and out of him in deep moves of his lungs.

"Tell me," she said, after a time. "What is the one place where you have not been that you will go before you leave town next week?''

He took a deep breath, let it hiss out slowly.

"The catacombs," he said.

The graveyard was at the top of the hill. It looked over all of the town. The town was hills—hills that issued down in trickles and then creeks and then rivers of cobblestone into the town, to flood the town with rough and beautiful stone that had been polished into smooth flatness over the centuries. It was a pointed irony that the very best view of the town could be had from the cemetery hill, where high, thick walls surrounded a collection of tombstones like wedding cakes, frosted with white angels and iced with ribbons and scrolls, one against another, toppling shining cold. It was like a cake confectioner's yard. Some tombs were as big as beds. From here on freezing evenings you could look down at the candlelit valley, hear dogs bark sharp as tuning forks banged on a flat stone, see all the funeral processions coming up the hill in the dark, coffins balanced on shoulders.

Roby Cibber stood halfway up the hill, looking at the cemetery wall.

"Don't go up today," said Celia. "Can't you wait until tomorrow?''

His voice was flat. "No. Now that I've thought of it, it's the one place. It was in my mind all the time, but I wouldn't go look. I wouldn't let myself believe until today. I had to look everyplace else first. The last place I wanted to look was in the catacombs. I've heard of that horrible place and those mummies standing wired against the walls."

He walked up the hill slowly and looked at a little soft-drink stand. He laughed wearily. "It's warm. Celia, have an Orange Crush with me. We need something."

"You look sick."

"I'm going to be a whole lot sicker. I'm going to be sick all the rest of my life, after today."

They stood in the sunlight, drinking down the bottled drinks, making foolish sucking noises on the bottle necks with their lips, not thinking anything.

He finished his bottle and looked at the little girl who tended the stand. She held a little candy corpse in her hand. She was eating it.

He didn't move. He watched her eat it.

Then he turned sighing, and walked up the hill, not talking, with Celia's shadow moving long and easy beside his own shadow, up and up to where the wrought-iron gates swung, squealing, opening on ancient hinges to the graveyard.

By the church, by the plaza, under the dark green trees, the people sat waiting. They waited for something to happen. When it happened they would get up and run around and be part of it. The sun was lowering over the many hills, showing in dull flashes the tin sidings of the silver mines high up. The people waited in the square until finally it was very dark.

Roby Cibber came down the street slowly. He stopped and looked in the many windows. He went in one place and had a beer. Celia was with him, would not leave him. He didn't think of her, though. It wasn't important.

Douglas McClure was up on top of that hill, right now. In the catacombs.

You walked up the hill and paid the graveyard attendant a peso and he flung back a steel door and you went down a spiral stone stair into the earth, into the catacombs. You entered a long dim hall with one hundred twenty-five mummies facing each other, standing against the walls, their mouths open, their beards intact. Looking as if they had leaped up at your entrance, screaming silently.

You walked along the line of standing dead. You looked into the bony, tight-skinned faces.

Until you came to the body of Douglas McClure.

Roby Cibber walked up the slanting street until it gave into the plaza before the church. Somewhere he lost Celia.

A brass band with five busy members marched briskly up one alley, flinging off a tune with the vicious, unpredictable centrifuge of a musical wheel. The men in handwoven pants beat drums, spat into trumpets, or chewed lovingly their long black clarinets. Roby heard them dully, with no appreciation, as they moved by him.

What will you do now?

I don't know. I'm sick. I'm afraid. Tonight, I need people all around me, on all sides, to protect me. I need noise. I'm going to stay here, in the middle of the fiesta, until Celia comes. I won't go up any dark alleys. I won't be alone one moment. I'll stand here in the plaza where *he* can't get me!

Who?

The person who killed Douglas McClure.

The band marched up on the bandstand, played *Yankee Doodle*. It came out of the horns with a strange loss, changed by the breath that blew it and the minds that thought it before the blowing. It was not quite *Yankee Doodle*; it was something frightening.

I'm going to be killed, thought Roby Cibber.

Don't talk like an ass. Go to the police.

What good would that do? Maybe they already know about McClure's body being in the catacombs but kept it quiet so as not to get in trouble with the American government. Those things happen.

A bull was carried into the square, a papier-mâché bull carried on the shoulders of Old Tomás, grunting, charging about. The bull rested on a reed frame, or what appeared to be reeds.

How did Douglas McClure die?

He had a strange hole between his eyes.

A bullet hole?

No. A *strange* kind of hole. I don't know.

The people jumped up from the benches. Something exploded. Old Tomás, lighting fuses on the bamboos and reeds under his papier-mâché bull, ran about the plaza, chasing people before him.

The bull erupted. Involuntarily Roby cried out. The bull gave off great balls of flame. From tubes under the bull shot out, one after another, brilliant, round, blazing fireballs that hit, streamed, gushed into the crowd! The crowd buckled, fell back, closed in. Old Tomás shuffled forward, the bull on his shoulders, laughing. The bull's eyes glowed, flashed, banged out loud traces of yellow-and-orange fire. There were hidden Roman candles, dozens of them, in and under the bull. All these stabbed the air, spurting, beating the children mercilessly with swift fire. The children waved red kerchiefs. The bull charged. Everyone screamed and laughed.

Under the green unmoving trees people stumbled and fell over benches to get out of the way of the fire-throwing bull. A little boy caught a fireball in his shirtfront, leaped into a trough, splashing. Now the bull was all fire, all aglow, all illumination. People held onto each other, panting, holding their sides, gasping for breath from the game.

Roby Cibber let himself be taken into the crowd. He began to run, first slowly, his face ashen, then more swiftly. He felt the need to be at their very center, to whirl, to fall, to laugh, to clutch at them, to use them as shields for himself against whoever might be watching and waiting for him. And he wanted to forget. He ran and laughed. At first it was not a very good laugh. Then it was hysterically exhausted, but he kept leaping hedges as the bull charged first at him, then at someone else. The bull whirled in all directions, booming out firecrackers. An immense cloud of smoke filled the air. Somebody set off a dozen rockets that pierced the sky and blew out into a grand high architecture of red across the stars.

The bull charged again. The crowd parted away from Roby Cibber. He turned, crying out in confused delight. For a moment there was no fear but the simple fear of the firecracker bull and old shambling Tomás. A fireball caught him on the ear. He cried out. There were explosions. He felt something hit him in the arm. He dogged. He laughed. He stumbled over somebody.

Celia was there.

He saw her in the crowd at the edge of the square, standing, watching his wild gyrations.

He freed himself by pushing and shoving and shouting all through the rolling mob until he made a path through to her.

He almost fell as he reached her.

She looked at him with a look of ancient, tired horror.

She was looking at the blood pouring from his arm, warm and constant.

"You've been shot," she said.

The band blared away in a mechanical tumult.

He fell down upon his knees and held onto Celia, and her arms came down to hold him and try to lift him up. . . .

Doctors are no use in Mexico. If you are hysterical, they are so calm and quiet in their inefficiency that you want to scream. Maybe you do, a little. The doctor bandages your wound quietly. It is the fiesta, señor. No more, no more. Some happy man fired a gun. Simply an accident. You will not prosecute, señor? Who is there to prosecute. No one. And this—this wound of the señor's—perhaps only a Roman candle made it, eh? No? Well, it *is* deeper. Yes, I will admit, a bullet. But only from a happy soul. Forget it, señor, forget it!

Roby Cibber came from the doctor's office, Celia with him.

"Did you see who fired the shot, Celia?"

"I saw nothing. Nobody saw. There was so much running and noise. But you are lucky, only a flesh wound."

"That doctor! Sitting there, philosophizing on death! You're not safe anywhere in Mexico, alone or in a crowd."

"Perhaps it would be better if you went back to the United States."

"No. I'll stay. I've got to get Douglas out of the catacombs and shipped home where he belongs. Then there'll be the investigation. In the morning, though—I'm bushed." He looked at her coldly. She was alien. Everything was frightening and alien. He wasn't even certain of her now. Maybe she—

"You're tired," she said. "You'd better get to bed."

He returned to his hotel.

The funeral awaited him.

It was on a little shingle, lying on his bed, the funeral.

He closed the door after switching on the light and he lay against the door looking at the funeral.

It was a tiny funeral. There was a tiny priest with a tiny nut for a head, holding a tiny black book and raising a tiny hand in a holy gesture. There were little altar boys bearing small banners. There was a small coffin and a small sugar-candy corpse in it. And there was an altar with a picture of the corpse on it.

The picture was of Roby Cibber.

He looked around. Someone had gone through his luggage, found an old photo of his, clipped it small and pasted it on the little altar.

There was no note with the funeral. The funeral was enough. These little shingles with tiny figures were sold in the market for *el Día de Muerte*. But this one was just a little out of place on his bed in the waiting, silent room, and he was cold, very cold, and he began to shiver.

There was a tapping on the door behind him. He started. Then, coldly, he opened the door.

"*Señor!*" A hiss. Old Tomás stood in the dim hall. There was the smell of sweat and wine. "It is important that I see you."

"I'm tired."

Tomás looked in at the bed, at the little funeral.

"It is about *that*, señor." Tomás pointed at the funeral. "A little while ago I came through the hall. I saw someone go in your room with that small funeral. I thought you would want to know this."

Roby blinked several times. "Did you see his face?"

"It was no man, señor. It was a woman."

"A woman?"

"Señorita Celia. I saw her."

"You'd better go downstairs. I'm cold and you're drunk."

"She did not see me. She held the funeral in her hands and went in and came out a few minutes later. You are not well, señor?"

Roby held on to the door, shutting his eyes. "I am not well."

"Señor, I have watched the señorita each day, with you. This is not a thing for Mexican women to do. It is not our custom for a woman to be on the streets with a man, or to see a man alone, or to walk alone. And yesterday, Señora Licone, who makes sugar skulls, said to me, 'Ah, that Celia woman, she is insane. She came to me and asked me to make a sugar skull and put the name of the *americano* on top of it: Roby.' I thought nothing of this thing, señor, until tonight, when I saw her take the funeral in, and then, when you were hurt at the fiesta. I thought all of these things over and came to you."

Roby sat down heavily, careful of the bandage along the right side of his chest. "Can you take me to Señora Licone tonight?"

"*Sí, señor.*"

"I must talk to her about the sugar skull."

"*Sí.*" Old Tomás wet his lips. His dark face grew darker, his dark eyes glowed. "I thought all of this strange, señor, for in the past, there was another *americano*—"

"Another!"

"Sit down, señor. You look very pale. Yes, another *americano*, at this hotel, a year ago. He and the señorita were together much. I saw them go in and out of the hotel together—"

Roby talked quietly to the floor. "Celia, Celia—"

"And then one day that other *americano*, he vanished!"

"Yes, I know."

"And this Celia, she showed surprise at his being gone. A clever woman. She removed his luggage herself, of this we may be certain."

"Why didn't you go to the police?" Roby studied the man.

"For what, señor? An *americano* goes away, perhaps to the United States. Is that murder? Is that bad, señor? No, it is only this week, and the things I have seen that make me think. The woman Celia with you, your injury tonight, the sugar skull, the little funeral. Then I think back. I remember this other *ameri-*

cano. Then I come to you. Will you see Señora Licone now, señor?''

"I'll see her. Where do we go?"

"A little way."

They went down the street of the coffin makers. Even this late at night there was a tapping and sawing of wood. Through the open door you saw the coffin makers joking at their work.

Celia, thought Roby Cibber, sweet, gentle-eyed Celia. What happened? Did you love Douglas McClure and did he do something to you that was not of your Mexican logic and custom? And then did you kill him, in some sudden passion, as most killings occur in Mexico? Oh, death is quick down here. It's not the slow brooding poison and the plan. It is the instant act for which, a moment later, you are sorry. A blow, a knife, a gun— quick, and over. Did Douglas say or do something, try to hold or kiss you? Did your family dislike him? Was your reputation hurt by being seen with him? A simple thing to us Americans, but not to you—was that it, Celia? And so you killed him, in one passionate instant, took his luggage from his room. It looked simply as if he'd gone away. Then you let an unidentifiable naked body be found, to be put in the catacombs. Maybe so you could go down and laugh at him once in a while, I don't know. And then I came, and you tried to warn me away, but I'm not going.

"This way, señor."

They turned down a dark alley. The stars were clear and cold. A dog barked across the stone valley. A guitar picked out a fine, clear, crystal chord. A voice sang somewhere, sadly.

"How much farther, Tomás?"

"A little way, señor."

They went up a hill in the moonlight. . . . There was no way to get McClure's body out of the catacombs, was there, Celia? thought Roby. It was found and put down there, but you couldn't bribe anyone to get it out; it would have given you away. Maybe you didn't *want* to get it out. Maybe you've been playing with me. Maybe you *wanted* me to find Douglas there.

The moon was a white pallid eye staring over the sky and the empty land. Their shadows hung under them; they breathed hard with climbing.

They turned in at a familiar-looking building. There were banners on the outside fence, played by the wind.

"This is the bullring, Tomás?"

"Yes, the bullring."

"Does Señora Licone live here?"

"She has no home. She lives beneath the bullring and there she makes her sugar skulls and the little shingle funerals. *Here.*"

They walked out into the clear, moon-filled silent space of the bullring. The sand was a white dimpled sea and the *barreras*—the stands—went around in moon-drenched circles, empty and quiet.

"How do you feel, señor?"

"Not so good. That was a climb."

"Look over there," said Tomás.

They looked. Tomás walked to a black bundle that lay on the sand. "Why, señor, someone has left a bullfighter's equipment here."

There was a scarlet cape. There was a little *birreta* and there were some tiny black ballet slippers and a sword that shone in the light.

"Someone forgot them," said Roby uneasily.

Tomás bent to touch the articles. "It is a shame these were forgotten. These are good things." He picked up the *birreta* and handled it carefully. "Have you seen the bullfight, señor?"

"A few times. I didn't like it."

"Señor, you *americanos.*" Tomás fitted the *birreta* to his head. In the moonlight his body straightened. He held his hands down. "How do I look, señor?"

"Fine, fine. Now if you'll take me to Señora Licone—"

"Do I not look fine?"

"Fine indeed, but—"

"Did you know that once, many years ago, señor, I was the best bullfighter in all of Mexico?"

"Undoubtedly, but—"

"Please, señor, to listen." Tomás was very tall suddenly, with the moon over him casting his shadow long on the sand.

Suddenly he was not hunched, the muscles were released, the dark chin was up, the old eyes flashed with new fire. "Once I fought three bulls here—in one day!" he cried. "Oh, there were people in all the *barreras* to the sky. When I was done they cut off the ears of the bulls and gave them to me. The people threw down hats and gloves and purses at me. It was like a rain." He said it proudly.

Roby looked at him and said not a word. They both stood looking at one another coldly.

Tomás bent and took up the sword and the cape. "I handled the veronicas so, and so—" He whirled to show how it was done. "Beautifully." He bent and put on the little ballet slippers in place of the *huaraches* he had kicked off. "Now, señor—" He walked toward Roby.

"Señora Licone?"

"Yes, yes, the maker of candy skulls." Tomás pointed. "There she is now, you see?"

Roby turned. Simultaneously Tomás struck him a blow on the back of the neck. "Señor!"

Roby cried out. He leaped back and almost fell. He clapped his hand to his neck and discovered it was pierced by three tiny needles to which were attached little fluttering ribbons, red, white, and green. He pulled them out and cast them down. "Tomás!"

"Señor!" cried Tomás. "The banderillas. The pikes for the neck of the bull. Have you seen the bullfight, señor, in which the bandilleros stick the banderillas into the neck of the bull? This I have just done!"

"Tomás, Tomás!" shouted the American, backing up.

Tomás struck at him with the sword. The sword went through Roby's leg, in and out. He collapsed and fell bleeding.

"Tomás!"

Tomás bent over him in the moonlight.

"Do you know what happened tonight, señor?"

"Tomás," gasped the sprawled man.

"I tried to kill you in the fiesta. It was easy, with my gun

193

hidden under the framework of the charging bull. But you escaped, señor!''

"Take me to the candy woman, Tomás!" Roby could not breathe. His mouth opened and shut violently. He was sick.

"There is no candy woman. Do you know what will happen tomorrow morning, señor?" He shouted. "Tomorrow the woman Celia will ask for you. And you will be gone from the hotel. Your luggage gone. *You*, gone!"

Roby tried to get up.

"Get up," said Tomás. "I am ready for you."

Roby gained his feet. Pain was firing his wounded leg. He stood, swaying. "Tomás, you're crazy. Put down the sword, you fool."

"No."

"Why should you want to kill me?"

"Because."

Tomás adjusted the *birreta* on his head. It would have been ridiculous, save for the pain and the blood and the stark moonlight and the clear sky. "I'll shout," said Roby. "People will hear."

"You would not do that, and spoil the game, señor. Then I would have to kill you quickly. The sword between the eyes."

Roby shivered. He saw Douglas McClure in the catacombs again. Now the strange hole in the skull was understood. The hole of a bullfighter's sword. This was how McClure had died.

"We shall have a little game, señor. I am the greatest toreador in the world. You, señor, will be the bull. You will charge me, I will lead you on. You will charge again. I will nick your arms, your legs, your chest. The moon will watch. And the stars will fill the *barreras*."

"What have I done, Tomás?"

"Each day I have watched you go in and come out of the hotel. I have seen Celia with you. She is of us; she is not of you." Tomás stood there, tall and proud. "In the sunlight you walked and laughed and did not speak to me. Each day, each day I saw you touch her and laugh with her, and I hated you, señor, yes, even as I hated the other one. The one last year who went in and out of the hotel—the young *yanqui*, the ridiculous tourist. And Celia had only eyes for him, as now it is only you she sees. She has no eyes for Tomás. Tomás who was once the toast of all Mexico, from Oaxaca to Guadalajara and Monterrey! No, Tomás is old now, no longer can he dance in the ring. No bull would look at him, much less a woman. Tomás is not fit for swine. People spit on him. Tomás was gored by a bull many years ago—"

He made a jerking motion of his hand. The smooth flat of his belly was revealed under the shirt, the scarred, flat, brown belly with the gore mark deep-puckering it.

"See, señor? See? My mark of honor! My profession! But what are scars to young women? You walked and laughed with her. I watched. I watched her with the other. And when I could no longer see them together, I guided him here one night, I the toreador, and he the silly animal, and I killed him. Now you have come, and you too shall die!"

"Tomás, I hold nothing against you, old man—"

"I am not old!" raged Tomás, running lightly forward, making a vicious sweep with the sword. "She thinks me old, yes. That Celia one! Each day she passes me on my bench and does not look at me, and each day of each year I have gazed at her beauty as she walked. And I said to myself, these *yanquis* shall not have her. As many as come to walk with her will I kill. One and then two and then three, and perhaps a dozen before I am caught. *They* shall not have her. *I* will have her." He cut the air with the sword. "Now, move, *yanqui*! Do not stand; move, run, charge me! Give me a fight!"

"My leg, I can't move."

"I will *make* you move!" And Tomás beat him across the face with the sword until the anger made Roby leap forward on his agonized leg. Tomás dodged. "Good!" he cried, swirling the cape. "Another!" Roby stumbled forward. "And another! Good, good!"

Roby stood panting. Tomás looked at the moon. "It is late. It is time for the finish. You will run and I will put the sword in your brain." He held the cape, so, fluttering in the cold wind. The moonlight lay over all.

Roby's leg was pulsing like a massive heart. He could not see well. The earth tilted and the stars tilted. "Tomás," he said, gently.

"Come," said Tomás, waving the cape, the sword out, cold, shining in the wind.

"All right," said Roby.

"Now," said Tomás.

"Now!" Roby leaped.

The sword glittered.

Roby fell, rolled sidewise, kept rolling. He struck the legs of the toreador. He grabbed. Tomás shrieked. Tomás fell. They were together on the white sand, wild, and in the cape, with the sword held now by one, now by another.

Then one of them got clear, stood up, the sword in his hand. The sword sank down through, pinning the other to the white moonlit sand. "This is for *me*," said the one with the sword wildly, swaying. He pulled the sword out and put it in the squirming body again. "And this is for Celia!" Out and in again.

"And *this* is for Douglas McClure!"

When Celia met Roby he was coming down the street, limping, in the early morning, limping, fresh from the doctor's office, carrying something small and white and sugary in his hand. It was very early. The sun was just rising among the blue hills and the church bells were sounding as she saw him from a distance. Roby stopped, stood, took a deep breath of the incredibly sweet charcoal air. Then he lifted the little white sugar skull with the name Roby on it, and he broke it into several fragments and finished eating it even as she walked up and said good morning. Chewing and swallowing, he smiled and answered her.

The Killer

•

Norman Mailer

*Norman Mailer is generally acknowledged as being the most
significant and probably the most talented living American writer.
One of his nonfiction works,* The Armies of the Night *(1968),
earned him the National Book Award and a shared Pulitzer Prize;
and he was the recipient of a second Pulitzer, in the category of
fiction, for* Executioner's Song, *his study of the life and death
of convicted murderer Gary Gilmore. "The Killer," a relatively
early (midfifties) short story, has all the power in microcosm of
Mailer's first crime novel, the bestselling* Tough Guys Don't
Dance *(1984).*

"**N**ow," he said to me, "do you think you're going to bear
up under the discipline of parole?"

"Yessir," I said.

He had white hair even though he was not more than fifty-
two. His face was red. He had blue eyes. He was red, white,
and blue. It was a fact I noticed before. They had this coloring.
Maybe that was why they identified with the nation.

"In effect you're swearing that you won't take a drink for
eight months."

"I know, sir, but I haven't had a drink inside for four years."
Which was a lie. Three times I had come in with my cellmate
on part of a bottle. The first time I was sick. The second time
we had a fight, a quiet fight that I lost. He banged my head on
the floor. Without noise. The third time we had sex. Democratic
sex. We did each other.

"You understand that parole is not freedom."

"Yessir."

They asked these questions. They always asked the same questions, and they always got the same answers. It had nothing to do with what you said. It had nothing to do with how you shaved or how you combed your hair because you combed your hair the way everybody else did, the day you went up to the Board you shaved twice. Maybe it had to do with how many shaving cuts you had, but I didn't have any. I had taken care, wow. Suppose it had to do with the way you moved. If two of the three men on the parole board liked the way you moved, you were all right, provided they didn't like the way you moved too much. Sex. No matter who I'm with, man or woman, I always get a feeling off them. At least I used to. I always could tell if they were moving inside or moving away, and I could tell if anything was going on inside. If we ever touched, I could tell better. Once I was in a streetcar and a girl sat down next to me. She was a full barrel. A very fat girl. Pretty face. I don't like fat. Very fat people have no quick. They can always stop. They can stop from doing a lot of things.

This girl and me had a future, however. Her hip touched. I could feel what I did to her. From side of my leg, through my pants, and her dress, through some kind of corset, cheap plastic corset, something bad, through that, through her panties, right into her, some current went out of me, and I could feel it in her, opening up future. She didn't do a thing, didn't move. Fixed.

Well, five minutes, before I got off at my stop. In those minutes I was occupied by a project with that girl where we projected five years. I knew what I could do to her. I say without exaggeration I could take her weight down from one hundred eighty to one-eighteen in a year and it would have been a pleasure because all that fat was stored-up sugar she was saving. For somebody. She was stingy, congealed like lard, but I had the current to melt that. I knew it would not be hard to pick her up. If I did, the rest would happen. I would spend a year with her. It is difficult to pick up a fat girl, but I would have used shock treatment. For example, I would have coughed, and dropped an oyster on her skirt. I think it is revolting to do something like that, but it would have worked with this fat girl because disgust would have woke her up. That's the kind of dirt sex is, in the mind of somebody fat and soft and clammy. Sex to them is spit and mucus. It would have given me the opportunity to wipe it off. I could trust my fingers to give a touch of something. The point to the entire operation (people watching in the streetcar, me standing with my handkerchief, apologizing) would be that my fingers would be doing two things at once, proper and respectful in the part of my hand everybody else could see, flame through the handkerchief on her lap. I would have begun right there. For the least I would get her name. At the end of the five minutes I turned to take a look at her, and under that fat face, in the pretty face which could be very attractive, I could see thee was a dumb look in her eyes that nothing was going to improve. That stopped me. Putting in a year on a girl like that would be bad unless she was all for me at the end. Stupidity is for nothing, not even itself. I detest stupidity in women—it sets me off. So I got off the car. Didn't even look at the girl. After she gets married to somebody fat and stupid like herself she will hate any man who looks like me because of that five minutes. Her plastic corset must have had a drugstore smell after I got off the trolley car. Think of plastic trying to smell.

I tell this as an example. On the outside it used to be that I never sat down next to anybody that I didn't feel them even when we didn't touch and two or three times a week, or even a day, I would be close to the possibilities of somebody like the fat girl. I know about certain things. I know with all policemen, detectives, correction officers, turnkeys, hacks, parole-board officials that sex is the problem with them. Smartest cellmate I had said one time like a philosopher, "Why, man, a judge will forgive any crime he is incapable of committing himself." My friend put it right. Sex is a bitch. With police. They can't keep their hands off. They do, but then it builds tension. For some it's bad. They can get ready to kill. That's why you comb your hair. Why you must look neat. You have to be clean. Above sex. Then a cop can like you. They ask you those questions knowing how you will answer. Often they know you are lying. For example they know that you will take a drink in the next six months. What is important is not that you are lying, but the kind of lie they hear in your voice. Are you afraid of them? Are you afraid they will see down into your lying throat? Then you are OK. They will pass you. If you are afraid of them, you're a good risk. But if you think they are stupid, faintest trace of such a thought in yourself, it comes through. Always one of them will be sensitive to condescension. It gets them ready to kill. A policeman never forgives you when you get him ready to kill. Obviously he can't do it, especially in a room performing official duty with a stenographer at the side. But the adrenaline goes through him. It is bad to take a flush of adrenaline for nothing. All that murder and nowhere to go. For example when you're standing up talking to a parole board it's important the way you stand, how tight your pants are. Good to be slim, trim, shipshape, built the way I am, provided you are modest. Do not project your groin forward or your hips back. It is best if your pants are not tightfit. Younger juvenile delinquents actually make this sort of mistake. It is not that they are crazy so much as egotistical. They think older men will like them so much they will give them parole in order to look them up. A mistake. Once read in the newspapers about a Russian soldier who picked up a German baby and said, "It's beautiful," but then he got angry because he remembered the baby's father had been shooting his children, so he killed the baby. That's a cop. If you strut, even in good taste and subtle, they will start to get a glow where it is verboten, and they will like you, they will get a little rosy until they sense it goes nowhere, and wow the sex turns. Gets ready to kill you. If cops have an adrenaline wash for their trouble, you are remembered badly. It is much better to be slim, trim, shipshape, and a little peaked-looking, so they can see you as a thrifty son, which is the way they must have seen me because they gave parole that day, and I was out of there in a week. Out of prison. Out of the can. I think I would have died another year. Liver sickness or go berserk.

Now you may ask can police be so dumb as to let me go on an armed-robbery sentence, six years unserved out of ten? Well, they saw me as thrifty. I was careful that day with voice and posture. But how can police be so stupid as to think in categories like thrifty? That's easy, I can answer. Police are pent up, they're apes, they're bulls. Bulls think in categories.

2

Well, I've been feeling small for four years now. Prison is a bitch for people like me. It cuts your—I don't want to use doubtful language. It's a habit you build up inside. Some do use language that way. Some lifers. Spades. People who don't give a damn. They're playing prison as if it is their life, the only one they are going to have. But I am conservative in temperament. I comb my hair every morning, I comb it the same way. Minor matter you may say, but it isn't for me. I like to comb my hair when I feel like it. Animal of the woods. I have the suspicion— some would call it superstition—that combing my hair can spoil some good ideas. I would never say this to a hack, but why is it not possible that some ideas live in your hair, the way the hair curls. I have very wavy hair when it is left to itself. Whenever I get a haircut, I have the feeling I'm losing possibilities I never got around to taking care of. Put it this way: when I comb my hair, it changes my mood. So naturally I prefer to comb it when I want to. In prison forget that. Comb your hair the same time same way every day. Look the same. If you're smart, keep your mood the same way. No ups. Nor downs. Don't be friendly. Don't be sullen. Don't offer company. Don't keep too quiet. If you stay safe, in the middle, and are the same thing every day you get a good report. The reason I get parole first time out, six years off a ten-year sentence is that I was a model prisoner, which means just this: you are the same thing every day. Authorities like you if you are dependable. Be almost boring. I think what it may be about is that any man in authority finds his sleep important to him. People in authority can't stand the night. If you wear a uniform and you go to bed to sleep and a certain prisoner never bothers your dreams, you'll say a good word for him when it comes time to making out reports.

Of course, you are not popular. Necessarily. My bunky shakes my hand when I get this news, but I can see he is not happy in every way. So I complain about details. I am not to possess liquor at home, nor am I to frequent any bar even once, even at

Christmas. Moreover, I am not to eat in any restaurant which serves liquor.

"What if you don't drink? But just eat there?"

"I'm not to go into any premises having a liquor license."

"A restaurant that don't serve liquor is a tearoom or a hash house."

"Crazy," I say. I don't like such expressions, but this is perfect to express my sentiments.

"Well, good luck."

It is possible we are thinking of the same things, which is the three times he got a bottle into the cell and we drank it together. The first time sick, second time we had a fight, third time sex. I remember I almost yelled in pain when my rocks got off, because they wouldn't stop. I was afraid I'd hurt myself. It had been so long. It seemed each time I took liquor something started in me that was different from my normal personality. By normal I mean normal in prison, no more. You wouldn't want a personality like that on the outside any more than you would want to smell like a laundry bag. But so far as inside personality went, I couldn't take liquor and keep the same. So if I started drinking on the secret when outside, I was in trouble. Because my style of personality would try to go back to what it was before, and too many eyes would be on me. My parole officer, people in the neighborhood. The parole board was getting me a job. They just about picked out the room where you lived. They would hear about it even if I didn't get into a rumble when I was drunk. If I kept a bottle in my room, I would have to hide it good. The parole officer has been known to come around and pay a friendly visit, which is to say a sneak visit. Who could enjoy the idea of him sniffing the air in my room to see was there liquor on the breeze? If they caught me drinking in the eight months, back I would be sent to here. A gamble, this parole. But I was glad to take it, I needed out. Very much. Because there was a monotony in me. It had been coming in day after day. I didn't have the feeling of a current in me anymore, of anything going. I had the feeling if I sat down next to a girl like the fat girl now, and our legs touched, she would move away 'cause there was a blank in me which would pass into her. Something repulsive. There was something bad in me, something very dull. It wasn't in my body, it wasn't even in my mind, it was somewhere. I'm not religious, but it was somewhere. I mean I didn't know if I could keep control or not. Still, I couldn't have done it the other way. Eight more months. I might have flipped. Talking back to a hack, a fight. I'd have lost good time. There is only one nightmare in prison. It's that you don't get out, that you never get out because each time you come close the tension has built up in you so that you have to let it break out, and then your bad time is increased. So it's like being on the wrong escalator.

"Take it slow, take it easy," said my bunky. "Eight months goes by if you get yourself some sun."

"Yeah, I'm going to sleep in the sun," I said. "I'm going to drink it."

"Get a good burn your first day out, ha-ha. Burn the prison crap out of your pores."

Maybe the sun would burn the dullness away. That's what I was thinking.

The People Across the Canyon

·

Margaret Millar

Margaret Millar's distinguished career has spanned nearly fifty years, beginning with the publication of her first novel, The Invisible Worm, *in 1941. Such outstanding novels of psychological suspense as* Beast in View *(1955),* Stranger in My Grave *(1960),* Beyond This Point Are Monsters *(1970), and* Spider Webs *(1986), have led many readers, writers, and critics to praise her work as equal to—and perhaps better than—that of her late husband, Kenneth Millar (Ross Macdonald). She has published only a trio of short stories, but each is as superbly crafted as her novels; and of the three, "The People Across the Canyon" is certainly the most chilling.*

The first time the Bortons realized that someone had moved into the new house across the canyon was one night in May when they saw the rectangular light of a television set shining in the picture window. Marion Borton knew it had to happen eventually, but that didn't make it any easier to accept the idea of neighbors in a part of the country she and Paul had come to consider exclusively their own.

They had discovered the site, had bought six acres, and built the house over the objections of the bank, which didn't like to lend money on unimproved property, and of their friends who thought the Bortons were foolish to move so far out of town. Now other people were discovering the spot, and here and there through the eucalyptus trees and the live oaks, Marion could see half-finished houses.

But it was the house directly across the canyon that bothered her most; she had been dreading this moment ever since the site had been bulldozed the previous summer.

"There goes our privacy." Marion went over and snapped off the television set, a sign to Paul that she had something on her mind which she wanted to transfer to his. The transference, intended to halve the problem, often merely doubled it.

"Well, let's have it," Paul said, trying to conceal his annoyance.

"Have what?"

"Stop kidding around. You don't usually cut off Perry Mason in the middle of a sentence."

"All I said was, there goes our privacy."

"We have plenty left," Paul said.

"You know how sounds carry across the canyon."

"I don't hear any sounds."

"You will. They probably have ten or twelve children and a howling dog and a sports car."

"A couple of children wouldn't be so bad—at least, Cathy would have someone to play with."

Cathy was eight, in bed now, and ostensibly asleep, with the night light on and her bedroom door open just a crack.

"She has plenty of playmates at school," Marion said, pulling the drapes across the window so that she wouldn't have to look at the exasperating rectangle of light across the canyon. "Her teacher tells me Cathy gets along with everyone and never causes any trouble. You talk as if she's deprived or something."

"It would be nice if she had more interests, more children of her own age around."

"A lot of things would be nice *if*. I've done my best."

Paul knew it was true. He'd heard her issue dozens of weekend invitations to Cathy's schoolmates. Few of them came to anything. The mothers offered various excuses: poison oak, snakes, mosquitoes in the creek at the bottom of the canyon, the distance of the house from town in case something happened and a doctor was needed in a hurry . . . these excuses, sincere and valid as they were, embittered Marion. *"For heaven's sake, you'd think we lived on the moon or in the middle of a jungle."*

"I guess a couple of children would be all right," Marion said. "But please, no sports car."

"I'm afraid that's out of our hands."

"Actually, they might even be quiet *nice* people."

"Why not? Most people are."

Both Marion and Paul had the comfortable feeling that something had been settled, though neither was quite sure what. Paul went over and turned the television set back on. As he had suspected, it was the doorman who'd killed the nightclub owner with a baseball bat, not the blonde dancer or her young husband or the jealous singer.

It was the following Monday that Cathy started to run away.

Marion, ironing in the kitchen and watching a quiz program on the portable set Paul had given her for Christmas, heard the school bus groan to a stop at the top of the driveway. She waited for the front door to open and Cathy to announce in her high thin voice, "I'm home, Mommy."

The door didn't open.

From the kitchen window Marion saw the yellow bus round the sharp curve of the hill like a circus cage full of wild captive children screaming for release.

Marion waited until the end of the program, trying to convince herself that another bus had been added to the route and would come along shortly, or that Cathy had decided to stop off at a friend's house and would telephone any minute. But no other bus appeared, and the telephone remained silent.

Marion changed into her hiking boots and started off down the canyon, avoiding the scratchy clumps of chapparal and the creepers of poison oak that looked like loganberry vines.

She found Cathy sitting in the middle of the little bridge that Paul had made across the creek out of two fallen eucalyptus trees. Cathy's short plump legs hung over the logs until they almost touched the water. She was absolutely motionless, her face hidden by a straw curtain of hair. Then a single frog croaked a warning of Marion's presence and Cathy responded to the sound as if she was more intimate with nature than adults were, and more alert to its subtle communications of danger.

She stood up quickly, brushing off the back of her dress and drawing aside the curtain of hair to reveal eyes as blue as the periwinkles that hugged the banks of the creek.

"Cathy."

"I was only counting waterbugs while I was waiting. Forty-one."

"Waiting for what?"

"The ten or twelve children, and the dog."

"What ten or twelve chil—" Marion stopped. "I see. You were listening the other night when we thought you were asleep."

"I wasn't listening," Cathy said righteously. "My ears were hearing."

Marion restrained a smile. "Then I wish you'd tell those ears of yours to hear properly. I didn't say the new neighbors had ten or twelve children, I said they *might* have. Actually, it's very unlikely. Not many families are that big these days."

"Do you have to be old to have a big family?"

"Well, you certainly can't be very young."

"I bet people with big families have station wagons so they have room for all the children?"

"The lucky ones do."

Cathy stared down at the thin flow of water carrying fat little minnows down to the sea. Finally she said, "They're too young, and their car is too small."

In spite of her aversion to having new neighbors, Marion felt a quickening of interest. "Have you seen them?"

But the little girl seemed deaf, lost in a water world of minnows and dragonflies and tadpoles.

"I asked you a question, Cathy. Did you see the people who just moved in?"

"Yes."

"When?"

"Before you came. Their name is Smith."

"How do you know that?"

"I went up to the house to look at things and they said, hello, little girl, what's your name? And I said, Cathy, what's yours? And they said Smith. Then they drove off in the little car."

"You're not supposed to go poking around other people's

207

houses," Marion said brusquely. "And while we're at it, you're not supposed to go anywhere after school without first telling me where you're going and when you'll be back. You know that perfectly well. Now why didn't you come in and report to me after you got off the school bus?"

"I didn't want to."

"That's not a satisfactory answer."

Satisfactory or not, it was the only answer Cathy had. She looked at her mother in silence, then she turned and darted back up the hill to her own house.

After a time Marion followed her, exasperated and a little confused. She hated to punish the child, but she knew she couldn't ignore the matter entirely—it was much too serious. While she gave Cathy her graham crackers and orange juice, she told her, reasonably and kindly, that she would have to stay in her room the following day after school by way of learning a lesson.

That night, after Cathy had been tucked in bed, Marion related the incident to Paul. He seemed to take a less serious view of it than Marion, a fact of which the listening child became well aware.

"I'm glad she's getting acquainted with the new people," Paul said. "It shows a certain degree of poise I didn't think she had. She's always been so shy."

"You're surely not condoning her running off without telling me?"

"She didn't run far. All kids do things like that once in a while."

"We don't want to spoil her."

"Cathy's always been so obedient I think she has *us* spoiled. Who knows, she might even teach us a thing or two about going out and making new friends." He realized, from past experience, that this was a very touchy subject. Marion had her house, her garden, her television sets; she didn't seem to want any more of the world than these, and she resented any implication that they were not enough. To ward off an argument he added, "You've done a good job with Cathy. Stop worrying . . . Smith, their name is?"

"Yes."

"Actually, I think it's an excellent sign that Cathy's getting acquainted."

At three the next afternoon the yellow circus cage arrived, released one captive, and rumbled on its way.

"I'm home, Mommy."

"Good girl."

Marion felt guilty at the sight of her: the child had been cooped up in school all day, the weather was so warm and lovely, and besides Paul hadn't thought the incident of the previous afternoon too important.

"I know what," Marion suggested, "Let's you and I go down to the creek and count waterbugs."

The offer was a sacrifice for Marion because her favorite quiz program was on and she liked to answer the questions along with the contestants. "How about that?"

Cathy knew all about the quiz program; she'd seen it a hundred times, had watched the moving mouths claim her mother's eyes and ears and mind. "I counted the waterbugs yesterday."

"Well, minnows, then."

"You'll scare them away."

"Oh, will I?" Marion laughed self-consciously, rather relieved that Cathy had refused her offer and was clearly and definitely a little guilty about the relief. "Don't you scare them?"

"No. They think I'm another minnow because they're used to me."

"Maybe they could get used to me, too."

"I don't think so."

When Cathy went off down the canyon by herself Marion realized, in a vaguely disturbing way, that the child had politely but firmly rejected her mother's company. It wasn't until dinner time that she found out the reason why.

"The Smiths," Cathy said, "have an Austin-Healey."

Cathy, like most girls, had never shown any interest in cars, and her glib use of the name moved her parents to laughter.

The laughter encouraged Cathy to elaborate. "An Austin-Healey makes a lot of noise—like Daddy's lawn mower."

"I don't think the company would appreciate a commercial

from you, young lady," Paul said. "Are the Smiths all moved in?"

"Oh, yes. I helped them."

"Is that a fact? And how did you help them?"

"I sang two songs. And then we danced and danced."

Paul looked half pleased, half puzzled. It wasn't like Cathy to perform willingly in front of people. During the last Christmas concert at the school she'd left the stage in tears and hidden in the cloak room . . . Well, maybe her shyness was only a phase and she was finally getting over it.

"They must be very nice people," he said, "to take time out from getting settled in a new house to play games with a little girl."

Cathy shook her head. "It wasn't games. It was real dancing—like on Ed Sullivan."

"As good as that, eh?" Paul said, smiling. "Tell me about it."

"Mrs. Smith is a nightclub dancer."

Paul's smile faded, and a pulse began to beat in his left temple like a small misplaced heart. "Oh? You're sure about that, Cathy?"

"Yes."

"And what does Mr. Smith do?"

"He's a baseball player."

"You mean that's what he does for a living?" Marion asked. "He doesn't work in an office like Daddy?"

"No, he just plays baseball. He always wears a baseball cap."

"I see. What position does he play on the team?" Paul's voice was low.

Cathy looked blank.

"Everybody on a ball team has a special thing to do. What does Mr. Smith do?"

"He's a batter."

"A batter, eh? Well, that's nice. Did he tell you this?"

"Yes."

"Cathy," Paul said, "I know you wouldn't deliberately lie to me, but sometimes you get your facts a little mixed up."

He went on in this vein for some time but Cathy's story remained unshaken: Mrs. Smith was a nightclub dancer, Mr. Smith a professional baseball player, they loved children, and they never watched television.

"That, at least, must be a lie," Marion said to Paul later when she saw the rectangular light of the television set shining in the Smiths' picture window. "As for the rest of it, there isn't a night club within fifty miles, or a professional ball club within two hundred."

"She probably misunderstood. It's quite possible that at one time Mrs. Smith was a dancer of sorts and that he played a little baseball."

Cathy, in bed and teetering dizzily on the brink of sleep, wondered if she should tell her parents about the Smiths' child—the one who didn't go to school.

She didn't tell them; Marion found out for herself the next morning after Paul and Cathy had gone. When she pulled back the drapes in the living room and opened the windows she heard the sharp slam of a screen door from across the canyon and saw a small child come out on the patio of the new house. At that distance she couldn't tell whether it was a boy or a girl. Whichever it was, the child was quiet and well behaved; only the occasional slam of the door shook the warm, windless day.

The presence of the child, and the fact that Cathy hadn't mentioned it, gnawed at Marion's mind all day. She questioned Cathy about it as soon as she came home.

"You didn't tell me the Smiths have a child."

"No."

"Why not?"

"I don't know why not."

"Is it a boy or a girl?"

"Girl."

"How old?"

Cathy thought it over carefully, frowning up at the ceiling. "About ten."

"Doesn't she go to school?"

"No."

"Why not?"

"She doesn't want to."

"That's not a very good reason."

"It is her reason," Cathy said flatly. "Can I go out to play now?"

"I'm not sure you should. You look a little feverish. Come here and let me feel your forehead."

Cathy's forehead was cool and moist, but her cheeks and the bridge of her nose were very pink, almost as if she'd been sunburned.

"You'd better stay inside," Marion said, "and watch some cartoons."

"I don't like cartoons."

"You used to."

"I like real people."

She means the Smiths, of course, Marion thought as her mouth tightened. "People who dance and play baseball all the time?"

If the sarcasm had any effect on Cathy she didn't show it. After waiting until Marion had become engrossed in her quiz program, Cathy lined up all her dolls in her room and gave a concert for them, to thunderous applause.

"Where are your old Navy binoculars?" Marion asked Paul when she was getting ready for bed.

"Oh, somewhere in the sea chest, I imagine. Why?"

"I want them."

"Not thinking of spying on the neighbors, are you?"

"I'm thinking of just that," Marion said grimly.

The next morning, as soon as she saw the Smith child come out on the patio, Marion went downstairs to the storage room to search through the sea chest. She located the binoculars and was in the act of dusting them off when the telephone started to ring in the living room. She hurried upstairs and said breathlessly, "Hello?"

"Mrs. Borton?"

"Yes."

"This is Miss Park speaking, Cathy's teacher."

Marion had met Miss Park several times at P.T.A. meetings and report-card conferences. She was a large, ruddy-faced, and unfailingly cheerful young woman—the kind, as Paul said, you wouldn't want to live with but who'd be nice to have around in an emergency. "How are you, Miss Park?"

"Oh, fine, thank you, Mrs. Borton. I meant to call you yesterday but things were a bit out of hand around here, and I knew there was no great hurry to check on Cathy; she's such a well-behaved little girl."

Even Miss Park's loud, jovial voice couldn't cover up the ominous sound of the word *check*. "I don't think I quite understand. Why should you check on Cathy?"

"Purely routine. The school doctor and the health department like to keep records on how many cases of measles or flu or chicken pox are going the rounds. Right now it looks like the season for mumps. Is Cathy all right?"

"She seemed a little feverish yesterday afternoon when she got home from school, but she acted perfectly normal when she left this morning."

Miss Park's silence was so protracted that Marion became painfully conscious of things she wouldn't otherwise have noticed—the weight of the binoculars in her lap, the thud of her own heartbeat in her ears. Across the canyon the Smith child was playing quietly and alone on the patio. *There is definitely something the matter with that girl*, Marion thought. *Perhaps I'd better not let Cathy go over there any more, she's so imitative.* "Miss Park, are you still on the line? Hello? Hello—"

"I'm here." Miss Park's voice seemed fainter than usual, and less positive. "What time did Cathy leave the house this morning?"

"Eight, as usual."

"Did she take the school bus?"

"Of course. She always does."

"Did you see her get on?"

"I kissed her goodbye at the front door," Marion said. "What's this all about, Miss Park?"

"Cathy hasn't been at school for two days, Mrs. Borton."

"Why, that's absurd, impossible! You must be mistaken." But even as she was speaking the words, Marion was raising the binoculars to her eyes: the little girl on the Smiths' patio had a

213

straw curtain of hair and eyes as blue as the periwinkles along the creek banks.

"Mrs. Borton, I'm not likely to be mistaken about which of my children are in class or not."

"No. No, you're—you're not mistaken, Miss Park. I can see Cathy from here—she's over at the neighbor's house."

"Good. That's a load off my mind."

"Off yours, yes," Marion said. "Not mine."

"Now we mustn't become excited, Mrs. Borton. Don't make too much of this incident before we've had a chance to confer. Suppose you come and talk to me during my lunch hour and bring Cathy along. We'll all have a friendly chat."

But it soon became apparent, even to the optimistic Miss Park, that Cathy didn't intend to take part in any friendly chat. She stood by the window in the classroom, blank-eyed, mute, unresponsive to the simplest questions, refusing to be drawn into any conversation even about her favorite topic, the Smiths. Miss Park finally decided to send Cathy out to play in the schoolyard while she talked to Marion alone.

"Obviously," Miss Park said, enunciating the word very distinctly because it was one of her favorites, "obviously, Cathy's got a crush on this young couple and has concocted a fantasy about belonging to them."

"It's not so obvious what my husband and I are going to do about it."

"Live through it, the same as other parents. Crushes like this are common at Cathy's age. Sometimes the object is a person, a whole family, even a horse. And, of course, to Cathy a nightclub dancer and a baseball player must seem very glamorous indeed. Tell me, Mrs. Borton, does she watch television a great deal?"

Marion stiffened. "No more than any other child."

Oh, dear, Miss Park thought sadly, *they all do it; the most confirmed addicts are always the most defensive.* "I just wondered," she said. "Cathy likes to sing to herself and I've never heard such a repertoire of television commercials."

"She picks things up very fast."

"Yes. Yes, she does indeed." Miss Park studied her hands,

which were always a little pale from chalk dust and were even paler now because she was angry—at the child for deceiving her, at Mrs. Borton for brushing aside the television issue, at herself for not preventing, or at least anticipating, the current situation, and perhaps most of all at the Smiths who ought to have known better than to allow a child to hang around their house when she should obviously be in school.

"Don't put too much pressure on Cathy about this," she said finally, "until I talk the matter over with the school psychologist. By the way, have you met the Smiths, Mrs. Borton?"

"Not yet," Marion said grimly. "But believe me, I intend to."

"Yes, I think it would be a good idea for you to talk to them and make it clear that they're not to encourage Cathy in this fantasy."

The meeting came sooner than Marion expected.

She waited at the school until classes were dismissed, then she took Cathy into town to do some shopping. She had parked the car and she and Cathy were standing hand in hand at a corner waiting for a traffic light to change; Marion was worried and impatient, Cathy still silent, unresisting, inert, as she had been ever since Marion had called her home from the Smiths' patio.

Suddenly Marion felt the child's hand tighten in a spasm of excitement. Cathy's face had turned so pink it looked ready to explode and with her free hand she was waving violently at two people in a small cream-colored sports car—a very pretty young woman with blonde hair in the driver's seat, and beside her a young man wearing a wide friendly grin and a baseball cap. They both waved back at Cathy just before the lights changed and then the car roared through the intersection.

"The Smiths," Cathy shouted, jumping up and down in a frenzy. "That was the Smiths."

"Sssh, not so loud. People will—"

"But it was the *Smiths*!"

"Hurry up before the light changes."

The child didn't hear. She stood as if rooted to the curb, staring after the cream-colored car.

With a little grunt of impatience Marion picked her up, carried her across the road, and let her down quite roughly on the other side. "There. If you're going to act like a baby, I'll carry you like a baby."

"I saw the Smiths!"

"All right. What are you so excited about? It's not very unusual to meet someone in town whom you know."

"It's unusual to meet *them*."

"Why?"

"Because it is." The color was fading from Cathy's cheeks, but her eyes still looked bedazzled, quite as if they'd seen a miracle.

"I'm sure they're very unique people," Marion said coldly. "Nevertheless they must stop for groceries like everyone else."

Cathy's answer was a slight shake of her head and a whisper heard only by herself: "No, they don't, never."

When Paul came home from work Cathy was sent to play in the front yard while Marion explained matters to him. He listened with increasing irritation—not so much at Cathy's actions but at the manner in which Marion and Miss Park had handled things. There was too much talking, he said, and too little acting.

"The way you women beat around the bush instead of tackling the situation directly, meeting it head-on—fantasy life. Fantasy life, my foot! Now we're going over to the Smiths right this minute and talk to them and that will be that. End of fantasy. Period."

"We'd better wait until after dinner. Cathy missed her lunch."

Throughout the meal Cathy was pale and quiet. She ate nothing and spoke only when asked a direct question; but inside herself the conversation was very lively, the dinner a banquet with dancing, and afterward a wild, windy ride in the roofless car . . .

Although the footpath through the canyon provided a shorter route to the Smiths' house, the Bortons decided to go more formally, by car, and to take Cathy with them. Cathy, told to comb her hair and wash her face, protested: "I don't want to go over there."

"Why not?" Paul said. "You were so anxious to spend time

216

with them that you played hooky for two days. Why don't you want to see them now?"

"Because they're not there."

"How do you know?"

"Mrs. Smith told me this morning that they wouldn't be home tonight because she's putting on a show."

"Indeed?" Paul was grim faced. "Just where does she put on these shows of hers?"

"And Mr. Smith has to play baseball. And after that they're going to see a friend in the hospital who has leukemia."

"Leukemia, eh?" He didn't have to ask how Cathy had found out about such a thing; he'd watched a semidocumentary dealing with it a couple of nights ago. Cathy was supposed to have been sleeping.

"I wonder," he said to Marion when Cathy went to comb her hair, "just how many 'facts' about the Smiths have been borrowed from television."

"Well, I know for myself that they drive a sports car, and Mr. Smith was wearing a baseball cap. And they're both young and good-looking. Young and good-looking enough," she added wryly, "to make me feel—well, a little jealous."

"Jealous?"

"Cathy would rather belong to them than to us. It makes me wonder if it's something the Smiths have or something the Bortons don't have."

"Ask her."

"I can't very well—"

"Then I will, dammit," Paul said. And he did.

Cathy merely looked at him innocently. "I don't know. I don't know what you mean."

"Then listen again. Why did you pretend that you were the Smiths' little girl?"

"They asked me to be. They asked me to go with them."

"They actually said, Cathy, will you be our little girl?"

"Yes."

"Well, by heaven, I'll put an end to this nonsense," Paul said, and strode out to the car.

It was twilight when they reached the Smiths' house by way

217

of the narrow, hilly road. The moon, just appearing above the horizon, was on the wane, a chunk bitten out of its side by some giant jaw. A warm dry wind, blowing down the mountain from the desert beyond, carried the sweet scent of pittosporum.

The Smiths' house was dark, and both the front door and the garage were locked. Out of defiance or desperation, Paul pressed the door chime anyway, several times. All three of them could hear it ringing inside, and it seemed to Marion to echo very curiously—as if the carpets and drapes were too thin to muffle the sound vibrations. She would have liked to peer in through the windows and see for herself, but the venetian blinds were closed.

"What's their furniture like?" she asked Cathy.

"Like everybody's."

"I mean, is it new? Does Mrs. Smith tell you not to put your feet on it?"

"No, she never tells me that," Cathy said truthfully. "I want to go home now. I'm tired."

It was while she was putting Cathy to bed that Marion heard Paul call to her from the living room in an urgent voice, "Marion, come here a minute."

She found him standing motionless in the middle of the room, staring across the canyon at the Smiths' place. The rectangular light of the Smiths' television set was shining in the picture window of the room that opened onto the patio at the back of the Smiths' house.

"Either they've come home within the past few minutes," he said, "or they were there all the time. My guess is that they were home when we went over, but they didn't want to see us, so they just doused the lights and pretended to be out. Well, it won't work! Come on, we're going back."

"I can't leave Cathy alone. She's already got her pajamas on."

"Put a bathrobe on her and bring her along. This has gone beyond the point of observing such niceties as correct attire."

"Don't you think we should wait until tomorrow?"

"Hurry up and stop arguing with me."

Cathy, protesting that she was tired and that the Smiths

weren't home anyway, was bundled into a bathrobe and carried to the car.

"They're home all right," Paul said. "And by heaven they'd better answer the door this time or I'll break it down."

"That's an absurd way to talk in front of a child," Marion said coldly. "She has enough ideas without hearing—"

"Absurd, is it? Wait and see."

Cathy, listening from the back seat, smiled sleepily. She knew how to get in without breaking anything: ever since the house had been built, the real estate man who'd been trying to sell it always hid the key on a nail underneath the window box.

The second trip seemed a nightmarish imitation of the first: the same moon hung in the sky but it looked smaller now, and paler. The scent of pittosporum was funereally sweet, and the hollow sound of the chimes from inside the house was like the echo in an empty tomb.

"They must be crazy to think they can get away with a trick like this twice in one night," Paul shouted. "Come on, we're going around to the back."

Marion looked a little frightened. "I don't like trespassing on someone else's property."

"They trespassed on our property first."

He glanced down at Cathy. Her eyes were half closed and her face was pearly in the moonlight. He pressed her hand to reassure her that everything was going to be all right and that his anger wasn't directed at her, but she drew away from him and started down the path that led to the back of the house.

Paul clicked on his flashlight and followed her, moving slowly along the unfamiliar terrain. By the time he turned the corner of the house and reached the patio, Cathy was out of sight.

"Cathy," he called. "Where are you? Come back here!"

Marion was looking at him accusingly. "You upset her with that silly threat about breaking down the door. She's probably on her way home though the canyon."

"I'd better go after her."

"She's less likely to get hurt than you are. She knows every inch of the way. Besides, you came here to break down the doors. All right, start breaking."

But there was no need to break down anything. The back door opened as soon as Paul rapped on it with his knuckles, and he almost fell into the room.

It was empty except for a small girl wearing a blue bathrobe that matched her eyes.

Paul said, "Cathy. Cathy, what are you doing here?"

Marion stood with her hand pressed to her mouth to stifle the scream that was rising in her throat. There were no Smiths. The people in the sports car whom Cathy had waved at were just strangers responding to the friendly greeting of a child—had Cathy seen them before, on a previous trip to town? The television set was no more than a contraption rigged up by Cathy herself—an orange crate and an old mirror which caught and reflected the rays of the moon.

In front of it Cathy was standing, facing her own image. "Hello, Mrs. Smith. Here I am, all ready to go."

"Cathy," Marion said in a voice that sounded torn by claws. "What do you see in that mirror?"

"It's not a mirror. It's a television set."

"What—what program are you watching?"

"It's not a program, silly. It's real. It's the Smiths. I'm going away with them to dance and play baseball."

"There are no Smiths," Paul bellowed. "Will you get that through your head? *There are no Smiths*!"

"Yes, there are. I see them."

Marion knelt on the floor beside the child. "Listen to me, Cathy. This is a mirror—only a mirror. It came from Daddy's old bureau and I had it put away in the storage room. That's where you found it, isn't it? And you brought it here and decided to pretend it was a television set, isn't that right? But it's really just a mirror, and the people in it are us—you and Mommy and Daddy."

But even as she looked at her own reflection, Marion saw it beginning to change. She was growing younger, prettier; her hair was becoming lighter and her cotton suit was changing into a dancing dress. And beside her in the mirror, Paul was turning into a stranger, a laughing-eyed young man wearing a baseball cap.

"I'm ready to go now, Mr. Smith," Cathy said, and suddenly all three of them, the Smiths and their little girl, began walking away in the mirror. In a few moments they were no bigger than matchsticks—and then the three of them disappeared, and there was only the moonlight in the glass.

"Cathy," Marion cried. "Come back, Cathy! Please come back!"

Propped up against the door like a dummy, Paul imagined he could hear above his wife's cries the mocking muted roar of a sports car.

Iris

•

Stephen Greenleaf

Like his creator, John Marshall Tanner is a former lawyer from San Francisco—and a private eye in the classic tradition, though more closely akin to Ross Macdonald's Lew Archer than to Hammett's Sam Spade or Chandler's Philip Marlowe. "Iris" marks Tanner's first appearance in a short story, and a fine one it is— the grim and compelling tale of violent passions in rural northern California. Stephen Greenleaf's widely praised novels featuring Tanner include Grave Error *(1979),* State's Evidence *(1982),* Beyond Blame *(1986), and* Toll Call *(1987).*

The Buick trudged toward the summit, each step slower than the last, the automatic gearing slipping ever-lower as the air thinned and the grade steepened and the trucks were rendered snails. At the top the road leveled, and the Buick spent a brief sigh of relief before coasting thankfully down the other side, atop the stiff gray strap that was Interstate 5. As it passed from Oregon to California the car seemed cheered. Its driver shared the mood, though only momentarily.

He blinked his eyes and shrugged his shoulders and twisted his head. He straightened his leg and shook it. He turned up the volume of the radio, causing a song to be sung more loudly than it merited. But the acid fog lay still behind his eyes, eating at them. As he approached a roadside rest area he decided to give both the Buick and himself a break.

During the previous week he had chased a wild goose in the shape of a rumor all the way to Seattle, with tantalizing stops in Eugene and Portland along the way. Eight hours earlier, when he had finally recognized the goose for what it was, he had

222

headed home, hoping to make it in one day but realizing as he slowed for the rest area that he couldn't reach San Francisco that evening without risking more than was sensible in the way of vehicular manslaughter.

He took the exit, dropped swiftly to the bank of the Klamath River and pulled into a parking slot in the Randolph Collier safety rest area. After making use of the facilities, he pulled out his map and considered where to spend the night. Redding looked like the logical place, out of the mountains, at the head of the soporific valley that separated him from home. He was reviewing what he knew about Redding when a voice, aggressively gay and musical, greeted him from somewhere near the car. He glanced to his side, sat up straight and rolled down the window. "Hi," the thin voice said again.

"Hi."

She was blond, her long straight tresses misbehaving in the wind that tumbled through the river canyon. Her narrow face was white and seamless, as though it lacked flesh, was only skull. Her eyes were blue and tardy. She wore a loose green blouse gathered at the neck and wrists and a long skirt of faded calico, fringed in white ruffles. Her boots were leather and well-worn, their tops disappearing under her skirt the way the tops of the mountains at her back disappeared into a disc of cloud.

He pegged her for a hitchhiker, one who perpetually roams the roads and provokes either pity or disapproval in those who pass her by. He glanced around to see if she was fronting for a partner, but the only thing he saw besides the picnic and toilet facilities and travelers like himself was a large bundle resting atop a picnic table at the far end of the parking lot. Her worldly possessions, he guessed; her only aids to life. He looked at her again and considered whether he wanted to share some driving time and possibly a motel room with a girl who looked a little spacy and a little sexy and a lot heedless of the world that delivered him his living.

"My name's Iris," she said, wrapping her arms across her chest, shifting her weight from foot to foot, shivering in the autumn chill.

"Mine's Marsh."

223

"You look tired." Her concern seemed genuine, his common symptoms for some reason alarming to her.

"I am," he admitted.

"Been on the road long?"

"From Seattle."

"How far is that about?" the question came immediately, as though she habitually erased her ignorance.

"Four hundred miles. Maybe a little more."

She nodded as though the numbers made him wise. "I've been to Seattle."

"Good."

"I've been lots of places."

"Good."

She unwrapped her arms and placed them on the car door and leaned toward him. Her musk was unadulterated. Her blouse dropped open to reveal breasts sharpened to twin points by the mountain air. "Where you headed, Marsh?"

"South."

"L.A. ?"

He shook his head. "San Francisco."

"Good. Perfect."

He expected it right then, the flirting pitch for a lift, but her request was slightly different. "Could you take something down there for me?"

He frowned and though of the package on the picnic table. Drugs? "What?" he asked.

"I'll show you in a sec. Do you think you could, though?"

He shook his head. "I don't think so. I mean, I'm kind of on a tight schedule, and . . ."

She wasn't listening. "It goes to . . ." She pulled a scrap of paper from the pocket of her skirt and uncrumpled it. "It goes to 95 Albosa Drive, in Hurley City. That's near Frisco, isn't it? Marvin said it was."

He nodded. "But I don't . . ."

She put up a hand. "Hold still. I'll be right back."

She skipped twice, her long skirt hopping high above her boots to show a shaft of gypsum thigh, then trotted to the picnic

Iris

table and picked up the bundle. Halfway back to the car she proffered it like a prize soufflé.

"Is this what you want me to take?" he asked as she approached.

She nodded, then looked down at the package and frowned. "I don't like this one," she said, her voice dropping to a dismissive rasp.

"Why not?"

"Because it isn't happy. It's from the B Box, so it can't help it, I guess, but all the same it should go back, I don't care *what* Marvin says."

"What is it? A puppy?"

She thrust the package through the window. He grasped it reflexively, to keep it from dropping to his lap. As he secured his grip the girl ran off. "Hey! Wait a minute," he called after her. "I can't take this thing. You'll have to . . ."

He thought the package moved. He slid one hand beneath it and with the other peeled back the cotton strips that swaddled it. A baby—not canine but human—glared at him and screamed. He looked frantically for the girl and saw her climbing into a gray Volkswagen bug that was soon scooting out of the rest area and climbing toward the freeway.

He swore, then rocked the baby awkwardly for an instant, trying to quiet the screams it formed with every muscle. When that didn't work, he placed the child on the seat beside him, started the car and backed out. As he started forward he had to stop to avoid another car, and then to reach out wildly to keep the child from rolling off the seat.

He moved the gear to park and gathered the seat belt on the passenger side and tried to wrap it around the baby in a way that would be more safe than throttling. The result was not reassuring. He unhooked the belt and put the baby on the floor beneath his legs, put the car in gear and set out after the little gray VW that had disappeared with the child's presumptive mother. He caught it only after several frantic miles, when he reached the final slope that descended to the grassy plain that separated the Siskiyou range from the lordly aspect of Mt. Shasta.

The VW buzzed toward the mammoth mountain like a mad

225

mouse assaulting an elephant. He considered overtaking the car, forcing Iris to stop, returning the baby, then getting the hell away from her as fast as the Buick would take him. But something in his memory of her look and words made him keep his distance, made him keep Iris in sight while he waited for her to make a turn toward home.

The highway flattened, then crossed the high meadow that nurtured sheep and cattle and horses below the lumps of the southern Cascades and the Trinity Alps. Traffic was light, the sun low above the western peaks, the air a steady splash of autumn. He checked his gas gauge. If Iris didn't turn off in the next fifty miles he would either have to force her to stop or let her go. The piercing baby sounds that rose from beneath his knees made the latter choice impossible.

They reached Yreka, and he closed to within a hundred yards of the bug, but Iris ignored his plea that the little city be her goal. Thirty minutes later, after he had decided she was nowhere near her destination, Iris abruptly left the interstate, at the first exit to a village that was hand-maiden to the mountain, a town reputed to house an odd collection of spiritual seekers and religious zealots.

The mountain itself, volcanic, abrupt, spectacular, had been held by the Indians to be holy, and the area surrounding it was replete with hot springs and mud baths and other prehistoric marvels. Modern mystics had accepted the mantle of the mountain, and the crazy girl and her silly bug fit with what he knew about the place and those who gathered there. What didn't fit was the baby she had foisted on him.

He slowed and glanced at his charge once again and failed to receive anything resembling contentment in return. Fat little arms escaped the blanket and pulled the air like taffy. Spittle dribbled down its chin. A translucent bubble appeared at a tiny nostril, then broke silently and vanished.

The bug darted through the north end of town, left, then right, then left again, quickly, as though it sensed pursuit. He lagged behind, hoping Iris was confident she had ditched him. He looked at the baby again, marvelling that it could cry so loud, could for so long expend the major portion of its strength in unrequited pleas. When he looked at the road again the bug had disappeared.

He swore and slowed and looked at driveways, then began to plan what to do if he had lost her. Houses dwindled, the street became dirt, then flanked the log decks and lumber stacks and wigwam burners of a sawmill. A road sign declared it unlawful to sleigh, toboggan or ski on a country road. He had gasped the first breaths of panic when he saw the VW nestled next to a ramshackle cabin on the back edge of town, empty, as though it had been there always.

A pair of firs sheltered the cabin and the car, made the dwindling day seem night. The driveway was mud, the yard bordered by a falling wormwood fence. He drove to the next block and stopped his car, the cabin now invisible.

He knew he couldn't keep the baby much longer. He had no idea what to do, for it or with it, had no idea what it wanted, no idea what awaited it in Hurley City, had only a sense that the girl, Iris, was goofy, perhaps pathologically so, and that he should not abet her plan.

Impossibly, the child cried louder. He had some snacks in the car—crackers, cookies, some cheese—but he was afraid the baby was too young for solids. He considered buying milk, and a bottle, and playing parent. The baby cried again, gasped and sputtered, then repeated its protest.

He reached down and picked it up. The little red face inflated, contorted, mimicked a steam machine that continuously whistled. The puffy cheeks, the tiny blue eyes, the round pug nose, all were engorged in scarlet fury. He cradled the baby in his arms as best he could and rocked it. The crying dimmed momentarily, then began again.

His mind ran the gauntlet of childhood scares—diptheria, smallpox, measles, mumps, croup, even a pressing need to burp. God knew what ailed it. He patted its forehead and felt the sticky heat of fever.

Shifting position, he felt something hard within the blanket, felt for it, finally drew it out. A nippled baby bottle, half-filled, body-warm. He shook it and presented the nipple to the baby, who sucked it as its due. Giddy at his feat, he unwrapped his package further, enough to tell him he was holding a little girl and that she seemed whole and healthy except for her rage and fever. When she was feeding steadily he put her back on the floor and got out of the car.

The stream of smoke it emitted into the evening dusk made the cabin seem dangled from a string. Beneath the firs the ground was moist, a spongy mat of rotting twigs and needles. The air was cold and damp and smelled of burning wood. He walked slowly up the drive, courting silence, alert for the menace implied by the hand-lettered sign, nailed to the nearest tree, that ordered him to KEEP OUT.

The cabin was dark but for the variable light at a single window. The porch was piled high with firewood, both logs and kindling. A maul and wedge leaned against a stack of fruitwood piled next to the door. He walked to the far side of the cabin and looked beyond it for signs of Marvin.

A tool shed and a broken-down school bus filled the rear yard. Between the two a tethered nanny goat grazed beneath a line of drying clothes, silent but for her neck bell, the swollen udder oscillating easily beneath her, the teats extended like accusing fingers. Beyond the yard a thicket of berry bushes served as fence, and beyond the bushes a stand of pines blocked further vision. He felt alien, isolated, exposed, threatened, as Marvin doubtlessly hoped all strangers would.

He thought about the baby, wondered if it was all right, wondered if babies could drink so much they got sick or even choked. A twinge of fear sent him trotting back to the car. The baby was fine, the bottle empty on the floor beside it, its noises not wails but only muffled whimpers. He returned to the cabin and went onto the porch and knocked at the door and waited.

Iris wore the same blouse and skirt and boots, the same eyes too shallow to hold her soul. She didn't recognize him; her face pinched only with uncertainty.

He stepped toward her and she backed away and asked him what he wanted. The room behind her was a warren of vague shapes, the only source of light far in the back by a curtain that spanned the room.

"I want to give you your baby back," he said.

She looked at him more closely, then opened her mouth in silent exclamation, then slowly smiled. "How'd you know where I lived?"

"I followed you."

"Why? Did something happen to it already?"

"No, but I don't want to take it with me."

She seemed truly puzzled. "Why not? It's on your way, isn't it? Almost?"

He ignored the question. "I want to know some more about the baby."

"Like what?"

"Like whose is it? Yours?"

Iris frowned and nibbled her lower lip. "Sort of."

"What do you mean, 'sort of?' Did you give birth to it?"

"Not exactly." Iris combed her hair with her fingers, then shook it off her face with an irritated twitch. "What are you asking all these questions for?"

"Because you asked me to do you a favor and I think I have the right to know what I'm getting into. That's only fair, isn't it?"

She paused. Her pout was dubious. "I guess."

"So where did you get the baby?" he asked again.

"Marvin got it."

"From whom?"

"Those people in Hurley City. So I don't know why you won't take it back, seeing as how it's theirs and all."

"But why . . ."

His question was obliterated by a high glissando, brief and piercing. He looked at Iris, then at the shadowy interior of the cabin.

There was no sign of life, no sign of anything but the leavings of neglect and a spartan bent. A fat gray cat hopped off a shelf and sauntered toward the back of the cabin and disappeared behind the blanket that was draped on the rope that spanned the rear of the room. The cry echoed once again. "What's that?" he asked her.

Iris giggled. "What does it sound like?"

"Another baby?"

229

Iris nodded.

"Can I see it?"

"Why?"

"Because I like babies."

"If you like them, why won't you take the one I gave you down to Hurley City?"

"Maybe I'm changing my mind. Can I see this one?"

"I'm not supposed to let anyone in here."

"It'll be okay. Really. Marvin isn't here, is he?"

She shook her head. "But he'll be back any time. He just went to town."

He summoned reasonableness and geniality. "Just let me see your baby for a second, Iris. Please? Then I'll go. And take the other baby with me. I promise."

She pursed her lips, then nodded and stepped back. "I got more than one," she suddenly bragged. "Let me show you." She turned and walked quickly toward the rear of the cabin and disappeared behind the blanket.

When he followed he found himself in a space that was half-kitchen and half-nursery. Opposite the electric stove and Frigidaire, along the wall between the wood stove and the rear door, was a row of wooden boxes, seven of them, old orange crates, dividers removed, painted different colors and labelled A to G. Faint names of orchards and renderings of fruits rose through the paint on the stub ends of the crates. Inside boxes C through G were babies, buried deep in nests of rags and scraps of blanket. One of them was crying. The others slept soundly, warm and toasty, healthy and happy from all the evidence he had.

"My God," he said.

"Aren't they beautiful? They're just the best little things in the whole world. Yes they are. Just the best little babies in the whole wide world. And Iris loves them all a bunch. Yes, she does. Doesn't she?"

Beaming, Iris cooed to the babies for another moment, then her face darkened. "The one I gave you, she wasn't happy here. That's because she was a B Box baby. My B babies are always sad, I don't know why. I treat them all the same, but the B babies are just contrary. That's why the one I gave you should go back. Where is it anyway?''

''In the car.''

''By itself?''

He nodded.

''You shouldn't leave her there like that,'' Iris chided. ''She's pouty enough already.''

''What about these others?'' he asked, looking at the boxes. ''Do they stay here forever?''

Her whole aspect solidified. ''They stay till Marvin needs them. Till he does, I give them everything they want. Everything they need. No one could be nicer to my babies than me. *No* one.''

The fire in the stove lit her eyes like ice in sunlight. She gazed raptly at the boxes, one by one, and received something he sensed was sexual in return. Her breaths were rapid and shallow, her fists clenched at her sides. ''Where'd you get these babies?'' he asked softly.

''Marvin gets them.'' She was only half-listening.

''Where?''

''All over. We had one from Nevada one time, and two from Idaho I think. Most are from California, though. And Oregon. I thing that C Box baby's from Spokane. That's Oregon, isn't it?''

He didn't correct her. ''Have there been more besides these?''

''Some.''

''How many?''

''Oh, maybe ten. No, more than that. I've had three of all the babies except G babies.''

''And Marvin got them all for you?''

She nodded and went to the stove and turned on a burner. ''You want some tea? It's herbal. Peppermint.''

He shook his head. ''What happened to the other babies? The ones that aren't here any more?''

''Marvin took them.'' Iris sipped her tea.

''Where?''

''To someone that wanted to love them.'' The declaration was as close as she would come to gospel.

The air in the cabin seemed suddenly befouled, not breathable. "Is that what this is all about, Iris? Giving babies to people that want them?"

"That want them and will *love* them. See, Marvin gets these babies from people that *don't* want them, and gives them to people that *do*. It's his business."

"Does he get paid for it?"

She shrugged absently. "A little, I think."

"Do you go with Marvin when he picks them up?"

"Sometimes. When it's far."

"And where does he take them? To Idaho and Nevada, or just around here?"

She shrugged again. "He doesn't tell me where they go. He says he doesn't want me to try and get them back." She smiled peacefully. "He knows how I am about my babies."

"How long have you and Marvin been doing this?"

"I been with Marvin about three years."

"And you've been trading in babies all that time?"

"Just about."

She poured some more tea into a ceramic cup and sipped it. She gave no sign of guile or guilt, no sign that what he suspected could possibly be true.

"Do you have any children of your own, Iris?"

Her hand shook enough to spill her tea. "I *almost* had one once."

"What do you mean?"

She made a face. "I got pregnant, but nobody wanted me to keep it so I didn't."

"Did you put it up for adoption?"

She shook her head.

"Abortion?"

Iris nodded, apparently in pain, and mumbled something. He asked her what she'd said. "I did it myself," she repeated. "That's what I can't live with. I scraped it out of there myself. I passed out. I . . ."

She fell silent. He looked back at the row of boxes that held her penance. When she saw him look she began to sing a song.

232

"Aren't they just perfect?" she said when she was through. "Aren't they all just perfect?"

"How do you know where the baby you gave me belongs?" he asked quietly.

"Marvin's got a book that keeps track. I sneaked a look at it one time when he was stoned."

"Where's he keep it?"

"In the van. At least that's where I found it." Iris put her hands on his chest and pushed. "You better go before Marvin gets back. You'll take the baby, won't you? It just don't belong here with the others. It fusses all the time and I can't love it like I should."

He looked at Iris' face, at the firelight washing across it, making it alive. "Where are you from, Iris?"

"Me? Minnesota."

"Did you come to California with Marvin?"

She shook her head. "I come with another guy. I was tricking for him when I got knocked up. After the abortion I told him I wouldn't trick no more so he ditched me. Then I did a lot of drugs for a while, till I met Marvin at a commune down by Mendocino."

"What's Marvin's last name?"

"Hessel. Now you got to go. Really. Marvin's liable to do something crazy if he finds you here." She walked toward him and he retreated.

"Okay, Iris. Just one thing. Could you give me something for the baby to eat? She's real hungry."

Iris frowned. "She only likes goat's milk, is the problem, and I haven't milked today." She walked to the Frigidaire and returned with a bottle. "This is all I got. Now, git."

He nodded, took the bottle from her, then retreated to his car.

He opened the door on the stinging smell of ammonia. The baby greeted him with screams. He picked it up, rocked it, talked to it, hummed a tune, finally gave it the second bottle, which was the only thing it wanted.

As it sucked its sustenance he started the car and let the engine warm, and a minute later flipped the heater switch. When it seemed prudent, he unwrapped the child and unpinned her soggy diaper and patted her dumplinged bottom dry with a tissue from the glove compartment. After covering her with her blanket he got out of the car, pulled his suitcase from the trunk and took out his last clean T-shirt, then returned to the car and fashioned a bulky diaper out of the cotton shirt and affixed it to the child, pricking his finger in the process, spotting both the garment and the baby with his blood. Then he sat for a time, considering his obligations to the children that had suddenly littered his life.

He should go to the police, but Marvin might return before they responded and might learn of Iris' deed and harm the children or flee with them. He could call the police and wait in place for them to come, but he doubted his ability to convey his precise suspicions over the phone. As he searched for other options, headlights ricocheted off his mirror and into his eyes, then veered off. When his vision was re-established he reached into the glove compartment for his revolver. Shoving it into his pocket, he got out of the car and walked back to the driveway and disobeyed the sign again.

A new shape had joined the scene, rectangular and dark. Marvin's van, creaking as it cooled. He waited, listened, and when he sensed no other presence he approached it. A converted bread truck, painted Navy blue, with sliding doors into the driver's cabin and hinged doors at the back. The right fender was dented, the rear bumper wired in place. A knobby-tired motorcycle was strapped to a rack on the top. The door on the driver's side was open, so he climbed in.

The high seat was rotted through, its stuffing erupting like white weeds through the dirty vinyl. The floorboards were littered with food wrappers and beer cans and cigarette butts. He activated his pencil flash and pawed through the refuse, pausing at the only pristine object in the van—a business card, white with black engraving, taped to a corner of the dash: 'J. Arnold Rasker, Attorney at Law. Practice in all Courts. Initial Consultation Free. Phone day or night.'

He looked through the cab for another minute, found nothing resembling Marvin's notebook and nothing else of interest. After listening for Marvin's return and hearing nothing he went through the narrow doorway behind the driver's seat into the cargo area in the rear, the yellow ball that dangled from his flash bouncing playfully before him.

The entire area had been carpeted, ceiling included, in a matted pink plush that was stained in unlikely places and coming unglued in others. A roundish window had been cut into one wall by hand, then covered with plasticine kept in place with tape. Two upholstered chairs were bolted to the floor on one side of the van, and an Army cot stretched out along the other. Two orange crates similar to those in the cabin, though empty, lay between the chairs. Above the cot a picture of John Lennon was tacked to the carpeted wall with a rusty nail. A small propane bottle was strapped into one corner, an Igloo cooler in another. Next to the Lennon poster a lever-action rifle rested in two leather slings. The smells were of gasoline and marijuana and unwashed flesh. Again he found no notebook.

He switched off his light and backed out of the van and walked to the cabin, pausing on the porch. Music pulsed from the interior, heavy metal, obliterating all noises including his own. He walked to the window and peered inside.

Iris, carrying and feeding a baby, paced the room, eyes closed, mumbling, seemingly deranged. Alone momentarily, she was soon joined by a wide and woolly man, wearing cowboy boots and Levi's, a plaid shirt, full beard, hair to his shoulders. A light film of grease coated flesh and clothes alike, as though he had just been dipped. Marvin strode through the room without speaking, his black eyes angry, his shoulders tipping to the frenetic music as he sucked the final puffs of a joint held in an oddly dainty clip.

Both Marvin and Iris were lost in their tasks. When their paths crossed they backed away as though they feared each other. He watched them for five long minutes. When they disappeared behind the curtain in the back he hurried to the door and went inside the cabin.

The music paused, then began again, the new piece indistinguishable from the old. The heavy fog of dope washed into his lungs and lightened his head and braked his brain. Murmurs from behind the curtain erupted into a swift male curse. A pan clattered on the stove; wood scraped against wood. He drew his gun and moved to the edge of the room and sidled toward the curtain and peered around its edge.

Marvin sat in a chair at a small table, gripping a bottle of beer. Iris was at the stove, her back to Marvin, opening a can of soup. Marvin guzzled half the bottle, banged it on the table, and swore again. "How could you be so fucking stupid?"

"Don't, Marvin. Please?"

"Just tell me who you gave it to. That's all I want to know. It was your buddy Gretel, wasn't it? Had to be, she's the only one around here as looney as you."

"It wasn't anyone you know. Really. It was just a guy."

"What guy?"

"Just a *guy*. I went out to a rest area way up by Oregon, and I talked to him and he said he was going to Frisco so I gave it to him and told him where to take it. You *know* it didn't belong here, Marvin. You know how puny it was."

Marvin stood up, knocking his chair to the floor. "You stupid bitch." His hand raised high, Marvin advanced on Iris with beer dribbling from his chin. "I'll break your jaw, woman. I swear I will."

"Don't hit me, Marvin. Please don't hit me again."

"Who was it? I want a name."

"I don't *know*, I told you. Just some guy going to Frisco. His name was Mark, I think."

"And he took the kid?"

Iris nodded. "He was real nice."

"You bring him here? Huh? Did you bring the son-of-a-bitch to the cabin? Did you tell him about the others?"

"No, Marvin. No. I swear. You know I'd never do that."

"Lying bitch."

Marvin grabbed Iris by the hair and dragged her away from the stove and slapped her across the face. She screamed and cowered. Marvin raised his hand to strike again.

Sucking a breath, he raised his gun and stepped from behind the curtain. "Hold it," he told Marvin. "Don't move."

Marvin froze, twisted his head, took in the gun and released his grip on Iris and backed away from her, his black eyes glistening. A slow smile exposed dark and crooked teeth. "Well, now," Marvin drawled. "Just who might you be besides a fucking trespasser? Don't tell me; let me guess. You're the nice man Iris gave a baby to. The one she swore she didn't bring out here. Right?"

"She didn't bring me. I followed her."

Both men glanced at Iris. Her hand was at her mouth and she was nibbling a knuckle. "I thought you went to Frisco," was all she said.

"Not yet."

"What do you want?" Her question assumed a fearsome answer.

Marvin laughed. "You stupid bitch. He wants the *rest* of them. Then he wants to throw us in jail. He wants to be a hero, Iris. And to be a hero he has to put you and me behind bars for the rest of our fucking lives." Marvin took a step forward.

"Don't be dumb." He raised the gun to Marvin's eyes.

Marvin stopped, frowned, then grinned again. "You look like you used that piece before."

"Once or twice."

"What's your gig?"

"Detective. Private."

Marvin's lips parted around his crusted teeth. "You must be kidding. Iris flags down some bastard on the freeway and he turns out to be a private cop?"

"That's about it."

Marvin shook his head. "Judas H. Priest. And here you are. A professional hero, just like I said."

He captured Marvin's eyes. "I want the book."

"What book?" Marvin burlesqued ignorance.

"The book with the list of babies and where you got them and where you took them."

Marvin looked at Iris, stuck her with his stare. "You're dead meat, you know that? You bring the bastard here and tell him all about it and expect him to just take off and not try to *stop* us? You're too fucking dumb to breathe, Iris. I got to put you out of your misery."

"I'm sorry, Marvin."

"He's going to take them *back*, Iris. Get it? He's going to take those sweet babies away from you and give them back to the assholes that don't want them. And then he's going to the cops and they're going to say you *kidnapped* those babies, Iris, and that you were bad to them and should go to jail because of what you did. Don't you see that, you brain-fried bitch? *Don't you see what he's going to do*?"

"I . . ." Iris stopped, overwhelmed by Marvin's incantation. "Are you?" she asked, finally looking away from Marvin.

"I'm going to do what's best for the babies, Iris. That's all."

"What's best for them is with me and Marvin."

"Not any more," he told her. "Marvin's been shucking you, Iris. He steals those babies. Takes them from their parents, parents who love them. He roams up and down the coast stealing children and then he sells them, Iris. Either back to the people he took them from or to people desperate to adopt. I think he's hooked up with a lawyer named Rasker, who arranges private adoptions for big money and splits the take with Marvin. He's not interested in who loves those kids, Iris. He's only interested in how much he can sell them for."

Something had finally activated Iris' eyes. "Marvin? Is that true?"

"No, baby. The guy's blowing smoke. He's trying to take the babies away from you and then get people to believe you did something bad, just like that time with the abortion. He's trying to say you did bad things to babies again, Iris. We can't let him do that."

He spoke quickly, to erase Marvin's words. "People don't give away babies, Iris. Not to guys like Marvin. There are agencies that arrange that kind of thing, that check to make sure the new home is in the best interests of the child. Marvin just swipes them and sells them to the highest bidder, Iris. That's all he's in it for."

"I don't believe you."

"It doesn't matter. Just give me Marvin's notebook and we can check it out, contact the parents and see what they say about their kids. Ask if they wanted to be rid of them. That's fair, isn't it?''

''I don't know. I guess.''

''Iris?''

''What, Marvin?''

''I want you to pick up that pan and knock this guy on the head. Hard. Go on, Iris. He won't shoot you, you know that. Hit him on the head so he can't put us in jail.''

He glanced at Iris, then as quickly to Marvin and to Iris once again. ''Don't do it, Iris. Marvin's trouble. I think you know that now.'' He looked away from Iris and gestured at her partner. ''Where's the book?''

''Iris?''

Iris began to cry. ''I can't, Marvin. I can't do that.''

''The book,'' he said to Marvin again. ''Where is it?''

Marvin laughed. ''You'll never know, detective.''

''Okay. We'll do it your way. On the floor. Hands behind your head. Legs spread. Now.''

Marvin didn't move. When he spoke the words were languid. ''You don't look much like a killer, detective, and I've known a few, believe me. So I figure if you're not gonna shoot me I don't got to do what you say. I figure I'll just take that piece away from you and feed it to you inch by inch. Huh? Why don't I do just that?''

He took two quick steps to Marvin's side and sliced open Marvin's cheek with a quick swipe of the gun barrel. ''Want some more?''

Marvin pawed at his cheek with a grimy hand, then examined his bloody fingers. ''You bastard. Okay. I'll get the book. It's under here.''

Marvin bent toward the floor, twisting away from him, sliding his hands toward the darkness below the stove. He couldn't tell what Marvin was doing, so he squinted, then moved closer. When Marvin began to stand he jumped back, but Marvin wasn't attacking, Marvin was holding a baby, not a book, holding a baby by the throat.

''Okay, pal,'' Marvin said through his grin. ''Now, you want to see this kid die before your eyes, you just keep hold of that gun. You want to see it breathe some more, you drop it.''

He froze, his eyes on Marvin's fingers, which inched farther around the baby's neck and began to squeeze.

The baby gurgled, gasped, twitched, was silent. Its face reddened; its eyes bulged. The tendons in Marvin's hand stretched taut. Between grimy gritted teeth, Marvin wheezed in rapid streams of glee.

He dropped his gun. Marvin told Iris to pick it up. she did, and exchanged the gun for the child. Her eyes lapped Marvin's face, as though to renew its acquaintance. Abruptly, she turned and ran around the curtain and disappeared.

''Well, now.'' Marvin's words slid easily. ''Looks like the worm has turned, detective. What's your name, anyhow?

''Tanner.''

''Well, Tanner, your ass is mine. No more John Wayne stunts for you. You can kiss this world good-bye.''

Marvin fished in the pocket of his jeans, then drew out a small spiral notebook and flashed it. ''It's all in here, Tanner. Where they came from; where they went. Now watch.''

Gun in one hand, notebook in the other, Marvin went to the wood stove and flipped open the heavy door. The fire made shadows dance.

''Don't.''

''Watch, bastard.''

Marvin tossed the notebook into the glowing coals, fished in the box beside the stove for a stick of kindling, then tossed it in after the notebook and closed the iron door. ''Bye-bye babies.'' Marvin's laugh was quick and cruel. ''Now turn around. We're going out back.''

He did as he was told, walking toward the door, hearing only a silent shuffle at his back. As he passed her he glanced at Iris. She hugged the baby Marvin had threatened, crying, not looking at him. ''Remember the one in my car,'' he said to her. She nodded silently, then turned away.

Marvin prodded him in the back and he moved to the door. Hand on the knob, he paused, hoping for a magical deliverance, but none came. Marvin prodded him again and he moved outside, onto the porch then into the yard. "Around back," Marvin ordered. "Get in the bus."

He staggered, tripping over weeds, stumbling over rocks, until he reached the rusting bus. The moon and stars had disappeared; the night was black and still but for the whistling wind, clearly Marvin's ally. The nanny goat laughed at them, then trotted out of reach. He glanced back at Marvin. In one hand was a pistol, in the other a blanket. "Go on in. Just pry the door open."

He fit his finger between the rubber edges of the bus door and opened it. The first step was higher than he thought, and he tripped and almost fell. "Watch it. I almost blasted you right then."

He couldn't suppress a giggle. For reasons of his own, Marvin matched his laugh. "Head on back, Tanner. Pretend you're on a field trip to the zoo."

He walked down the aisle between the broken seats, smelling rot and rusts and the lingering scent of skunk. "Why here?" he asked as he reached the rear.

"Because you'll keep in here just fine till I get time to dig a hole out back and open that emergency door and dump you in. Plus it's quiet. I figure with the bus and the blanket no one will hear a thing. Sit."

He sat. Marvin draped the blanket across the arm that held the gun, then extended the shrouded weapon toward his chest. He had no doubt that Marvin would shoot without a thought or fear. "Any last words, Tanner? Any parting thoughts?"

"Just that you forgot something."

"What?"

"You left the door open."

Marvin glanced quickly toward the door in the front of the bus. He dove for Marvin's legs, sweeping at the gun with his left hand as he did so, hoping to dislodge it into the folds of the blanket where it would lie useless and unattainable.

"Cocksucker."

Marvin wrested the gun from his grasp and raised it high, tossing off the blanket in the process. He twisted frantically to protect against the blow he knew was coming, but Marvin was too heavy and strong, retained the upper hand by kneeling on his chest. The revolver glinted in the darkness, a missile poised to descend.

Sound split the air, a piercing scream of agony from the cabin or somewhere near it. "What the hell?" Marvin swore, started to retreat, then almost thoughtlessly clubbed him with the gun, once, then again. After a flash of pain a broad black creature held him down for a length of time he couldn't calculate.

When he was aware again he was alone in the bus, lying in the aisle. His head felt crushed to pulp. He put a hand to his temple and felt blood. Midst throbbing pain he struggled to his feet and made his way outside and stood leaning against the bus while the night air struggled to clear his head.

He took a step, staggered, took another and gained an equilibrium, then lost it and sat down. Back on his feet, he trudged toward the porch and opened the door. Behind him, the nanny laughed again.

The cabin was dark, the only light the faint flicker from the stove behind the curtain. He walked carefully, trying to avoid the litter on the floor, the shapes in the room. Halfway to the back his foot struck something soft. As he bent to shove it out of his way it made a human sound. He knelt, saw that it was Iris, then found a lamp and turned it on.

She was crumpled, face down, in the center of the room, arms and legs folded under her, her body curled to avoid assault. He knelt again, heard her groan once more, and saw that what he'd thought was a piece of skirt was in fact a pool of blood and what he'd thought was shadow was a broad wet trail of the self-same substance leading toward the rear of the cabin.

He ran his hands down her body, feeling for wounds. Finding none, he rolled Iris to her side, then to her back. Blood bubbled from a point beneath her sternum. Her eyelids fluttered, open, closed, then open again. "He shot me," she said. "It hurt so bad I couldn't stop crying so he shot me."

"I know. Don't try to talk."

"Did he shoot the babies, too? I thought I heard . . ."

"I don't know."

"Would you look? Please?"

He nodded, stood up, fought a siege of vertigo, then went behind the curtain, then returned to Iris. "They're all right."

She tried to smile her thanks. "Something scared him off. I think some people were walking by outside and heard the shot and went for help. I heard them yelling."

"Where would he go, Iris?"

"Up in the woods. On his dirt bike. He knows lots of people up there. They grow dope, live off the land. The cops'll never find him." Iris moaned again. "I'm dying, aren't I?"

"I don't know. Is there a phone here?"

She shook her head. "Down at the end of the street. By the market."

"I'm going down and call an ambulance. And the cops. How long ago did Marvin leave?"

She closed her eyes. "I blacked out. Oh, God. It's real bad now, Mr. Tanner. Real bad."

"I know, Iris. You hang on. I'll be back in a second. Try to hold this in place." He took out his handkerchief and folded it into a square and placed in on her wound. "Press as hard as you can." He took her left hand and placed it on the compress, then stood up.

"Wait. I have to . . ."

He spoke above her words. "You have to get to a hospital. I'll be back in a minute and we can talk some more."

"But . . ."

"Hang on."

He ran from the cabin and down the drive, spotted the lights of the convenience market down the street and ran to the phone booth and placed his calls. The police said they'd already been notified and a car was on the way. The ambulance said it would be six minutes. As fast as he could he ran back to the cabin, hoping it would be fast enough.

Iris had moved. Her body was straightened, her right arm outstretched toward the door, the gesture of a supplicant. The sleeve of her blouse was tattered, burned to a ragged edge above her elbow. Below the sleeve her arm was red in spots, blistered in others, dappled like burned food. The hand at its end was charred and curled into a crusty fist that was dusted with gray ash. Within the fingers was an object, blackened, burned, and treasured.

He pried it from her grasp. The cover was burned away, and the edges of the pages were curled and singed, but they remained decipherable, the written scrawl preserved. The list of names and places was organized to match the gaily painted boxes in the back. Carson City. Boise. Grant's Pass. San Bernardino. Modesto. On and on, a gazetteer of crime.

"I saved it," Iris mumbled. "I saved it for my babies."

He raised her head to his lap and held it till she died. Then he went to his car and retrieved his B Box baby and placed her in her appointed crib. For the first time since he'd known her the baby made only happy sounds, an irony that was lost on the five dead children at her flank and on the just dead woman who had feared it all.

About the Editors

MARTIN GREENBERG has compiled over two hundred anthologies, including nine in Fawcett's Best of the West series. He is a noted scholar and teaches at the University of Wisconsin in Green Bay.

BILL PRONZINI, in addition to collaborating with Martin Greenberg on several anthologies, is an award-winning mystery writer, the author of many novels and short stories. He lives in Sonoma, California.